PLAUSIBLE DECEPTION

To Amy –
Congratulations!
I hope you enjoy
the book!

12·5·24

PLAUSIBLE DECEPTION

DWAIN LEE

ISBN: 978-1-964530-02-4

Printed in the United States of America

Book design by Scott Stortz

Published by:
Butler Books
www.butlerbooks.com

To George, Erica, and Andrea, with all my love.

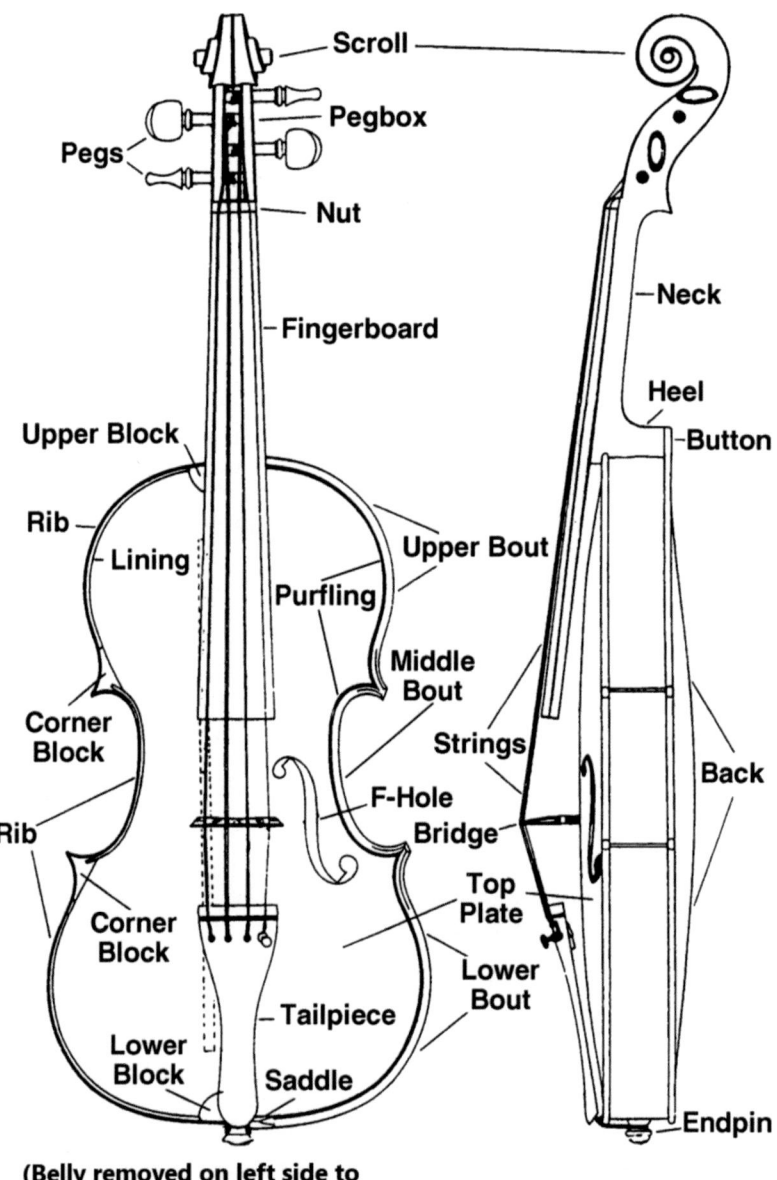

Scroll

Pegbox

Pegs

Nut

Fingerboard

Upper Block

Rib

Lining

Purfling

Upper Bout

Corner
Block

Middle
Bout

Rib

Strings

F-Hole

Bridge

Corner
Block

Top
Plate

Lower
Bout

Tailpiece

Lower
Block

Saddle

Neck

Heel

Button

Back

Endpin

(Belly removed on left side to
show interior construction)

Front and Side Views of a Violin

PROLOGUE

ANAHEIM

The hands held the violin up, almost reverently. Wood, varnish, and polish worked together to create a warm, golden-brown glow as the sunlight coming through the window bathed its surfaces.

"Still no developments in the theft of the famous 'Jackson Stradivarius' violin, which was stolen two days ago from a convention taking place here in the city." The televised report continued: "Local, federal, and even international law enforcement agencies are engaged in a far-reaching investigation, with little to show for it yet." The screen displayed several law enforcement officials conversing. "At this point, authorities are baffled as to how the rare violin could have been stolen, or who could have done it."

The hands gently caressed the violin's gracefully undulating surfaces—spruce, maple, ebony—edges all once crisp and new, now long since worn smooth and round and bearing the patina from centuries of use.

"This is really a first for our department," a police detective said on the screen. "The closest thing we've ever had to this was the theft of several Olympic gold medals, but nothing like this. That's why we're delighted and very grateful that the FBI has agreed to our request to assist in this case."

Liar. You didn't want the FBI here at all; I heard you say that myself. No matter. The hands continued to twist and turn the violin, causing the sunlight to flicker and dance along the flame pattern in the wood's grain, creating movement, depth, as it flowed across the contours and rippled textures of the surfaces, creating brilliance, shade, shadow. Fascinating. Mesmerizing.

". . . and yet the owner, a local surgeon, remains hopeful for a break in the case." The television now showed an elderly man in a hat, calm but clearly distraught, being interviewed by police inside a hotel lobby. *I've never understood why he wears that hat indoors. It's odd.*

After setting the violin down on a silk cloth, one of the hands hovered over its weathered spruce belly, paused for a moment, and then, haltingly, settled onto the wood. *I'll clean the skin oils off later.* The hand carefully, slowly moved along the surface. The subtleties of the wood grain, the sensuous, compound curvature of the surface, punctuated with beautifully carved openings, all transmitted not just tactile connection, but emotion, life. The instrument could sing, but it also spoke.

When the tree it was carved from was a sapling, Bernini's colonnade reaching from St. Peter's Basilica was brand new. The tree was already 20 feet tall when Vivaldi was born; 30 when Bach was just an infant. When this piece of wood was carved, Louis IV still ruled France, and there weren't even 13 English colonies in the New World yet, let alone a United States.

The violin had managed to survive for more than 300 years. *You've been played by some of the finest violinists to ever live, and your music has touched the souls of everyone from monarchs to mechanics. Throughout all you've experienced, all you've seen, all you've been, you aren't just a witness to history—you are history.*

News stories, even ones about the theft of a rare violin, a valuable cultural artifact of global significance, rarely exceed two and a half minutes. The newscast had already moved on to a remote from a local farmer's market and an update on an incoming cold front.

The hands gently wrapped the silk cloth up and around the instrument. *And now, your history starts a new chapter.*

CHAPTER 1

LOUISVILLE, THREE WEEKS EARLIER

"Are you going to eat one today, preacher man?"

Dan Randolph stopped on the sidewalk, surrounded by the aroma of cinnamon, brown sugar, butter, chocolate, and a half dozen other delightful smells. Through the doorway of the old wooden storefront, he saw Adimu Kimani, a Kenyan immigrant who had carved out her piece of the American Dream through her legendary cookies, standing behind a glass case filled with baked goods inside the small, inviting shop. It was only about 7:00 and the store wasn't open yet, but she and a helper had already been baking for several hours.

"Nope. You know I'm watching my weight," Dan said.

Adimu frowned. "Well, my friend, watching your weight is important and all, but a life without cookies is no life at all. Here, take one," she said, holding a fresh-baked snickerdoodle out toward

1

him. "I'll even give you a free one."

"Adimu," he joked, "I've stayed away from the goodies at all those church potlucks for two years now, but if I had one of your sweet, buttery calorie bombs, I know I'd fall completely off the wagon."

She offered him a scolding look, then laughed and said, "OK, OK. Keep walking, skinny man. I'll see you later!"

Dan offered her a wave and a smile and continued on his way, passing by Adimu's windows filled with the African decor and art reproductions that she sold in addition to her baked goods. He continued down Bardstown Road, one of Louisville's most well-known and eclectic streets, with its diverse selection of bars, restaurants, clothing stores, resale shops, tattoo parlors, head shops, and boutiques.

Walking almost every day was one of the few things that had kept Dan sane during the Covid lockdown. With all the stores closed, it sometimes seemed like he was wandering through a ghost town, and it was nice to occasionally encounter another person—even masked and having to do the pandemic pas de deux, waving but arcing around each other on the sidewalk to maintain distance while wondering if the other person had just inadvertently given you a lethal virus.

Today, Dan had plans to meet up with a friend and to include a walk around Louisville's iconic Cherokee Park as part of his route. Cherokee was the largest and most impressive of a series of parks in Louisville designed by the famed Frederick Law Olmsted, landscape architect of New York's Central Park and countless other noteworthy urban green spaces.

At the top of a rise not far into the park, he reached Hogan's Fountain, created by Enid Yandell, a noted female sculptor who had achieved international acclaim but little public recognition in her own country. The local landmark dated to the very early 20th century and featured a large round basin with a central stone pylon topped by a bronze sculpture of the Greek god Pan.

"Hey Dan, how's it going?" Standing next to the fountain was a man with salt-and-pepper hair, wearing a black and red jogging suit. It was his friend Rich Anderson, a member of the gay men's yoga class that Dan and his husband were part of.

"Hi, Rich. Pretty good, how about you?

"Not bad. I've got just enough time to do a quick walk around the park before cleaning up, eating, and heading into the office for a bit."

Rich gave Dan a quick once-over. "You know, I've meant to tell you that you've really done an amazing job losing all that weight. You're really looking good these days."

Dan smiled. "Well, thanks. I really lost it for health reasons, but after I did, people actually began to compliment me on my looks—

and without adding the dreaded *for your age*."

"Ah yes," Rich added knowingly, "the *for your age* kiss of death."

"And you know, when you're 62 years old, gay, straight, or otherwise, that feels pretty good."

"Far be it from me to quote the Bible to you, but doesn't it say somewhere in there 'all is vanity, and a chasing after wind'?"

"Screw you," Dan said with mock offense and a chuckle. "At least I own it." Then, thinking of Rich's husband, Dan asked, "So where's Mike today? He isn't joining us?"

"Not today, he decided to sleep in. It would have been nice if he'd come. On the other hand, he's big on Saturday morning breakfasts together, so I know I'll have a nice healthy breakfast waiting for me when I get home. And what's that husband of yours up to today?"

"Oh, he's already in the workshop this morning." Dan recognized the irony of two out gay men having a conversation about their husbands while standing in this particular place. Decades earlier, Hogan's Fountain had been one of the main meeting spots for closeted gay men to cruise and connect, using all the coded language and choreography that gay men in previous generations employed in a time when a simple glance or casual touch could, and often did, get a man arrested for supposed sexual perversion. *Thank God we're past all that*, Dan mused. *Or are we, given the past few years?*

The two men started around the trail, making small talk and

enjoying the park's beautiful combination of wooded areas, prairie meadows, rolling terrain, and broad vistas, occasionally punctuated with picturesque bridges and other structures. It all seemed completely natural, but in fact, every bit of the park's design was an intentional, carefully thought-out composition, a testimony to Olmsted's genius.

They eventually reached a sun-drenched meadow on a rise near the end of the loop, where they passed an exercise group working out on the pavement in front of a picturesque stone picnic pavilion. As they did, Rich asked, "So what exactly is Greg working on now?"

"I think he was doing some last-minute tweaks on a couple of instruments he's just finished. Late this week, he's headed to New York for a major exhibition featuring his work, and just a couple of weeks after that he'll be going to Los Angeles for a big competition."

Dan's husband, Greg Zhu, was a professional violin maker, or luthier, whose instruments were played by some of the finest professional musicians and the most promising conservatory students in the country. Greg had played the violin all his life, but he had spent more than a decade working as a systems engineer in the telecommunications industry. Eventually, though, he changed gears and went on to study violin making, where he discovered a perfect way to meld his love of music, science, and even history, along with his natural talent and love for woodworking. He'd truly found his dream job—his calling.

"Every year," Dan explained, "one of his dealers in New York hosts this exhibition featuring some of the top contemporary makers in the world. He's been part of that for a number of years. And every other year, the Violin Society of America hosts a competition where the top luthiers compete for awards. This just happens to be a year where they're both taking place, and they're spaced very closely together, so he's been swamped lately, getting ready for them. The instruments are ready to go, but he's already started on a new violin."

"Are you going to go with him?"

"Yeah, I'm tagging along on both trips," Dan answered. "A number of Greg's violin-making associates have become friends of mine too, and it's always good to catch up with them. And we usually try to mix business and pleasure, and turn these into little mini-vacations. But these days, I'm trying to take a lower profile at the events than I have in the past. I'll hang out at the actual event for a while, but then I'll make myself scarce. I really want Greg to be able to go full-on violin geek with his own tribe, without having to worry about me holding him back. Plus, I'm just the violin maker's spouse. I don't want any of his associates resenting me, and taking it out on him, because they feel like I'm inappropriately invading their space. I worry that I've unintentionally done that in the past sometimes, and I feel awful, so I'm really trying to be mindful about it."

Rich nodded his head. "I get that. When it comes to spouses and our professions, we all need to find that balance between being supportive and giving the right amount of space, and that can be really hard."

"Exactly," Dan agreed. "And I really can't complain. By far, he's got it tougher than I do—the difficulties of surviving as 'the pastor's spouse' are legendary, and being a same-sex spouse comes with its own special set of additional landmines to navigate. So I'm going to go with him to New York, and to Los Angeles—hopefully to help him celebrate if he receives any awards. But still, I'm going to try to stay in the background as much as I possibly can."

As they continued, Rich changed the topic. "So how exactly did you end up being a minister? Were you always very religious?"

Dan laughed. "Not at all. In fact, I didn't really have anything to do with religion until I was a teenager, when some fundamentalist youth group advertised events through the high school. I really only went at first because some friends were going and there was going to be free food. I didn't care about the religious aspect at all. I only gradually got sucked into the God-talk that they slipped in between everything else."

Rich smirked. "So you're saying that a bunch of conservative Christians 'groomed' you?"

"I know, kind of ironic, isn't it? Anyway, that's how it all started, but I got tired of the fundies after several years, and for a long time I just walked away from religion altogether."

"Well, that kind of makes sense. I mean, you had to know you were gay by then. How did you square that with all the antigay hellfire-and-brimstone they were probably spewing and all those fundamentalist burger bashes?"

Dan thought for a moment. The answer to his friend's question was complex. "Yeah, I always knew there was something different about me compared to other boys, even when I was maybe five or six years old. Long before I could understand anything specific about it, I knew I was intrigued by men's bodies in a way I couldn't explain." He looked over at Rich and said, "You were probably the same way."

"Most of us were," his friend agreed. "Hah! I remember when I was really little, I always got a strange feeling and was completely mesmerized by John-Boy Walton on TV."

Dan stopped in his tracks and looked incredulously at his friend. "John-Boy Walton? Really?"

Rich shrugged his shoulders. "Hey, the heart wants what the heart wants, even if the heart's only five."

"I will never look at you the same way again. John-Boy Walton. Pfft."

Dan took a breath before continuing. "I knew I was different, but I just didn't have any language, any vocabulary for it. I didn't know much about gay people, but everything I'd heard indicated that they were all supposed to be these immoral, sick, horrible people, and flamboyantly effeminate, so I told myself that whatever I was feeling, I couldn't be gay, because I wasn't any of those things."

"So you were in so much denial that you just didn't think you fit into the category of people they were criticizing."

"Well kind of, but it wasn't that cut-and-dried," Dan answered honestly. "Even while I didn't call myself gay, I still knew that what I was thinking and feeling was wrong in their eyes. I was completely filled with shame over it, and I knew I had to keep all that a secret, tucked deep down, away from everyone, even from myself, as much as possible."

"You clearly aren't a fundamentalist now," Rich observed.

Dan chuckled. "Obviously. The whole process of reconnecting with religion in a different way, and then giving up being an architect to become a minister, took a long time. And coming out as gay is a whole other story."

"So how old were you when you finally came out?"

"I was 54, and I had an ex-wife and two teenaged daughters by then."

By this time, the two had come full circle to the entry of the park, where another Yandell sculpture stood, this one of Daniel Boone. "Hey, good walking with you, Dan; let's do it again soon. Next time, you'll have to tell me more of that story."

"It's a deal," Dan promised. "I'll see you and Mike at yoga this week. Tell him I said hi, and enjoy that nice breakfast!"

Dan walked west on Eastern Parkway, back over Bardstown Road, and headed toward home. Eventually, normal sidewalks were replaced by a single asphalt pathway in a broad green space between the opposing lanes of traffic, turning the street into a picturesque boulevard lined with mature trees. The road was also part of Olmsted's grand vision for the city.

It was late October, and fall was unfolding slowly this year. The trees were just now grudgingly giving up their leaves, filling the air with that wonderful autumn fragrance and lightly stippling the pathway, offering a pleasing crunch under Dan's feet. As he walked, he thought about his conversation with Rich. *There's so much more to the story.* How his architectural firm had risen and collapsed. How his first marriage, and family life, had risen and collapsed. How they'd been financially wiped out by the recession of 2008, and how his head was just getting back above water. *How I eventually rediscovered my faith and the Church, and how I went from being a hardcore right-wing political extremist to being about as progressive, theologically and politically, as a person could be.*

How he'd finally come out as gay, and the fallout from that. *Parts of the story for another day.*

Turning north on Goss Avenue, Dan quickly reached the Schnitzelburg Café, a small, locally owned coffee shop and restaurant housed in a hundred-year-old corner storefront. It had a cozy vibe and friendly staff and was a popular gathering place for the eclectic mix of residents of the two adjacent Louisville neighborhoods of Schnitzelburg and Germantown, where Dan and Greg lived. The café was one of Dan's favorite neighborhood hangouts—he'd written literally hundreds of sermons there. The front windows were always plastered with posters advertising upcoming local concerts, art shows, lectures, and so on. Dan didn't think he and Greg had ever attended any of the events promoted in the window, but he still took comfort in knowing that there was so much going on in the neighborhood that they could take part in, if they wanted to.

This morning, Dan decided to stop in for a cup of coffee. He hopped up the few stairs to the old wooden corner door and pushed it open. The aged, exposed wooden floorboards creaked as he stepped into the high-ceilinged front room of the café, and the rich aroma of freshly roasted coffee beans filled the space. He quickly got a basic cup of the daily brew and found a place to sit. Almost as soon as he did, his phone rang. It was Michelle, his younger daughter.

"Well, this is odd. You usually text," Dan offered. "Is there something wrong?" Dan himself had long ago shifted to a general preference for text messages, and his daughters definitely had that preference, so he was expecting some kind of bad news when he saw the incoming call.

"Hey, Pops—no, nothing wrong here, everything's fine. I just thought I'd call for a change; sometimes it's good to hear an actual voice. So what's new there?"

"Not much with me; pretty much same old, same old. The church is all good; work's good; life's good. The big stuff here now is really Greg's; he's got these events coming up in New York and LA shortly." Dan paused for a moment, then continued. "And I haven't said this to Greg, but I have to be honest, I'm really worried, even frightened, about his LA trip."

"Why's that?"

"This big international competition only comes up every other year. When we met, he was starting to win awards, and his star in the violin-making world was rising, but then he hit a dry spell. His instruments are still wonderful—in fact, his dealers and customers say they're better than ever. But his work hasn't received a single award from his violin-making peers since we got together, and I just worry that there's a correlation between the two."

"Come on, I really doubt that's the case."

"No, I'm serious. I mean, now that we're together, I think that overall, Greg is happier and more fulfilled in general than he was before—at least, I hope he is. But am I just a boat anchor to his career? I know I've got more than my share of personal quirks. Am I such an emotional drain, do I create so much stress in his life, that he can't concentrate on his work?"

"Well, you really aren't exactly the easiest person to live with."

Ouch. There were volumes embedded in the short comment. Dan knew that in the moment, Michelle was joking—mostly—but the words still stung. Financial and marital difficulties, along with Dan's transitioning from one profession to another—one that no one else in the family was happy about—made family life very stressful in the last years of his first marriage, even without factoring in Dan's depression while struggling to come to terms with his sexuality. Michelle had stopped speaking to him following the divorce, but they had finally reconciled. Then Dan came out, and Michelle had almost completely erased him from her life. Eventually, the two made peace, and they seemed to be on good terms, now. But Dan knew that he'd carry the guilt from having hurt both of his daughters for the rest of his life.

After an awkward pause that felt longer to Dan than it probably was, Michelle seemed to soften the blow a bit by adding, "I wouldn't worry about it. You know that awards are very subjective, especially in the world of the arts. Look at how many great movies never won a single Oscar. And think of how many world-famous artists died broke and unappreciated, and 50 years later their work is worth millions. Don't worry; Greg will do fine."

"I suppose you're right," Dan said. "His dry spell is probably just coincidence, or the quirks of particular judges, or whatever. I'm sure he'll do well this year." His words projected more conviction than really lay beneath them. This competition in Los Angeles was always a big thing, and this time it would be even more so— certainly for Greg, but this time around, it was as big a deal for Dan's sense of well-being. He was really hoping this would be the year the dry spell was finally broken. *Knowing that I'm not an actual curse to my husband would let me sleep better at night.*

Their conversation shifted from Greg and the competition to other family news and chitchat. They enjoyed the time reconnecting, but eventually they both knew they needed to get on with the day.

"I need to run now, honey. I'll talk, or at least text, with you again soon."

"Talk to you soon. I love you, Pops."

"I love you too, honey, more than you can ever know."

Dan sat quietly for a few minutes after ending the call, thinking about Michelle, and her older sister, Nicole, and even Laura, his ex-wife. So much love. So much hurt. *And it's all on you, jackass. Damn.*

Dan left the café and headed up Goss Avenue, passing by scores of the cute 19th-century "shotgun" houses that gave the neighborhood much of its character. Originally, these modest little homes were built to house workers, mostly German immigrants, at a large cotton mill and yard good factory that the neighborhood was built around. These days, the houses were filled with a more diverse collection of longtime residents and newer transplants like Dan and Greg. Interspersed with the houses were a number of nice restaurants and watering holes, a couple of overpriced snob bars for the conspicuous-consumption crowd, and a diverse mixture of other shops and businesses that made Dan love the quirky little neighborhood. The old mill, now looming just ahead of Dan, had been tastefully converted into industrial loft apartments. Reaching the long, imposing brick building, Dan turned down a small side street and within a few minutes, still alone in his thoughts, he arrived home.

CHAPTER 2

Dan kicked off his shoes and passed through the house into the kitchen. Before anything else he washed his hands, part of the mandatory household reentry ritual. "Hey honey, I'm home!" Dan called, so he wouldn't startle Greg.

Greg often worked into the wee hours of the morning and then slept in much later than Dan, but this day he'd gotten an early start. Dan dried his hands, walked to the workshop—formerly one of the bedrooms—and knocked at the open doorway.

"Come on in."

Woodworking machinery and heavy wooden workbenches lined the walls, with additional equipment filling a center island that at the moment concealed Greg from Dan's view. The whole room was filled with the comforting scents of raw wood, hide glue, varnish, French polish, and a half dozen other pleasant smells.

"Did you wash your hands?"

Dan frowned. "You know that I did; I'm sure you heard the water running."

"It's just really important right now. If you touch any of the wood in here, you could get dirt on it, or just leave sweat or oil from your fingers on it, and the wood won't take its finish properly."

"I know, I know, I promise! I'm not going to touch anything," Dan said. He also knew there was more to the handwashing than just that.

Dan came around the center island and his husband came into view. Surrounded by small wood shavings covering the floor, Greg was sitting at his workbench in wrinkled old khakis and a stained, stretched-out-of-shape T-shirt. To his left was a work surface filled with woodworker's traditional chisels, planes, and other hand tools. A large computer monitor sat at the rear edge of the bench in front of him; one window on the screen displayed a large spreadsheet filled with what looked like enough mathematical data and other notes to run a mission to Mars. Another open window was playing Bach's Brandenburg Concerto no. 5 while visually tracking the score. Several pairs of reading glasses of various strengths perched on the top edge of the monitor. Over Greg's head was a wooden wall cabinet with glass-paneled doors housing numerous reference books, unfinished violins in progress, and several beautiful finished violins hanging on hooks. This was Greg Zhu's his inner sanctum, his Holy of Holies.

"How's work going this morning?"

"Things are going really well, today," he said enthusiastically. "I got my ribs bent and glued into place on the corner blocks, and I just took the clamps off after gluing the linings."

As Greg spoke, he held up a dark brown wooden form, shaped like the body of a violin. Around its perimeter were thin, curved strips of maple, no more than a millimeter thick—the side walls, or ribs, of a future violin—very carefully mitered and glued to small, solid-wood blocks at the intersections. Dan knew from previous discussions that the ribs were so thin that they didn't have enough surface area on their edges to adequately glue to the back and belly of the violin, so violin makers glue additional very small strips of wood—linings—inside the ribs for added surface area.

The Vieuxtemps Amati rib structure, still on its mold

"It looks great," Dan said, and he meant it. He was always in awe of the fact that there were people in the world who could create things like this with their hands.

Greg beamed. "Thanks, honey. Here, look at this," he said as he turned the rib structure back and forth under a task light, showing off the three-dimensional cat's-eye reflection, or chatoyancy, of the maple grain. "I had to recut the maple to just the right direction in relation to the grain to get that effect, but the extra work was definitely worth it. This is going to be beautiful once it's all varnished. I'm just glad I'm able to start another new one, now that those two are done." He pointed to two violins sitting on the adjacent workbench. "I did some really fine tonal adjustments to both of them while you were out. They're sounding really, really good now, and they're ready to go."

"I'm glad they're done, too," Dan teased, "since I've been living the life of 'the violin maker's widow' for the last few months." Greg shot him a disapproving glance.

The two violins sitting in front of Dan were truly beautiful. The warm, varnished finish on their spruce bellies and maple backs glowed in the sunlight coming through the workshop window. The precision of the joinery, the intricacy of their carved scrolls, the fine inlaid detailing of the tuning pegs—everything about these instruments was stunning.

But while they looked beautiful, one thing they didn't look was new. Even though they'd been completed just days earlier, they both looked like they'd seen centuries of use—and for good reason. The violin maker's work is art, but it isn't art for art's sake. Their instruments need to sell, so a maker has to respond to the preferences of their intended clientele. And beyond demanding that an instrument have the very best tone and ease of playability, most professional-level violinists prefer having an instrument that looks like it has some age and pedigree to it. Greg had once explained another important benefit of antiquing the instruments:

"Think about how the owner of a brand-new BMW feels when it gets its first scratch. It's the exact same thing with a pristine, professional-level violin. If the violin is antiqued from the very beginning, that's never a concern." That made sense to Dan.

"The end result is really beautiful," Dan said as he looked at the two violins on the bench, "but you know I cringe every time I see you take a beautiful new instrument and start antiquing it."

Greg offered an ornery smile. "Why? You don't like watching me rolling pebbles all over it to scratch and chip the varnish, or wearing down all the nice crisp corners?"

"Nope. Even after all this time I can't bear to watch you do it. As I said, I know it all comes out well in the end, but it's still painful to watch. I do like one thing about it, though."

"What's that?"

"Well, what you do isn't just random. The antiquing has a logic to it that makes it all believable."

"Oh, absolutely," Greg said. "Every bit of the antiquing is very carefully thought out. You have to understand how a violin actually ages over time. I'll put light scratches in the varnish in just the right place to look like years of accumulated stray bow scratches. I'll punch little pockmarks on the belly under the tailpiece to make it look like it's endured countless restringings. I'll wear down the backside of the scroll more, to replicate the wear it would have gotten in old-fashioned cases. I'll even wear away the varnish in just such a pattern that mimics the distressed finish a violin got from beard-grizzle back in the days when players didn't use chin rests."

Dan carefully picked up one of the violins by the neck and end button. Where to touch a violin, and especially where *not* to touch it, were lessons Dan had learned early on. He held the instrument up in the sunlight, carefully turning it and admiring it.

"I like how you keep very faint tool marks on some of the surfaces," Dan said, "so it's obvious it's something made by hand and not cranked out on some machine. And I like your fake dirt, too." Greg had spent years perfecting the complex blend of multiple pigments and sometimes waxes that he used to replicate the subtleties of the residue that accumulates over time in the crevices and scratches of even the most lovingly cared-for violin.

Greg nodded. "Dirt isn't just dirt. It's got patina—character. In any case, whether it's the detailing, the tooling, the finishing, or even the 'dirt,' the whole antiquing process has to be believable. It's all a deception," he said, "but it has to be a plausible deception."

"See, that's what I like about your violins—they're actually crafting a visual story." By vocation and personality, Dan was a storyteller. His master-storytelling grandfather, Tom Randolph, would often say "Never let the truth get in the way of a good story." He didn't originate the dictum, but he'd certainly lived by it, and many of his more than 30 grandchildren, including Dan, had inherited that gene as well. His storytelling abilities had helped him develop countless sermons over the years. Similarly, while he was still an architect, Dan had developed a complete fictional back story that guided the creation of the house he'd designed for his family. It had been designed as if it were originally a simple four-room, two-story farmhouse that had been expanded and extended in all directions over the years as the farmer's family and fortunes grew. It was the same with Greg's violins, Dan thought. Whether consciously or not, there always needed to be a believable, fictional backstory that guided the deception of the antiquing.

Just then, the Brandenburg background faded and was replaced by the familiar notification that Greg had an incoming video call.

Greg turned and looked at the computer screen.

"Oh wow, it's Bill Sloan!" Quickly accepting the call, Greg greeted his old friend. "Hey Bill, it's good to see you. How are you?"

"I'm great, thanks Greg. How have you and Dan been?"

"Oh, pretty well here; I finally got everything ready to go for both June's exhibition and the competition; Dan and I were just talking about them." Dan waved to Bill from behind Greg's shoulder.

"Good! I'm really looking forward to finally seeing you again in person when you get out here—both of you, I hope; it's been too long. Dan, are you coming out?"

"Yep; it will be great to catch up with you!"

"It's still pretty early for you out there; what prompted the call?" Greg asked.

"Well, I wanted to tell you that I'll be staying at the hotel to avoid all the commuting back and forth across town. While I'm there, I'm going to have the Jackson with me. I don't want to broadcast that; I'm only telling a few people: Konstantin, Eric Morrison, Alana Marino, and Hanna Sullenberger—and you, of course." Dan knew Konstantin, and he had heard Greg mention the others numerous times. "I definitely wanted to let you know and invite you to stop by and play it sometime."

The "Jackson" Bill was referring to was the Leonora Jackson Stradivarius, crafted by Antonio Stradivari in 1714—a beautiful instrument, and tonally, one of the finest Stradivarius violins in existence. Bill and his wife Judy owned the Jackson and were very generous in lending it to fine professional violinists to play, and to a limited number of luthiers to study. Greg had spent hours studying the Jackson in person and analyzing CT scans of its construction. He'd had the opportunity to play it a number of times in the past, but it was always a special treat.

"I'd love that Bill, thanks!" Greg replied. "We'll definitely make arrangements to do that."

"That's all I really wanted to tell you. I just wanted to give you a heads-up about the Jackson being here. Have a good time in New York, and we'll see you both out here in just a few weeks."

Greg closed the call and the Brandenburg resumed.

"Well, that's awfully nice of him," Dan said. "It will be great to see him again." Several years earlier, Bill and Judy had come to Louisville to be part of Dan and Greg's wedding, not only as guests, but as participants, playing the Méditation from Thaïs by Massanet as part of the service—Judy on piano, and Bill on the Jackson.

Dan was still holding one of the violins. "That one you're holding is headed for New York. It's actually another 'Jackson Amati,'" Greg explained.

"You've had real success with this pattern in the past, and it's one of your favorites."

"Each of them has looked great, had beautiful tone, and ended up being purchased quickly. But it's also a favorite of mine just because of its connection to the Jackson."

"It isn't just a great sounding instrument, and it isn't just an homage to a wonderful historical instrument," Dan said. "It's also an homage to Bill."

Greg didn't say anything, but Dan could see that he was thinking warmly of their friend.

Modern violin makers often base their work on that of the original masters of violin making, especially the work of three violin-making family dynasties from the 17th and 18th centuries—all three based in and around the city of Cremona, Italy. Most people are familiar with Stradivarius violins, created by Antonio Stradivari and his offspring. But of at least equal importance were two other family dynasties: Amati and Guarneri. The first—generally considered the "inventor" of what would be thought of as the modern violin—was Andrea Amati. The third family dynasty was the one begun by Andrea Guarneri, who, before launching his own workshop, had served as an apprentice to Nicolò Amati, Andrea Amati's grandson and arguably the most talented of the all the Amati family.

Greg had always been particularly drawn to the precise, crisp detailing and beauty of the Amati family's instruments. Because of this, his violins invariably incorporated the overall shape, dimensioning, and much detailing, of an Amati violin. But he would often take the back and belly geometry of some excellent-sounding non-Amati violin, and proportionally modify that geometry through complex mathematical modeling to fit within the Amati outline. The combination of the outer contours—the "arching"— and the inner ones—the "graduations"—of a violin back or belly can be mapped, like the contours on a topographical map or isobars on a weather map, and then recreated via meticulous carving and planing of the wood. Combined, these contours create a back or belly with very specific varying thicknesses, causing it to resonate in particular ways. This aspect of a violin's design is one major determinant of the instrument's tone. Through Greg's grafting process, he created instruments that were completely unique, while still firmly rooted in the so-called golden age of violin making.

"So what's the pattern of this one?" Dan asked, setting the first violin down and picking up the other one.

"Oh, the one for the competition? This is actually a brand-new pattern, a 'Vieuxtemps Amati.' It's a Brothers Amati pattern, but the belly and back are based on the Vieuxtemps Guarneri del Gesù, obviously."

"Well obviously, anyone could see that," Dan deadpanned with more than a touch orneriness.

"Smartass," Greg chuckled. Despite his wisecrack, Dan actually was familiar with the violin Greg was referring to. The 1741 Vieuxtemps, a remarkable instrument, had made news in the violin world in 2012, when it sold for more than $16 million, the highest price ever paid for a violin, at the time.

Greg's tone became more serious. "It seems like forever since I've been to either of these events, since Covid canceled them both for the past two years—and honestly, it makes me all the more nervous about them. It's been a while since I've actually made a sale, too; things are getting pretty tight."

"Honey, relax." Dan rubbed his shoulders. "You've done everything you possibly could to be ready for these events. And yeah, I know I'm just a fly on the wall of your world, but still, from what I've seen, there is no one—no one—whose instruments are more beautiful, physically or tonally, than yours." He held up one of the violins, turning it so its bass-side f-hole was at Greg's eye level. "Look at your label in there. What's the Latin inscription that you put inside every one of your instruments?"

"*Cantet anima mea fervorem Dei salvificantem,*" Greg said from memory. " 'Let my soul sing God's passionate healing.' "

"They do. Every single one of them. Your violins are still going to be around making wonderful music hundreds of years from now. Don't ever lose sight of the fact that you are truly creating something special, something for the ages. I could only dream

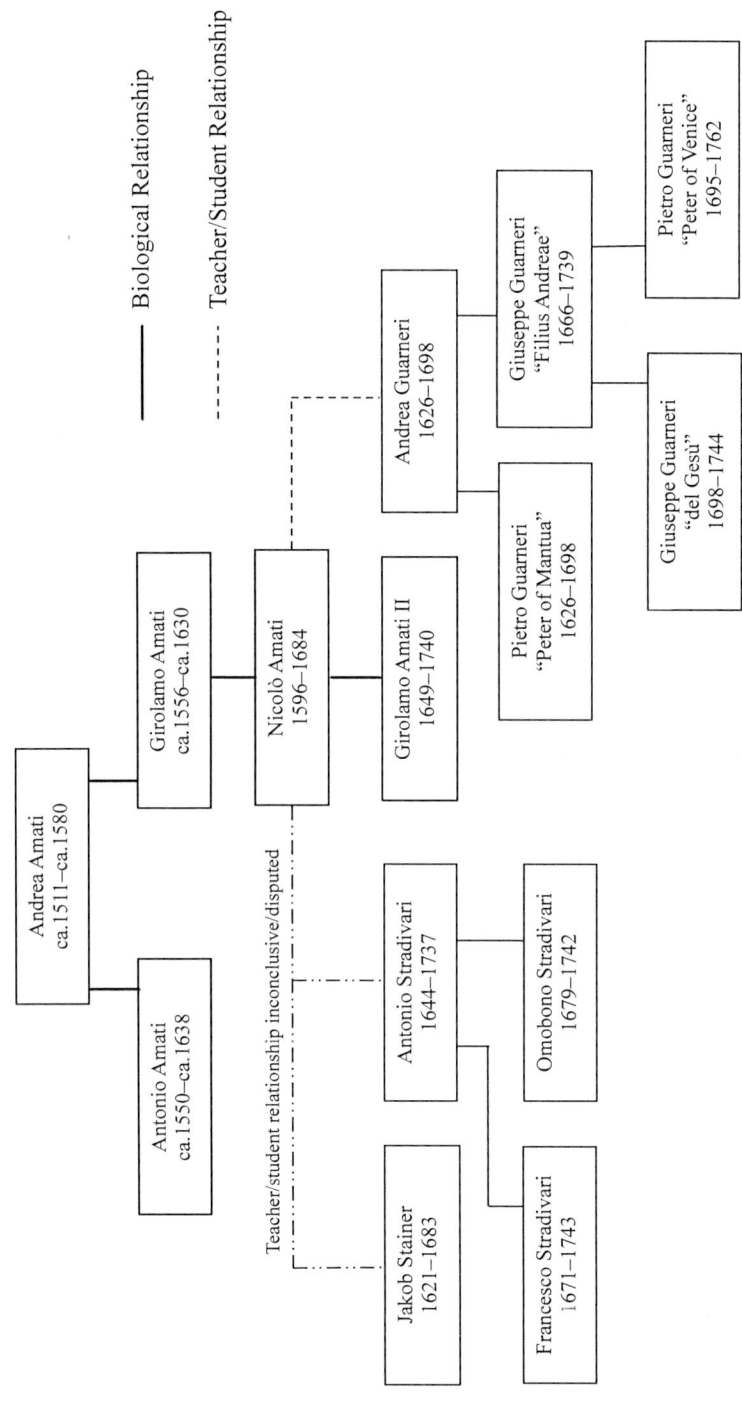

— Biological Relationship

----- Teacher/Student Relationship

Andrea Amati
ca.1511–ca.1580

Antonio Amati
ca.1550–ca.1638

Girolamo Amati
ca.1556–ca.1630

Nicolò Amati
1596–1684

Girolamo Amati II
1649–1740

Andrea Guarneri
1626–1698

Pietro Guarneri
"Peter of Mantua"
1626–1698

Giuseppe Guarneri
"Filius Andreae"
1666–1739

Pietro Guarneri
"Peter of Venice"
1695–1762

Giuseppe Guarneri
"del Gesù"
1698–1744

Teacher/student relationship inconclusive/disputed

Antonio Stradivari
1644–1737

Omobono Stradivari
1679–1742

Jakob Stainer
1621–1683

Francesco Stradivari
1671–1743

Biological and teaching relationships among various early violin makers.

that I'd ever do something in my life that would make lasting a difference in the world."

The stress on Greg's face eased a bit. "I hope so."

"I know so." Dan assured him. "And as far as sales, June told you that several customers know you've got a new violin coming to town, and they're already scheduling time to try it out, just based on how highly they regard your work."

The day before, Greg had spoken by phone with June Reynolds-Yakubu, one of his New York dealers and the organizer of the exhibition. She had told him about the excitement surrounding his latest instrument.

"You're right. I've done all I can do. I'll take my mind off of it by just moving on and working on this next one." He pointed to the rib structure he'd shown Dan a few minutes ago.

"Sounds like a plan," Dan replied. "And relax, you've got this." It was said with at least as much hope as it was assurance.

CHAPTER 3

UPPER EAST SIDE, MANHATTAN, TWO
WEEKS BEFORE THE COMPETITION

"Well, finally, here we are. Man, I've missed this place!" Greg exclaimed. He and Dan had hopped off the Metro at the Hunter College stop and walked the short distance to the exhibition venue, a facility larger and more suited to this type of event than June's shop. They opened the heavy wooden doors of the impressive stone building and stepped into the two-story reception hall. A monumental spiral staircase ran along one side of the hall, leading up to the main exhibition space. Here on the main level, a number of attendees were socializing while a string quartet played classical music in one corner of the room. A bar and comfortable seating occupied most of the rest of the first room. Just beyond, an artistic display of light refreshments blanketed the massive oak table in the center of an impressive wood-paneled room.

"We can hit the food and drink in a bit," Greg said, "but right now, let's go up to the exhibition space."

"Sounds good to me." The two scaled the grand marble staircase to a large salon with a parquet floor. Warm wood paneling bore paintings in ornate gilt frames. Much of the room was dominated by tables showcasing violins and violas, each of them accompanied by a bio of its maker. Cellos were displayed in front of a massive marble fireplace, while neighboring tables exhibited dozens of bows crafted by top makers from around the world. Throughout the space, musicians were trying out the instruments.

Almost as soon as they arrived at the top of the stairs, Greg heard his name called out. Turning toward the voice, he and Dan saw June Reynolds-Yakubu and Ping Yi, the organizers of the exhibition, approaching.

June smiled broadly. "It's so good to see you again Greg, and you too, Dan; I hope you're both well! Thanks so much for stopping by the showroom yesterday to drop your violin off; we brought it over to the exhibition hall early this morning, and it's already getting a lot of attention." She pointed toward Greg's violin; someone was playing it as they spoke.

"Oh wow, that's great!" Greg exclaimed. "It looks like a fantastic turnout this year, too!" He was right. This was opening night of the exhibition, and the hall was filled with musicians, luthiers, and a handful of industry insiders, all milling about and moving between the salon and the main level, below.

"Do you have any plans to go back to Taiwan anytime soon?" Ping Yi asked. Greg was a Canadian citizen, born in Hong Kong to Taiwanese and Chinese parents. He'd spent his toddler years in Taiwan before emigrating to Canada, and still had many relatives living there. Ping Yi was born in Taiwan and emigrated to the United State as an "Exceptional Alien," to use the odd terminology of the United States Citizenship and Immigration Service, which grants priority visa processing to people who exhibit 'extraordinary ability' in the arts, sciences, business, or some other field."

"Not any time soon, but I'd like to go back sometime in the near future and bring Dan. The last time I was there, all my relatives told me to bring him along next time; they all want to meet him."

"Well, when you go, you know you're going to stick out like a sore thumb," she said.

"Why, because we're a gay couple?"

"No, because you speak Chinese with a Canadian accent," she teased. "They'll know immediately that you're a tourist."

Dan smiled. "They'll figure it out right away when you speak Mandarin but end every sentence with 'eh?' "

"By the way," June said, "I have to take care of some business over in the showroom this afternoon. Why don't you two come over while I'm there? I have something really special that I think you'll both be interested in seeing- the Lipinski Strad is in the shop right now."

"Oooh, how cool! I've never actually seen it," Greg said. "Count us in. What time should we be there?

"Make it 2:30. I'll have coffee and some pastries for you from a great shop around the corner. See you then!" She and Ping Yi drifted off to mingle with other attendees. Within moments, Greg had joined them, while Dan, true to intention, largely tried to recede into the background, watching from the corner of the room near the top of the staircase.

"We've spent a lot of time in this room over the years, haven't we?" Dan looked up to see that Ping Yi had walked back over.

"Yes, we have," he answered. "And you know, I think that over the years, I've memorized half of the paintings in this room while Greg was busy doing his thing. Did you know that this one—" He pointed to the massive painting on the wall in front of them. "—is 'The Blessing of the Waters among the Hutzuls,' by the famous Polish painter Teodor Axentowicz?"

"Funny—with everything else I've been concerned with during the exhibitions, I never paid much attention to it, even though it is pretty hard to miss."

"Several years back, I was watching an episode of 'White Collar,'" Dan said. "The characters played by Matt Bomer and Tim DeKay walked up a monumental staircase, and I had to laugh. I thought the staircase looked familiar, but I knew they'd filmed the scene right here as soon as they got to the top of the stairs and I saw that painting on the wall behind them."

"Really? That's pretty cool."

"In order to catch a thief, Bomer's character had to create a masterful forgery of a very famous and rare bottle of wine, one that was supposedly impossible to duplicate. It was about to be sold at auction. They used this room as the setting for the auction house. The auctioneer was over there, just about where Greg's violin is."

"Hmm," Ping Yi said with a smile, "I know that he plays for your team and not mine, but that Matt Bomer is really a tall drink of water, isn't he? I wouldn't mind seeing him show up here again today."

"Hah! You and me both." Dan winked.

"Are you going out to LA with Greg for the convention?"

"Yeah, for a while. He'll go out for the whole week; I'll follow him out and be there for the last few days."

"Great. Be sure to stop by the exhibit we'll have out there. We're going to have a really nice collection of antique instruments."

"Oh, we'll be there. I know that's one of the things that Greg is really looking forward to."

Dan spent the next few hours making small talk with some of the people he knew, watching musicians taking instruments into private, adjacent rooms to try them out, and periodically checking in with Greg—but staying out of his way as much as possible. He and Greg slipped down into the East Village to their favorite Ukrainian restaurant for a late lunch. There, they filled themselves on *pierogi*, *halupki*, and other traditional Eastern European fare.

"Ah, this is my soul food!" Dan exclaimed as he dug into the large platter.

"What are you talking about? You're English, Scottish, Irish, and Italian. You don't have a drop of East European ancestry."

"Doesn't matter," Dan said, his mouth full of the best cabbage roll he'd had in a long time. "This is the food you grow up with in southwestern Pennsylvania." Smiling, he added, "I'm an honorary Eastern European."

"You're an honorary goofball." Greg rolled his eyes. "But the food is really good. As soon as we're done here, we go to June's showroom to see the Lipinski," he said. "After that, I'm going back to the exhibition hall. Do you want to come with me?"

"No, by that point I'll be violin-ed out. I'm going to get in some walking, probably through Central Park, and then just around the city. I've run the calorie count. I need to walk a little more than a mile to work off each *pierogi* and cabbage roll I've eaten."

"Based on that, you're going to need to walk to Newark," Greg teased.

"Actually, you're about right. In any case, it would be worth it—

this is incredible!"

A short while later, they made their way to June's violin shop, located in a mid-rise art-moderne office building just down the street from Carnegie Hall.

"Hey guys. Welcome!" June greeted them. "Let's go into my office, and I'll bring the Lipinski out, since we all have a lot on our plates today." She ushered Dan and Greg through the main showroom space, past several private listening rooms, to her office.

"Have a seat." June gestured to the conference table. "Hang on, let me get it from the instrument vault." She returned momentarily, the Lipinski Strad in hand.

"We're actually doing some minor repair work and tonal adjustments on it for the owner," she said. "I thought you'd like to look it over since you're here."

"Oh, absolutely," Greg said. "I love having the chance to study golden period instruments in person. I got to do that at the violin makers' workshops in Oberlin, at the Smithsonian, and the Library of Congress—and here, of course—but I've never seen the Lipinski." He held it up, carefully studying its detailing.

He turned to Dan. "This violin is noteworthy not just because it's a Strad—and a pretty good one, at that—but because it was famously stolen several years back." He set the instrument down on the workbench, carefully placing it in a velvet-lined cradle contoured to match a violin back.

"Wow, how did that happen?" Dan asked.

"It was really crazy. In fact, it's the only time a rare violin was the target of an actual armed robbery. The owner had set up a long-term loan of the instrument to a violinist in Milwaukee. As he was coming out of a performance and walking to his car, he was approached by someone who tasered him and ran off with the violin. The local police, the FBI, and Interpol got involved right away, since they worried it was going to be smuggled out of the country and sold on the international black market."

"Wow! How did they recover it?

"Neither of them was particularly bright. The biggest break in the case came quickly. When a Taser is fired, it releases a burst of tiny ID tags imprinted with bar-coded serial numbers that coat the victim and the surrounding area. It didn't take long for the police to scan the tags and track the Taser's serial number back to the purchaser. After that, the theft unraveled within days, with the two quickly confessing. They admitted to stashing the violin in a friend's attic, wrapped in a baby blanket, and that's where the authorities found it. They retrieved it just nine days after it was stolen. Thankfully, it hadn't been damaged in the process."

"Incredible." Dan looked at the instrument. "What did they think they were going to do with it once they stole it? I mean, stealing something this high-profile is hard to profit from."

"Exactly," Greg said. "They're just so identifiable. These instruments have been so thoroughly photographed, videotaped, even scanned by CT, that they just can't hide, at least not for long." He smiled and added, "As one media person in the violin world put it, a rare violin has been photographed from more angles than a porn star."

June laughed and picked up the story. "One of the culprits had been in prison before, for stealing a valuable statue from a museum and then offering to ransom it back to the owner. The FBI assumed that they were going to try to do the same thing with the Lipinski, since they hadn't picked up any chatter in the art-crime world about the theft. In any case," she added, "it's back in good hands now."

"Thanks for allowing us to see it, June," Greg said after several more minutes of examining the notorious violin.

"Yes, thanks. It's a beautiful violin with a fascinating story," Dan added.

"Oh, you're very welcome." She took the violin back to the vault, then ushered the two back toward the shop's entry. In the showroom, they saw a strikingly beautiful woman examining a violin. Greg's face brightened, recognizing her immediately.

"Alana, how are you? I haven't seen you for so long!" he said.

Alana Marino was an internationally acclaimed violinist, and currently a member of the Los Angeles Philharmonic. She was also quite beautiful: slight of build with flowing brown hair and olive skin framing piercing blue eyes—an uncommon feature in her hometown of Reggio Calabria, a small coastal city at the southernmost tip of Italy.

Her eyes sparkled, and her smiling face exuded warmth when she looked up to see Greg. "Oh, my dear friend," she cried. "How have you been? It's a delight to see you."

"Your name came up in a conversation I had with Bill Sloan about a week ago," Greg told her. "So what brings you to town and to June's shop?" he asked. "Are you looking for a new violin?"

"No, no, I'm very happy with the instruments I've got now," she replied. "But it's always fun to window shop. I was actually just over at Carnegie Hall, and since I was in the neighborhood, I thought I'd stop by."

"Are you going to the exhibition too?" Greg asked her.

"I wouldn't miss it. I know you've got your latest violin over there; I can't wait to try it out."

"On that note," Julie said, "I need to get back over to the exhibition. Alana, I hope to see you there. Greg, you're probably planning on going over for a while this afternoon too."

"Yes," Greg replied. "I'd like to spend a little more time there today, since we'll be heading back to Louisville mid-morning tomorrow."

"Well, I'll see you over there shortly," she said. "Dan, it's always good to see you; if I don't see you before you go, have a safe and pleasant trip."

After June departed, Alana continued. "As much as I'd like to spend more time at the exhibition, I'm afraid I'll only be able to be there a short while. I need to catch the train to Philadelphia, where I plan to reconnect with some of my old teachers and friends at the Curtis Institute." With a bit more seriousness, she added, "And I need to take care of some family business while I'm there. But then," she said, smiling again, "it's back to LA for me. We've got several performances scheduled before the VSA."

Greg nodded. "I heard that you're going to be one of the tone judges in the competition."

"I know that can be a very subjective thing," Dan said, "but could you help a non-violinist understand just what you look for when you're judging the tone of an instrument?"

"Well, probably the best way to do that is to play a good violin a bit and then explain how to hear it—what to listen for." She picked up the violin she'd been looking at earlier. "This one, for example. It's an antique instrument, and a very good one—an 1845 Jean-Baptiste Vuillaume. He was highly influenced by the violins of Guarneri del Gesù."

Greg explained, "Vuillaume is probably the most famous French violin maker ever, and yes, he rigorously studied the antique violins of his time, measuring them down to the smallest detail for his own work. In fact, he once made a replica of 'Il Cannone' del Gesù that was such a perfect copy, its owner, the great Italian violinist Niccolò Paganini, couldn't tell the difference between the two of them, visually. He could only tell which was which based on very, very subtle differences in tone."

"And that," Alana said to Dan, "brings us back to your question." Taking a bow from the counter, she played a bit of the Bach Chaconne for Solo Violin. "OK," she said as she set the bow back down. "Before I say anything, Mr. Non-Violinist," she joked, "tell me the strings on a violin, from the lowest to highest in pitch."

Dan chuckled. "You can't live with a violin maker without knowing that—G, D, A, E."

"Very good. Remembering that, some of what I'm looking for in a violin's tone is a power, a kind of warmth, on the low end of the G string, so it sounds appropriately 'deep,' if that makes sense. I'm also looking for a ringing sweetness from the D and A strings, and on the E string, I want to hear a brightness, but without a tinny or metallic sound. Having said all that, I still want to hear, and feel, a general evenness of tone across all of the strings—if that doesn't sound contradictory."

"No, I think I understand what you're saying," Dan said thoughtfully.

"But that isn't the whole story, either," she stressed. "Beyond just that, tone is also partly defined by the violin's responsiveness. It needs to 'speak,' immediately and clearly, over the full range of bow strokes, dynamics, string crossings, and so on."

"And I imagine that beyond an instrument's tone," Dan suggested, "the violin has to just feel right, in a physical, tactile sense, to the player."

"Yes," Alana agreed. "It might sound odd, but if the instrument doesn't feel right under my chin, it won't sound right to my ear. Plus, if it doesn't feel right to my fingers—if it makes me work harder than I'd otherwise need to in order to achieve that wonderful tone—then that wouldn't be the violin for me."

"And that," Greg interjected, "is a function of the height of the strings above the fingerboard, the spacing between them, the overall back length of the corpus, the smoothness of the joint of the neck and fingerboard—all differences of fractions of a millimeter—and other things, as well. There are a number of antique instruments that have wonderful tone, but based on those sorts of things, it can be exhausting for the violinist to actually get that tone out of them."

Nodding her head in agreement with Greg, Alana set the Vuillaume back down in its cradle. "Remember, though, that what we've just been discussing, including the 'feel' of the instrument, are relatively technical matters. 'Tone,' though, is actually a complex concept that transcends all of those particulars. Ultimately, a truly excellent violin has a tone with character, sophistication—a complexity like a fine Barolo wine. And this one," she said with a smile, "is a particularly good vintage."

Once the men made their way back down to the building's lobby, Greg headed back to the exhibition, while Dan set off for his post-*pierogi* walk through Central Park. A fan of Frederick Law Olmsted since his days in architecture school, he marveled at the man's ability here, just as in Cherokee Park, to create something that appeared to be a completely organic, naturally occurring landscape, but which was actually a painstakingly orchestrated composition. Olmsted used terrain, trees, and rocks the same way a painter works in oils, Dan thought, or that Greg works with pigments, wax, and scratches.

The rest of the day and night passed uneventfully, and before long, Dan and Greg were boarding their flight home. Much to Dan's liking, they'd opted to upgrade for a bit more legroom. Greg didn't particularly need it, but Dan had come to dread having his knees smashed into the seatback ahead of him in standard economy seating. As soon as they sat down, Greg pulled out a small bottle and squirted his hands with hand sanitizer, rubbing them together until the alcohol evaporated. With silent resignation, and without Greg even looking at him, Dan held out a hand, knowing that Greg was about to dispense some for him, too, whether he thought he needed it or not. *If I didn't hold out my hand he'd probably never even notice and just squirt some onto my thigh.*

"See, you've learned," Greg teased. Dan grunted.

The alcohol had barely dried from their hands when Greg turned and started talking with the man next to him. Dan wasn't surprised. *Greg could strike up a conversation with a brick wall.*

"Looks like it's going to be a packed flight. We've been visiting and are headed back home to Louisville. How about you, are you from here in the city?" Greg asked.

"No, I'm actually from upstate."

Hearing the man's answer, Dan rolled his eyes behind closed eyelids and smiled. It wouldn't have mattered where the man had mentioned; the same thing was about to unfold.

"Oh, really? Whereabouts? Catskills? Capital region? The Adirondacks?"

"Oh—capital region."

"What part? Albany? Schenectady? East Greenbush?"

"You know East Greenbush?"

"Sure, it's not far from Fort Crailo; that's where the lyrics for Yankee Doodle were written."

"I didn't even know that," the man said.

"So, in East Greenbush, are you close to . . ."

Dan smiled, knowing that this would go on for some time. Greg had an impressive, sometimes almost preternatural, memory about a number of things, and geography was one of them. *He's a living, breathing GPS system. Before we get to Louisville, he'll know the poor guy's whole life story and they'll be sharing family photos,* Dan thought. He drifted off to sleep shortly after the flight attendant had retaught them the tricky process of fastening a safety belt.

CHAPTER 4

LOUISVILLE, SATURDAY, 6:50 A.M.

Just two weeks after their return from New York, Dan and Greg arrived at the airport again. Momentarily double-parked in the chill of the predawn November morning, they both hopped out of the car outside the departures area.

"Here, let me help you," Dan said. He pulled Greg's suitcase out of the trunk while Greg slipped his carry-on backpack over his shoulders.

"Honestly honey, that thing is so old and ratty looking," Dan complained. "People look at that damned thing and think you're a homeless person or something. People judge you based on first impressions, and that crappy old thing is making you look bad. I want people to see you in your best light."

Greg looked at the tattered bag. "I know, I need to get a new one someday."

"Someday. I've offered to buy you a new one dozens of times. All you have to do is pick out one that you'd like, and I'll get it for you."

"I know, I know. I've compared at least 20 of them; I set up a spreadsheet comparing all their features, and I've already eliminated at least 10 or 12 of them. I just need to know that I've picked the exact right one."

"Honey. I've been asking you to pick one for three years now," Dan complained. "How much longer do you need?" *I'd have looked at four of them, maybe five, and picked one in ten minutes*, he thought to himself.

"Just give me a couple more weeks," Greg said tersely, looking down at the sidewalk.

Dan realized he'd overstepped. He'd pushed too hard and at the wrong time. He quickly backed off and changed the subject.

"I'm sorry; that was stupid of me. What matters right now is that I know you're going to have a great time out there. And be sure to tell Bill I said hi when you see him."

The momentary cloud passed from Greg's face. "Oh, I absolutely will." He stood on the curb with his suitcase in one hand and the "Vieuxtemps Amati" in the other, beaming like a little boy about to hop on the bus for his first day of the new school year. "I'm really looking forward to all of it, and especially the competition, but one of the things I'm looking forward to the most is the luncheon the VSA is having to honor Bill and Judy on Tuesday. They really deserve it."

"I agree; that should be one of the high points of the whole convention," Dan said. "Safe travels. I'll see you in a few days." He reached out and gave Greg a big hug and a kiss.

"Aren't you worried about homophobes?" Greg teased as he returned the embrace.

"No, you're my husband, and I love you. I'll miss you, so I'm going to kiss you goodbye. If anyone standing around here doesn't like it, screw 'em."

"That isn't very nice," Greg chided. "I don't think I'd put it that way."

"Whatever words you want to use, the sentiment would be the same," Dan replied.

"Well, that's true. But it still isn't very nice."

They parted ways, and before long, Greg had cleared security and was boarding his plane. As he stepped into the cabin, he got the attention of one of the flight attendants.

"Excuse me, by any chance could you please see if you've got room in the crew closet for my violin? I hope I don't have to stow in in the overhead compartment. It isn't really a typical carry-on shape; plus, I don't want other people crushing it as they try to cram their bags in on top of it."

The flight attendant replied, "I can't promise anything, but let's take a look. . . . Oh, sure, we've got room this time." The attendant carefully took the case from Greg and stowed it in the closet.

"Thank you so much! I don't want to be a pain, but I just can't have anything happen to this violin, especially now. I'm a violin maker, and that one is about to go into a very important violin-making competition."

"Really? That's so cool! I don't know if I've ever met a violin maker before." The flight attendant smiled and reassured him. "Trust me, I get your concern. I know that there are hundreds of horror stories about musicians' instruments and air travel. I used to play the violin in a youth orchestra myself when I was younger, so I'm glad I was able to help."

With that detail resolved, Greg settled into his seat. Several hours later, after an uneventful flight, the plane finally arrived at LAX. While waiting for the passengers ahead of him to deplane, Greg quickly texted Dan to let him know he'd arrived. Once the aisle was clear, he grabbed his backpack and moved forward, stopping briefly to retrieve the violin.

"Here you go," the flight attendant said, pulling it out of the closet. "Thanks for flying with us today, and good luck at your competition!"

"Thank you!" Greg replied. He moved quickly down the jetway, into the terminal, and toward baggage claim. Several minutes later, he'd reclaimed his bag. He needed to get from the airport to the hotel in Anaheim, where the convention was taking place. Before leaving Louisville, he'd mapped out a route that would get him there inexpensively, using public transit, and now he called the route back up on his phone. Not familiar with the airport, he walked up to a man who appeared to be an information agent.

"Excuse me, could you help me? I need to take the bus to Anaheim, and I'm not sure where I board one." He held up his phone for the guard to see and explained the route. "I need to take this first bus to here, then transfer to another bus to here, then transfer to another bus that will take me very near the hotel. GPS says this is the best route."

The man looked at the route on Greg's phone, and then back at Greg. "Well, you could do this if you really want to, but let me give you some advice: GPS is smart, but it doesn't know everything. That route is having you transfer in some pretty sketchy places. I can tell you, I wouldn't want anyone in my family taking that route; I'd be afraid they'd get mugged. And if you don't mind my saying so, you look like a pretty easy mark, dragging a suitcase behind you, and, what is that, a violin?" the man asked, pointing to the case sitting next to Greg.

Greg's face fell. "I don't know what to do then. I looked at the ride share prices, and they're ridiculous."

The agent shrugged his shoulders. "Worth it if it saves your life.

Plus, you'd get to the hotel a lot faster."

Greg realized that he should probably take the man's advice. "I guess it would be money well spent. I'll do a ride share. Where do I do that from here?"

The man gestured to the glass doors just ahead of them. "You'll need to take one of the shuttle buses over to the remote pickup lot, where you can get one. And look, you're in luck: there's one loading up right now; you can still catch it if you hurry."

"Thanks very much for your help!" Greg said, and he hurried to the bus. He hopped aboard, stowed his suitcase on the storage rack, and sank into his seat, relieved that he'd taken the guard's advice and was on his way. For a moment, he closed his eyes and breathed deeply.

"You look like you just had a big load taken off your shoulders." Greg opened his eyes to see an old older man sitting next to him.

"I guess I have," Greg answered. Over the next couple of minutes, Greg told the man about why he was in town, and why this time in particular it was so important.

"I always pay a lot of attention to the violins I make, but it's been so long since we've had a competition, I've paid even more to this one. Even after the painstaking detail I put into the actual construction, I've spent hours and hours of work fine tuning it—different strings, cutting and recutting the bridge, repositioning and retightening the tailpiece, recutting and repositioning the soundpost to tolerances of thousandths of a millimeter."

"I had no idea that so much went into it," the man said, listening intently.

"Oh, all that and more," Greg said. "It's been a lot of hard work. But now, I can relax, or at least I should, anyway. The violin is ready to go. I've done everything I can to make it the very best it can be."

"That's the right attitude."

Feeling even more relaxed, Greg added, "Yes. It's a great instrument, and as far as whether it ends up receiving any awards or not, that's all in the judges' hands."

It was when he said the word *hands* that it hit him: he wasn't holding the violin!

Instantly, Greg's chest and throat constricted and his head pounded. In one horrible, panicked moment, he let out a terrible scream, startling everyone on the bus, and he jumped up, out of his seat. He lunged at the luggage rack and pawed through all the bags, even though he knew he hadn't put the violin there. He knew that in his rush to catch the bus, he'd left the violin sitting in the terminal.

Hardly able to speak, hardly able to breathe, he managed to yell out to the driver, "Stop! Wait! Stop! I have to get back to the terminal! I left my violin back there! No, no, how could I have done that?! I need to get back there!!!"

The driver tried to calm Greg down, but the bus kept moving. "It's OK, it's OK. I can't stop the bus here, and honestly, where we are now, the quickest way to get you back to the terminal is to finish this route—really, we're just about a minute away. We'll get you on the next bus back."

Greg's mind was racing. "Oh no, no, no, I have to get that violin back!" he groaned, his hands squeezing the sides of his head. "Hurry! Please hurry!"

"I promise, I'm doing my best," the driver told him. "In the meantime, I'm going to call dispatch and tell them to be sure to hold one of the buses headed back to the terminal for an emergency priority boarding."

"Thank you! Please, hurry, hurry!" Greg's body was literally shaking. True to the driver's word, it was just another minute before they pulled into the remote lot.

"Folks, obviously you've all heard what's going on here. Please just stay put for a second while we get this gentleman out first," the driver said. Greg collected his suitcase and backpack and made his way up the aisle to the exit, and the driver hopped off with him. Putting his hand on Greg's shoulder, he turned him toward the bus parked directly in front of the one they'd just gotten off and quickly guided him over to its driver, who was standing at the door.

"This is my friend Bandit," the driver said. "She's going to take care of you from here. I promise you, she'll get you there as fast as she can."

As Greg climbed on the bus, he told Bandit what had been left behind.

In a calm and confident voice, she told him, "Try not to worry. Like Carl, your first driver, said, I'll get you there as quick as I can."

But it was impossible for him to not worry. *How could I have done that?* he thought to himself. His feet tapped nervously, and he kept smacking his thigh with his hand as he impatiently waited for the bus to get him back. *All of that time and effort, and now it could be gone forever!*

As they rode back, Greg excitedly told Bandit about the violin, the convention, and the competition, as much to burn off nervous energy as to make conversation. Even though he was talking with Bandit, everyone on the bus heard what was going on. After several minutes that seemed like hours to Greg, Bandit pulled the bus back up to the terminal. Greg fidgeted, looking out the windows of the bus and trying to see through the glass doors into the terminal, trying to see if—

"Yes!!! Yes!!! It's still there!!!" he shouted. Against all odds, the violin case was still sitting, untouched, right where he'd set it down while talking with the information agent.

His whole body was shaking. Halfway between laughter and

tears, he babbled "Oh, Bandit, thank you so much for getting me back here so quickly! Thank you, thank you!!!"

Bandit smiled. "Hey, it's nothing; just doing my job."

Greg practically bounced off the bus.

"And good luck!" Bandit called after him. "I hope everything goes well for you from here on out!"

"Thanks, I sure hope so, too!" Greg called over his shoulder as he ran to the terminal.

With the violin in sight, Greg was starting to regain his composure. By the time he reached it, his pulse had stopped racing, and he was feeling much more at ease. He bent to snatch it up, but as he did, a voice behind him barked, "Sir, what are you doing?"

Greg spun around to see a middle-aged man in black dress slacks and a short-sleeved white shirt staring at him very seriously.

"This is my violin; I accidentally left it here when I got on the shuttle bus," he explained.

"I need you to show me some ID, and then you need to very slowly and carefully open the bag for me to inspect it."

"Well, OK, but before that, I think I need to see some ID from you," Greg replied.

The man grasped the lanyard hanging from his neck and flashed a badge, identifying him as part of airport security. As an unattended bag, Greg's violin case had become a matter of concern.

"Here, I'm serious, it's my violin," Greg explained, picking up the case and setting it on a nearby countertop. "Look," he offered as he slowly opened it. "Here's my ID." The man compared Greg's driver's license to the tag attached to the case. "This is really my violin. And it isn't just my violin; it's literally *my* violin. Look!" He lifted the violin and pointed through one of the f-holes on its belly, showing the man the maker's label inside bearing his name. "It's a brand-new violin I'm taking to a major competition, and—"

"Hold on, it's OK, I get it. Before you say anything else though, let me make a phone call. I need to call off the police and the bomb squad; they're actually on their way here right now." The man made the call while Greg conjured nightmare images of an evacuated terminal building, a SWAT team surrounding the violin that he'd poured so much of himself into, and a remote-controlled robot approaching the case to blow it to smithereens.

"Oh, I'm so glad I got back here in time!" Greg said to the security officer.

"Well, we were concerned, but we thought it was probably an accident. I mean, it was just sitting out in the open like that, where you'd expect to see a bag. There wasn't any attempt to hide it, and it didn't look unusual. We had to call it in as a matter of protocol, but honestly, the only thing that gave me any real concern at all was that it had a funny, chemical-y smell coming from it."

The comment gave Greg pause, until he realized that what the man had smelled was benzoin. A key ingredient in the French polish that Greg applied to all of his instruments, benzoin is a highly aromatic rosin that's also found in the incense burned in many Catholic, Orthodox, and Anglican church services. Greg had applied the polish just days before, and the smell was still strong enough that it emanated from the case. *If he's a churchgoer, he's obviously a Protestant if he didn't recognize that smell.*

After everything was cleared up, Greg was allowed to go on his way. He headed back to the shuttle pickup spot to catch the next one back to the ride share area. As it turned out, it was Bandit coming back around the loop.

"Well, hey, stranger!" she laughed. "Feeling better now?"

"Yep! Now it's on to the competition!" he replied with a big smile.

"Well, I believe that things happen for a reason," Bandit told him. "I think the fact that your violin was still there is a sign that it's destined for something special. It was meant to be in that competition. I bet that you're going to win an award, and later on, some great violinist is going to buy it from you."

"Oh, I hope you're right on both counts," Greg said. His body relaxed and he settled into the hard orange fiberglass seat, finally able to breathe again.

"Now listen," Bandit said, handing him a business card, "We're a private company, and we run airport shuttles to and from the major hotels all the time. When it's time for you to leave town, just call the number on this card and schedule a return trip back, and you'll probably save some money, compared with the ride share companies."

"Oh," Greg said, "I wish I'd known about you earlier; I'd have scheduled a trip out to the hotel with you. But now that I know, I'll definitely call you when it's time for my return trip."

This time, though, Greg had booked a ride share, and once Bandit dropped him off in the designated pickup area, he quickly connected with his driver. The hour-long ride from the airport to the convention venue in Anaheim gave Greg a reminder of just how spread out the greater Los Angeles area is. If the length of the trip made him impatient, the feeling dissolved when he arrived at the hotel. After a long pandemic pause, the convention and competition had finally arrived, and violin makers were streaming in to be a part of it.

Given what he'd just been through, Greg was leery of letting go of anything. Luckily for him, since his hands were full, a hotel staffer held the large glass door open for him. He crossed the honed-granite floor to the registration desk. The sprawling, sun-drenched atrium lobby housed the usual assortment of accommodations: restaurant, bar, a souvenir shop. Greg noted that this one had an added amenity: a gelato stand. *It looks really good,* he thought, *but maybe I'll wait to try it out with Dan.* In any case, he had other priorities. Getting his room key, he dodged other hotel guests and luggage carts rolling through the lobby on the way to the elevators leading him up to his room.

After quickly getting settled into the room and freshening up, Greg brought the Vieuxtemps Amati back downstairs to the competition registration desk.

The Violin Society of America had been hosting this competition, one of the most prestigious luthiers' competitions in the world, for many years. Employing the most rigorous attempts at anonymity possible, it judged not only violins, but also violas, cellos, basses, and their bows. There were also categories for not just single instruments, but also quartets—one of each of the four types of instruments, all made and submitted by the same maker or team of makers. The instruments were judged on both tone and artisanship. The tone judges were all highly acclaimed professional violinists, and the artisanship judges were all prestigious and award-winning instrument makers who were not entrants in the competition—for obvious reasons.

Greg approached the registration desk with his instrument. After showing a staffer confirmation that he was registered for the competition and signing in, he moved to the next table. There, he had to apply tape over his maker's label inside the corpus, or body of the instrument. He carefully slid the tape through the bass-side f-hole and gently tamped the tape in place over the label. While Greg rarely did it, some makers also stamped their name on the bridge of the instrument; any who did had to cover that as well, at this point of the registration process. The cover-up complete, Greg handed the violin to a second staffer who confirmed that there were no personal identifiers visible on the instrument.

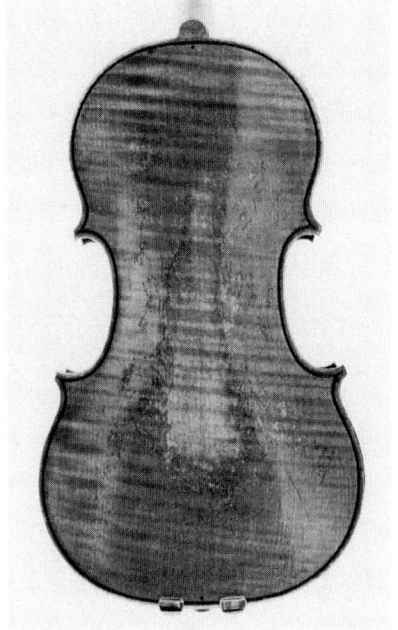

The Vieuxtemps Amati

The violin was then handed to a third staffer, who assigned it an entry number and placed a small label with just that number on an inconspicuous location on the instrument. That task completed, the staffer passed the instrument into the actual competition hall, via a fourth person behind double-baffle curtains. No one inside the hall would be able to see which maker was checking an instrument in.

It was a thorough system, and probably the best they could do to preserve anonymity. Still, the number of makers and industry professionals at this level comprise a relatively small universe, and while a layman might not be able to recognize subtle differences, those who were part of that universe could often look at these handmade instruments and recognize whose handiwork they were. Dan had commented that it wasn't even all that hard for him to recognize Greg's work. *After years of familiarity with my violins, Dan recognizes my scrolls and tuning pegs, if not other details.* Dan could easily pick Greg's work out of a lineup of a dozen or more makers' instruments.

Once he'd gotten his violin through the curtains and into the competition, Greg decided to make a quick stop in the vendors' hall to see which companies were attending. He had been wandering through the hall for a while when he saw a stall for The Violinist's Page, a bookseller specializing in modern, antique, and hard-to-find books related to violins and violin making. Greg had purchased a number of books from them in the past and had known its owner, Michael Page, for a number of years.

The Vieuxtemps Amati scroll

"Hi Michael, it's good to see you again," Greg said, greeting his old acquaintance, who was manning the booth. "I've been looking for a copy of a monograph about the Stauffer Amati viola put out by Cremona Books sometime in the 1990s. By any chance, do you happen to have a copy?"

Page thought for a moment. "We might. I'm pretty sure we have a copy or two of it in the store, but I'm not sure if I brought it with me for this event. If I've got it, it would probably be over here," he said, moving to a set of shelves on one side of the booth. Tipping his head back to better read through the bottoms of his bifocals, he scanned through several shelves of selections before announcing, "Yep, you're in luck. I do have one copy of it here. Do you want it?"

"Oh, absolutely," Greg said. He paid for the book and headed back out of the hall. *Well, that's a good find,* he thought. *That's getting the convention off on a good start.* He thought about taking the book up to his room before doing anything else, but as he stepped back out into the lobby, he saw the gelato shop again and thought better of his earlier decision. It was time for a treat. Dan could fend for himself when he got there.

"Greg!" He looked across the lobby toward the voice. There, dressed in khakis, a cardigan sweater, and his ubiquitous Trilby hat, was Bill Sloan.

Bill Sloan was a legend in the violin world. A very successful surgeon, he was both a gifted amateur violinist and a collector of fine violins. He made sure they were lovingly cared for by some of the most well-known violin dealers in the world. In addition to a number of extremely rare and valuable bows, Bill owned a beautiful 1742 Guarneri del Gesù violin, and even more impressively, the 1714 Jackson Stradivarius—one of the world's best known and finest sounding of all the surviving Strads.

Bill was also a talented amateur violin maker, and he graciously allowed both the Jackson and the del Gesù to be studied in great detail by a number of top makers. Greg had met him many years ago at another convention, and the two great minds, great talents, and even greater souls, quickly formed a lifelong friendship. From that time on, Greg and Bill were "benchmates" at the prestigious and exclusive violin makers' workshop held each year at Oberlin College in Ohio.

After three years of only connecting via emails and video conferencing, Greg was delighted to once again meet his old friend in person. He ran over to meet his friend, his face beaming. "Hey, Bill! It's so great to see you again!"

"Oh, you too, Greg! Hey, listen—I think the last time we were together, you, Dan, and I were eating ice cream at that great little shop in Oberlin. Let's pick up where we left off: let's get some from the stand, sit down, and talk."

"I was actually headed there myself," Greg laughed. After they'd each made a selection, the men sat down at a table in the lobby to talk about the convention schedule of events, catch up with each other's lives, and occasionally greet fellow convention-goers as they came through the lobby.

"Have you been to the rare instrument exhibit yet?" Greg asked, referring to the exhibit that Ping Yi had talked about in New York. It was actually one of the convention features Greg was most looking forward to, a showing of a dozen or so extremely rare and valuable antique instruments made by various members of the Amati,

Stradivari, and Guarneri clans. Under tight security, makers attending the event would have a chance to study these instruments up close.

"No, not yet," Bill replied. "They asked me if I'd put the Jackson and del Gesù in the exhibit, but most of the people here have seen them any number of times. In any case, I'd already agreed to lend the del Gesù to an amazingly talented young violinist for a concert this week. As I told you earlier, I did bring the Jackson, and I'll have the del Gesù here for most of the time, too." Even though he lived within the LA-metro area, given the sprawl and related travel times, Bill had booked a room at the hotel for the convention. "But as I said then, I want to keep it mostly under my hat that it's here. I've only mentioned it to a handful of people."

"No problem, Bill; I won't tell anyone. Are you looking forward to the luncheon?" In recognition of all of their generosity to the violin world, the VSA was hosting a special luncheon to honor him and his wife, Judy, at this year's convention.

"Actually, part of me wishes they weren't doing it," Bill said. "I mean, I'm genuinely honored, but I've always felt a little awkward receiving accolades like that."

"Really? You've earned it, you know—all that and more. I'm surprised that such an accomplished person hasn't gotten comfortable with receiving praise."

"No, I'm serious," Bill said. "Sure, it feels good, but it's also a little embarrassing, too."

Before Greg could reply, they were interrupted by Konstantin Pappas, a good friend of theirs. He was a distinguished-looking man with a thick crop of white hair, a friendly demeanor, and a sparkle in his eye. A native of Greece, Pappas was originally an engineer who had emigrated to the United States to work in the petroleum industry, and even now, decades later, his speech retained a heavy accent. Pappas had enjoyed a professional life that had been both personally and financially rewarding, but like Greg, Pappas had allowed his engineering expertise and his lifelong love of music to draw him into the luthier's world. And like Greg and Bill, Pappas was a regular at the Oberlin workshops. In the years following his career shift, he had produced instruments of great beauty and tone. In recent years, it was the rare competition where his instruments hadn't received some kind of recognition.

"Well, look at who I bump into," Pappas said with a smile, holding his hand out to Greg. "My friend, it's been far too long since I've seen you. Tell me, how have you been? How do you like living this side of the border, and being a Southerner, no less?" Greg had always liked Konstantin, not only because of the similarity of their engineering-to-violin-making trajectory, or the quality of his work, but especially because Konstantin was a genuinely nice person, and to Greg, that was more important than anything.

They pulled a chair over from an adjacent table, and the three of them spent most of the next hour catching up. Eventually, Bill decided to head back to his room for a while, and Greg wanted to attend a seminar about advances in violin-string manufacture. All three of them were walking through the lobby together when someone hailed them.

"Hi Bill, how have you been? Greg, long time no see! Isn't it great, all of us back together like this again?" It was Eric Morrison, a very talented luthier. A friendly, middle-aged man, he was a restoration expert with Stewart House Fine Violins, the London-based dealership that Bill retained to keep both the Jackson and del Gesù in top shape. In that capacity, Eric had known and been friends with Bill for over a decade, and Greg even longer, both men having graduated from the same violin-making school just a year apart.

"Hey Eric, I'm glad I bumped into you," Bill said. "Did you bring your tools?" Bill had told Eric a week earlier that he'd planned to bring the Jackson with him.

"Yep, I can make those adjustments for you while we're here," he replied. "I'm kind of tied up tomorrow, but how about sometime Tuesday?"

"That will be just fine," Bill said, "we'll figure out a time. I'll see you around later today." Bill waved goodbye and headed toward the elevators.

CHAPTER 5

LOUISVILLE, SUNDAY, 11:05 A.M.

The lobby area of Dan's church gradually filled as people flowed out of the worship service that Sunday morning, gathering in small clusters enjoying light refreshments, coffee, and conversation before they either made their way to the parking lot or to a Sunday School class. The small windows of time just before and just after the Sunday service were often the most hectic moments of Dan's week. He quickly moved through the building early in the morning, ensuring that all the logistical issues were resolved before the service began, making final adjustments to the sermon, getting buttonholed by parishioners asking that some last-minute announcement be made before the service, and so on. The time following the service was similarly chaotic. He routinely walked at least two miles just moving around the building on Sunday mornings. In the rush, he wasn't able to make the kind of deeper personal connections he'd have liked. But every Sunday, Greg worked the room in a way that Dan couldn't, and he provided Dan with important details of his conversations afterward. He was a godsend, and Dan was missing him intensely this morning.

Dan took care of necessary post-service duties as quickly as he could and joined the crowd in the gathering area, chatting and laughing with several parishioners before he had to slip into the adult Sunday School class he led. One of the parishioners was Ernie, an 80-year-old man of slight build who had just a wisp of hair left on the top of his head, a deep North Carolina accent, and the energy of someone 30 years younger. When visitors arrived at the church on Sunday, Ernie was often the first person to greet them, get them oriented, answer any questions, and just as often, to share some corny joke with them to help them feel at ease. Almost every Monday morning, Ernie would drop into Dan's office to offer his thoughts about the previous day's service or about something going on in the life of the church, or to just wisecrack a bit, laugh, and chew the fat. Ernie had been a bit uncertain about having a gay pastor when Dan first arrived, but the two of them quickly became friends—or the closest thing to friends that pastors can have with parishioners, since relationships between them always have to remain at arm's length. It was a requirement of the calling, one that resulted in many pastors being deeply lonely people. It isn't really being "friends" in the truest sense of the term, Dan often thought. Maybe call it being "friend-ish." Whatever it was, Dan had come to cherish the relationship with Ernie, and his Monday morning chats.

"So—not that I'm trying to get rid of you or anything, you know—but just when are you leaving?" Ernie teased.

"About 6:00 tomorrow morning," Dan replied. "I'll only be gone a few days. I'll be back before next Sunday, so you'll still have to put up with my smiling face in the pulpit next week. I know I'll have lots of interesting experiences on the trip. I'll be sure to work them all into the sermon, so bring a cushion and be ready for an extra-long one."

With mock dread on his face, Ernie groaned, "Gee, thanks for the warning; we'll be sure to go to the Methodist church next week. You know, we've been thinking about becoming members over there anyway."

"Oh, really? I have some of their brochures if you'd like. Here, let me get you one."

Ernie burst out laughing.

Across the room, Dan saw a visitor, a man in his mid-30s he'd noticed sitting in the pew with a stern look and his arms folded across his chest during the service. Dan walked across the room, smiled at the man, and reached out his hand as he introduced himself.

"Hi, welcome! I'm Dan, and you are . . . ?"

The man shook Dan's hand perfunctorily. "Cody."

"Well Cody, I'm really glad you visited with us today; it's nice to meet you."

"Do you think it's appropriate to use the house of God to spew liberal talking points like you did this morning?"

Well, good morning to you, too. "I'm sorry, Cody, what do you mean?"

"What I mean," the man said gruffly, "is that a supposed man of God should be preaching the blood of Jesus, shed to satisfy the wrath of God and to save sinners from eternity in hell. All I heard from you is that we should all be supporting leftist social programs and taking care of every illegal that swarms across our border. You need to forget all that and preach the Bible."

"That's exactly what I was doing. My sermon was based on those two texts we read from Matthew's Gospel. Do you remember Jesus's words in the first one: "You shall love the Lord your God with all your heart, and with all your soul, and with all your mind. This is the greatest and first commandment, and a second is like it: You shall love your neighbor as yourself. On these two commandments hang all the law and the prophets."

"Yeah," Cody complained. "But the most important way to love someone is to convict them of their sinfulness and get them to accept Jesus as their personal Lord and Savior so they'll go to heaven when they die, and you never once even mentioned that or had a time to give people a chance to do it."

"Well, no," Dan agreed, nodding his head, "you aren't likely to hear an altar call in most Presbyterian churches; that just isn't the way Reformed theology works. But to your point about salvation, we really did talk a lot about that, didn't we? That's what our second text, Matthew 25, was really all about. It's the only place in the Bible where Jesus talks about what that final judgment will be like, and it's fascinating. He says that we're actually going to be judged based on how we cared for the hungry, the stranger, the poor, the sick, the prisoner, all those who are suffering and in need, because we're all children of God. And while we need to do that in our personal lives, as a matter of faith, we also need to advocate for public policies that do those same things."

Cody huffed. "See, you're being political."

"Well," Dan said, "the truth is that Jesus's teachings are inescapably, unapologetically political. We really can't avoid it."

Cody shook his head. "You sound like some kind of woke 'social justice warrior.'"

Dan chuckled, "Well, I guess I am, Cody. Shouldn't all Christians be aware of other people's suffering and be concerned about social justice for all of God's people? I mean really, when did 'justice' become a bad word?"

Cody stood glaring at Dan with his arms folded across his chest. Dan smiled and said "Look, Cody, you and I may never agree about these things, but honestly, what I preached today came right from the Bible. It isn't a liberal thing or a conservative thing—it's a Jesus thing, and anyone who takes issue with it is just going to have to take it up with him. For better or worse, I'm just the messenger."

Cody turned and walked toward the door, mumbling that the Church had lost its way.

Ah well, if you aren't upsetting someone once in a while, you probably aren't really doing your job, Dan thought.

The man had barely gone when Dan felt a hand on his shoulder. He turned and saw Ernie again.

"What was up with that guy?" Ernie asked. "When he came in this morning, I greeted him and tried to joke with him, but he hardly said a word. He seemed like he had a chip on his shoulder about something."

"He probably did, Ernie. Personally, I think he already knew what our church was like, and he visited just so he could be offended. Some people just aren't happy unless they're unhappy, I guess."

Changing subjects, Ernie asked, "Since you're going to be gone, tomorrow, do you know what you want me to put on the sign this week?"

Dan joked, "Hmm, how about something like: 'Welcome

home, Pastor Dan, and special congratulations to his wonderful husband, master violin maker, Greg Zhu. Celebrate and enjoy your new gold medal!' "

Ernie laughed. "We only have four lines on the sign. Plus, we couldn't put that on both sides," he said while mentally counting. "It would take more E's than we have, and it always looks stupid when we have to use backward 3s."

Dan smiled. "Actually, I already wrote out what should go on the sign. It's in your mailbox."

That evening, Dan met up with a small group of friends that he and Greg had dinner with most Sunday evenings, in the home of Chet Hogarth and his wife, Shelly. Chet was the attorney who had handled the closing when Dan bought their house, and Shelly worked in the office alongside her husband. Chet had attended a well-known fundamentalist Christian college in Virginia before attending law school at the University of Louisville. Even though he wasn't religious at all these days, he could still talk the talk. He'd known at the closing that Dan was a minister in the Presbyterian Church—a liberal, apostate "false church" that was leading people into the very fires of eternal hell, according to the fundamentalists in both Chet's and Dan's pasts. Throughout the entire ballpoint ballet of signing, countersigning, and notarizing the mountain of legal documents, Chet had periodically dropped bits of Christian fundamentalism and the harshest bits of traditional Calvinist theology into the conversation, just to see how the liberal clergyman would respond. Dan had held his own in the conversation. He'd enjoyed the good-natured banter across the table. In addition to walking out of the room with a new home, he'd walked out with two new friends.

"Come on in!" Shelly called when Dan opened the front door. It had taken Dan at least a year before he felt comfortable just walking in without ringing the doorbell, but that ship had sailed long ago. Walking through the living room and around the corner into the kitchen, he saw Chet slicing a loaf of bread while overseeing several simmering pans on the cooktop. One of Chet's true passions in life was food. Whether it was something truly exotic or simple comfort food, what mattered most was that it be prepared in the best way possible, and shared with good friends.

"Hey, what's going on, folks?" Dan asked, giving Shelly a big hug. He turned to greet Jim and Cathy Findlay, and Jim's mother Liz, who were all seated around a small bar-height table.

He turned back toward Chet. "So, what's for dinner tonight, chef?"

"OK, so tonight," he said while intently working at the countertop, "in recognition of Greg being at a violin competition, and the fact that the city of Cremona was the home of the first great luthiers—"the birthplace of the violin"—we're going to enjoy a feast of traditional Cremonese dishes.

"Oh, that sounds intriguing," Liz Findlay said. "Sounds like we're in for a treat."

"Indeed, you are, Liz, and the first part is coming up right now," he said, rounding the granite counter and bringing a large wooden serving board to the table. "We start with a sampling of Cremonese cheeses."

Shelly pointed to the various items on the board, explaining, "OK, this is a Taleggio; then a Quartirolo Lombardo; and this harder one is Grana Padano, which is similar to a Parmigiano Reggiano but a little softer and delicate; I like it a little better. And finally, this is a smoked Provolone Valpadana." She grabbed a small cloth bag filled with precut pieces of a rustic, bakery bread from the counter and placed it next to the cheese board.

"And along with those," Chet said, ferrying more to the table, "we've got some absolutely to-die-for Salame Cremona, and a really nice Mostarda, which is basically a Cremonese chutney."

"It all sounds fantastic!" Cathy said. They dug into the delicious and wonderfully presented charcuterie.

Looking at Jim, Dan asked, "Did you swim this morning?"

Jim smiled and replied in a cheesy French accent, "But of course!" He continued without the accent. "Yeah, about a dozen of us swam eight miles in the river, around the island and beyond. Water wasn't really bad at all today, moderate current, temperature in the upper 50s."

Jim was a very accomplished cold-water swimmer who traveled around the world for various swim-run events and had even recently completed a team swim across the English Channel. He was one of Dan's parishioners and one of the top real estate agents in Louisville. He'd done an amazing job finding the perfect house for Dan, and during that process, he'd become good friends with Jim and Cathy. Dan recognized that this friendship with a parishioner was bit of pastoral rule-bending—or was it just hypocrisy? Either way, having long since recognized that the world wasn't black and white, but filled with scores of gray tones, Dan had made peace with it.

Shelly laughed and shook her head. "Oh my gosh. I saw Greg's group text last night about the whole bomb-scare incident! He must have almost died. I hope he's had a better day today."

"Yes, things have settled down and gone pretty well. He got his violin entered in the competition, he's already reconnected with a lot of his friends, and he's picked the seminars he wants to attend. He's basically in violin heaven at this point. I'm really looking forward to getting out there tomorrow."

"Well good," Jim said. "Now that all that's over, the rest of his week should be smooth sailing. I'm sure there won't be any excitement to top the competition."

"Did you all get the link for the livestream of the competition from Greg?" Dan asked.

"Yep. We'll be watching," Shelly said. "We're all pulling for him, because, well, you know, he's just so talented. And adorable; adorable, too."

"OK, everything's ready to go; it isn't getting any warmer!" Chet stood behind the beautiful spread facing the table from the peninsula counter. "First up, we've got a radicchio salad and several freshly made dressings, if you'd like. Then we move on to two different traditional Cremonese pasta dishes: Marubini Cremonesi, pasta stuffed with a blend of beef, veal, and a little bit of that Grana Padano, and soup— Marubini ai Tre Brodi—which has a slightly different blend of filling and pasta, and is served in a combination of chicken, beef, and pork broth. You really should try a bit of both of them.

"Next comes the main course: the definitive Cremonese entrée, Gran Bollito Misto."

"What's that?" Dan asked.

"Literally, a bunch of mixed boiled meats. I know; it sounds so much more exotic in Italian," Chet said, shrugging his shoulders apologetically. "So, you've got ox tongue, beef brisket, veal, chicken, and a Cotechino sausage. The Cotechino is maybe the most important ingredient in the whole dish, and it is just wicked hard to find anywhere outside of Italy. I actually had this shipped in from an amazing Italian deli in New York, and even at that, I had to know a guy just to get it," he said, with a bit of self-satisfaction. All the meats have to be boiled for hours, and all for different times, so I've been working on those bad boys for a lot of the day. You want to make sure you try a bit of all of them, along with a bit more of the Mostarda."

The group quickly filled their plates with the dinner, and their glasses with a wonderful hardy red that Shelly had selected to pair perfectly with the meal.

"Oh, this is delicious!" Dan said. "It's a non-violin Cremona masterpiece. I'm telling you, Nicolò Amati himself never ate so well."

"What lectionary text did you preach today?" Liz asked Dan. Liz was a lifelong, diehard Presbyterian, whose father had been a Presbyterian minister, and she and Dan always compared notes on the sermon he'd preached, and the one she'd heard in her own congregation.

"I actually went off-lectionary today, Liz. As you know, the news was filled this week with stories about horrible anti-immigrant, antiabortion, antigay, antiblack legislation being proposed in Washington and elsewhere, and all being loudly supported by radical Christian nationalists. I wanted to address that, and to do that best, I opted for some different texts."

"So, more to the point," Chet interjected, "what heresy did you preach today, you liberal apostate scum?"

Dan smiled. "Well, you'll be glad to know that I managed to tick off a visitor who called me a woke-snowflake-social-justice warrior before he stomped out of the building."

"Well, what do you expect? That's what happens when you stray too far from preaching the good old 'Romans Road,' " Chet said with mock indignation. "You progressives have strayed so far from your Calvinist roots—and of course, even *he* went to hell for his heresy. Election. Lack of free will. Predestination. Pfft."

"Let's just say I'm not going to lose any sleep over the incident. He wasn't the first, certainly won't be the last."

This group had become a very real, intentional family to Greg and Dan. Here, Dan could relax and be himself with little or no filter. Clergy can become exhausted by constantly being "on": portraying a version of themselves that is true, but tightly curated for public consumption. All clergy need a place, and a tribe, where they can feel completely at ease. For Dan, this was one of those. The fellowship and common meals enjoyed around this table was a different, but just as real, form of Communion for his own spiritual and mental well-being as anything served at the church.

After the dinner, Chet brought out dessert. "This is a Dulce Cremona," he announced as he presented a round, gear-shaped pastry baked golden brown, with a bit of turbinado sugar melted into the top. He cut the treat up and served it as Jim poured rounds

DWAIN LEE

of an exquisite 10-year bourbon that paired with it perfectly.

"When do you head out tomorrow?" Cathy asked before spooning a bite into her mouth.

"A little after six," Dan answered. "I'll have to get up pretty early. In fact," he said, pushing himself away from the table, "I should be leaving to get home and to bed." He gathered his coat, said goodbye to the group, and headed for the door. "Chet, tonight's meal was incredible! Greg is going to be so disappointed that he missed it."

"Oh, when you get out there, remind him to stop in at the House of Seasonings in Anaheim," Chet added. "He told me he'd swing by for me at some point. I've got a nice fava bean recipe that calls for winter savory, and I'm all out of it. I made a test batch of it with summer savory, but it just wasn't as good. Winter savory has an earthier, more subdued and less peppery taste that's just perfect with fava beans. If you aren't paying attention, it's easy to mistake one for the other since they look so much alike, but they're distinctly different. It isn't always easy to find, but I know Khalil, the manager there, and I know that they'll have it."

"Don't worry, we'll make sure to stop by," Dan said. "I wouldn't dream of forcing you to make fava beans with summer savory; that would be downright barbaric."

"Smartass," Chet deadpanned as Dan grinned. "Just make sure to get the savory, please."

82

CHAPTER 6

LOUISVILLE, MONDAY, 6:50 A.M.

Just as Greg had done days earlier, Dan boarded the plane and found his seat, next to a middle-aged woman apparently sending a few last-minute pre-flight text messages. Once she'd finished, she turned to Dan and asked, "So is LA your final destination?"

"Yes, it is," Dan said. "How about you?"

"Same here," she said. "I'm actually headed there for a conference for my work. So what do you do for a living?"

Dan hesitated ever so slightly before answering. "Well actually, I'm a Presbyterian minister."

An almost imperceptible smile crept over the woman's face. "I noticed you tensed up a bit before you answered. I think I know why, but relax, I actually work at the Center."

Dan focused more carefully on the woman's face. The Presbyterian Church (USA) is actually headquartered in Louisville, in a

downtown building that those in the know just called "the Center."
Dan had joked that given the ubiquitousness of denominational
big shots, mid-level managers, and staffers, serving as a minister in
Louisville was the Presbyterian equivalent of a Catholic priest filling
a position in the Vatican.

"Really? I know a lot of folks there, but I'm sorry, I don't think
we've ever met."

"No, I don't think so. I'm Angela Simpson-Lane; it's nice to
meet you."

"Likewise," Dan said with a warm smile.

"But you didn't want to tell a stranger on a plane that you're a
minister," she said in a manner that was half statement, half question.

"No, I didn't," Dan admitted. "Honestly, I considered just saying
I did something else, and you probably know why. When someone
asks what I do for a living and I tell them that I'm a minister,
they usually assume one of two things. They'll think I'm some
kind of radical right-wing extremist, or given the clergy sex abuse
scandals, they'll think I'm a child molester, or maybe even both.
Sometimes, it's the other option: the person who asked actually is
one of those right-wing extremists, and they get all excited and
start babbling a bunch of clichéd God-jargon, assuming that I
hold the same beliefs. Then when they learn that I'm a progressive
pastor, all bets are off."

Angela started to laugh. "Oh Lord, how many times I've been there."

"Of course, it only gets worse when they find out I'm gay, and horror of horrors, married to a man. They want to spend the rest of the flight locked in a theological debate aimed at getting me to see the error of my ways and renounce my flawed theology."

"And at some point," Angela said with a knowing sigh, "you know they're going to scold you and say, 'Read your Bible!!!' "

"Every. Single. Time." Dan shook his head. "I'd never actually do it, but there have been so many times when they've said that and I've been tempted to say, 'Well now, there's a thought. Oh wait—I do. Every day. In depth. Often in its original languages.' "

"The struggle is real," she agreed. "When I travel, if anyone asks what I do, I usually just tell them I'm a social worker or something, not an ordained minister, just to avoid those conversations. Ah, well." She paused for a moment, then continued, "What will you be doing out in LA?"

Dan told her about Greg and the competition.

"That's really interesting," she said. "I do have to say, 'Out, Gay, Presbyterian Minister' and 'World-Class Violin Maker' are both pretty small categories to be part of, and when you put them together as a couple, it's even more unique. Cool and interesting, but definitely unique."

Eventually the flight arrived at LAX. Dan said goodbye to Angela after they'd shared contact information and promised to connect once they were back in Louisville.

"Tell Greg I'm looking forward to meeting him, and good luck!"

Dan grabbed his gate-checked bag and made his way into the terminal. Greg had given him detailed instructions regarding where to get the shuttle to the ride share lot, and he headed in that direction. His path from the gates to the shuttles took him past the TSA security point for arriving passengers, where he heard "Dan! Hey, Dan!"

He was pleasantly surprised to see Nate and Charlotte Irving, a married couple from Louisville, just coming through the checkpoint along with another couple. Both Nate and Charlotte were academics, intellects, and visionaries, affiliated with two different universities in town, and both were very involved in racial- and other social justice initiatives. They were members of another church, but they were regular visitors, and he loved it when they'd show up on a Sunday morning.

"Hey, it's great to bump into you! What are you doing out here?" he asked.

"Believe it or not, we're out here for a Hollywood premiere," Nate told him. Introducing Dan to their friends, Nate explained that the friends' daughter was starring in a new movie, the second in a series of mysteries featuring a quirky but brilliant detective. *And not only brilliant, but ruggedly good looking, and it turns out, gay, too,* Dan thought. *All the better.*

"Wow, that's incredible!" Dan recognized the name of their friends' daughter. He turned to her parents and gushed, "It really is an honor and a pleasure to meet you. I think your daughter is an amazing actress. I love her previous work, and I'm really looking forward to seeing her in this film, too!"

"Oh, thank you, that's very kind," the actress's mother replied.

"I admit I've been looking forward to this movie ever since I heard there was a second one coming out. I accidentally stumbled across an online article filled with spoilers, so unfortunately the plot won't be a mystery, but I love how both this one and the first one play out as a concept."

"How do you mean?" the father asked.

"Well, it's how they deal with the suspects in the murder. They're all a collection of detestable people—horrible, parasitic underachievers—except for the one played by your daughter, in this movie. In most mysteries, the horrible characters are almost always red herrings, and the real villain almost always ends up being the likable, supposedly good one that no one suspects. These two films take a different course. The nice suspects actually remain nice, and innocent, to the end. And in this second one, the killer actually is one of the horrible people—the most horrible—who happens to be surrounded by other, merely garden-variety horrible people. Even in their detestability, they are underachievers."

"Ah, I see what you mean," Charlotte said. "Just when you think you know where to look, because you've become so jaded that you expect human goodness in these kinds of stories to be a deception, along comes a storyline that reverses the narrative, and at least to some degree, restores a person's faith in humanity."

"Exactly," Dan agreed. "Well, hey, I've got to run and catch up with Greg, but it's so nice to have bumped into you all out here. Safe travels home!"

Dan continued on to the curbside shuttle pickup. The next bus came along in just a few minutes, and he climbed aboard. He remembered Greg's experience on the bus and shuddered, imagining the panic Greg must have felt. The relief of getting his violin back must have been overwhelming. When he arrived at the ride share area, he asked the driver, "Do you know a driver called Bandit?"

The driver smiled. "Oh, yeah. Her real name is Felicia, but at work, she goes by Bandit."

"She did something really nice for my husband when he came through here the other day and left his violin behind in the terminal. Could you tell her that you bumped into that guy's husband, and he said thanks?"

"Oh, the violin? I heard all about that. As far as giving her your message, I don't need to. She's standing right over there." The driver pointed to a uniformed woman standing next to the bus parked just ahead of them. After hopping off the bus, Dan walked over and said "Hi, Bandit? I understand you helped my husband the other day when he forgot his violin."

Bandit burst into laughter. "That was your husband? Oh, dear sweet baby Jesus, he was about to blow a gasket until he got back to the terminal. But it was all OK; we got him taken care of."

"Well, it really meant a lot to him, and it means a lot to me, too. Thank you so much!"

"No need to thank me, but you are very welcome. You have a nice stay here in LA. Tell your husband you bumped into Bandit, and give him a big hug and a kiss for me."

Dan laughed. "Well, I'll do my best."

About an hour later, Dan arrived at the hotel. His architect's eye was immediately drawn upward to the sweeping steel structure that supported the sloped glass roof, forming a large triangular atrium lobby wedged between two towers of guestrooms. A few minutes before his arrival, Dan had texted Greg that he'd be there shortly, and just a minute or two after he'd arrived, he saw Greg smiling broadly and racing across the lobby.

"Hey honey, welcome to Anaheim!" Greg said as the two of them kissed and embraced, Dan making good on his promise to Bandit, and then some.

Suddenly, Greg winced. "Oh, I forgot to tell you—I found out about a shuttle that you could have taken to the hotel to save some money!"

"Well, it doesn't matter now. It's just good to finally be here." The two of them stood smiling at each other under the canopy of the large palm trees growing in the lobby. "So, what are you in the middle of right now?"

"Oh, I just stepped out of a lecture on the varnishing techniques of the Cremonese master luthiers. It's really fascinating."

"I'm glad you're finally able to get back in your element," Dan said. "What's on schedule later today?"

"Actually, for the first time ever, the VSA is hosting a reception for LGBTQ+ violin makers, and allies too, I guess. I thought we could go to that."

"Yeah," Dan agreed. "Let's plan on going. But for now, I think I'm going to get settled and maybe catch a quick nap. I'll let you get back to the fascinating world of Cremonese varnish." He winked playfully.

"Smartass. Oh, you'll need this," Greg said, reaching into his pocket. "Here's your room key." They kissed and headed their separate ways.

Later that afternoon, the two of them made their way to the hotel lobby. A large Progress Pride flag hung over the cash bar, where a good number of reception attendees were gathered, as an impromptu string quartet filled the reception area with Mozart's Hunt Quartet. They moved to the bar, where Dan ordered a gin and tonic for himself and a cola for Greg.

"Were any of the great historical violin makers gay?" Dan asked.

"Not as far as anyone knows, or even suspects."

"Darn. Would have been nice to have some 'family' in the violin-making pantheon somewhere."

"Well, there had to have been some," Greg offered. "We just don't know who they might have been. That's far less of a problem, now," he said, sweeping his arm outward at the people gathered at the reception.

While paying for their drinks, Dan noticed a poster displayed on an easel next to the bar. Most of it was a black-and-white, zoomed-in photograph of a violinist playing. Only the musician's chin, shoulder, and hands were visible. The featured violin had been edited to be rainbow-colored. Below the photo was the text: "Show Your Colors—A Place for the Queer Violin Community," along with a QR code leading to more information about the organization for LGBTQ+ luthiers, musicians, and others in the violin world.

Dan scanned the code with his phone and showed the site to

Greg. "Have you ever heard of them?"

"No, never," Greg said. "They must be new." Then he chuckled. "While I guess that graphic is kind of cool, I'd cringe if a violin were ever actually finished that way."

Dan sipped his drink. "I have to say, I'm still not totally comfortable with the term 'queer.' I mean, I don't mind using it when we're just among 'family,' but it's been a harmful slur for so long, I think I'll always have difficulty with using it in a more general setting."

"It's a generational thing, I guess. It's just a sign that you're getting old," Greg said with a twinkle in his eye.

Dan shot him a cold glance. "You're only two years younger than me."

"But you remember: however old we get, I'll always be younger."

"Screw you," Dan said in mock offense. Then smiling, he said, "Ah well, as long as we get old together; that's all that matters."

"Aw, that's so sweet—and so corny!" A woman's laughing voice broke into their conversation. They turned to see a thin woman in her early 30s with cropped and frosted blond hair. She was wearing black boots, skinny denim jeans, a black T-shirt, a denim jacket, and what appeared to be a hand-knitted scarf featuring muted, but beautiful, colors. A delicate silver nose ring adorned her right nostril; a less delicate single silver barbell passed through the upper half of her left earlobe. Next to her was an attractive brown-haired, similarly attired and accessorized woman of roughly the same age.

"Hanna, it's great to see you! Welcome back to the US—how have you been?" Greg turned to Dan. "This is Hanna Sullenberger, an incredibly talented violin maker. Hanna, this is my husband, Dan; I don't think you two have met before."

"No, I don't think we ever have," Dan said, extending his hand.

"It's nice to meet you," Hanna said to Dan as she shook his hand. Turning to the woman next to her she told him, "And this is my wife, Chloé Lavigne."

"Chloé, it's nice to meet you—and nice to meet another violin maker's spouse," he said.

Chloé rolled her eyes and smiled. "We'll have to swap horror stories over a drink."

"Hanna's a graduate of the Mittenwald school of violin making," said Greg.

"That's great," Dan said. "So I assume that you're originally from Germany?"

"Yes," Hanna replied. "I grew up in Kusel, a little town not far from Trier. But now, Chloé and I live in Paris." She mentioned the name of the very prestigious shop where she worked.

"Over my years of trailing Greg, I've met a number of really talented women makers," Dan said, "but the majority still seem to be men."

"Things are opening up a bit," Hanna said, "but worldwide, there's still a long way to go. When it comes to women gaining access to the highest levels, the violin-making world has its spruce equivalent to the corporate glass ceiling."

"Of course, being queer creates a second obstacle," Chloé added. Dan momentarily winced.

"I've obviously never had to deal with misogyny, but I've faced some homophobia from time to time," Greg said. "I made a violin once, shortly after Dan and I met, and on its label, I included the inscription, 'Dedicated to the man I love, Dan Randolph.' I got blowback from the dealer, who said the inscription would limit people interested in buying it. He told me I should replace the label."

Hanna shook her head. "So, what did you do?"

Greg offered a slight smile. "I replaced the dealer."

"Perfect!" Chloé said with a smile.

"Not only that, but within a couple of months of the violin being in another dealer's shop, it was bought by a member of the New York Phil, and it's being played routinely at Carnegie Hall to this day—with its original label intact."

"Isn't it nice when the good guys win once in a while?" Hanna asked.

Greg nodded. "Hanna, changing gears: Bill Sloan said that he told you he'd have the Jackson with him. Are you going to be looking it over while you're here?"

"Tomorrow, actually," she replied. "I'm currently making a violin that will be based a lot on the Jackson, and I wanted to look at it one more time, in person, while I've got the chance. I'm going to swing by the antique instruments exhibit early in the morning, and then I'll stop by Bill's room to spend a little bit of time studying it." She took a breath, then asked, "Will you both be at the awards banquet on Thursday?"

"Absolutely," Dan said. "Obviously, I'm not an actual attendee at the convention. I'm just here to sightsee and be arm candy for Greg," he joked. "But yes, we did buy two tickets to the banquet, and I'm really looking forward to it."

"Great!" Hanna said. "Chloé and I will both be there too; maybe we can sit together."

"We'd love to!" Greg offered enthusiastically.

"Well, that is something that I'm going to be very disappointed to miss." The group turned to see Eric Morrison, who had come up behind them.

"Hi, Eric." Hanna's voice was flat.

Eric responded tentatively. "Hanna, this is the first time we've seen each other since the job thing. We've always been friends, and I hope we can clear the air about that. I know that Malcolm strung you along, a lot, before giving me the job instead of you."

"His decision did come as a shock."

"I'm really sorry he did that to you. You deserved better treatment."

The opening of the impromptu string quartet's rendition of Schubert's "Death and the Maiden" filled the momentary pause in the conversation.

"Yes, I did," Hanna affirmed. "But you know, it ended up working out fine. I love the job I've got now, and to be honest, I much prefer living in Paris over London."

"In my completely unbiased opinion, I agree," Chloé said.

"Well, I just wanted to say that I'm sorry about all that, and I hope we can still be friends," Eric offered, more a question than a statement.

The quartet continued to provide background. Hanna sighed and smiled. "Eric, I'm not going to lie; I was really upset with you at first. But I could never stay mad at you for very long; I've known you too long. Plus, it wasn't you who screwed me over; it was Malcolm."

Eric nodded his head sadly. "Well for what it's worth, as you can undoubtedly figure, working for him is no picnic."

"How long have you been working for him?" she asked.

"Oh, for years now. And he actually dangled that position over my head like a carrot for a couple of years before it was even available. He told me I had to "dazzle" him to prove I deserved it, and I did. But when it did become available, he still tried to fill it from outside, and even once he did decide to hire me, he only paid me a fraction of what my predecessor had made. He said that part of my compensation was just the prestige of working for him and being able to work on the world-class instruments that his shop took care of."

"Eric, if I could wish anyone had that job other than myself, it would be you," Hanna said. "I'm sorry that it comes with the baggage of having to put up with him. For all that you do for him, Malcolm should be kissing your feet."

"Some days I'd like to tell him to kiss something, anyway."

"Why don't you just start your own shop?" Chloé asked. "Half of Stewart's clients would probably follow you."

"It's simple," Eric said. "Money. You can't survive just on rare and high-end repairs and restoration; you have to sell instruments, and to have the size and quality of inventory a shop like that would take, you've got to have very, very deep pockets—which I definitely don't." Dan certainly understood that; his own architectural firm started with just a couple thousand dollars, and while it eventually did all right, it always suffered from undercapitalization.

After a pause, Eric said, "It really isn't so bad, you know. In some ways, I really do feel fortunate to work in his shop—to work with the instruments, and the clients, that come through. Some days, it really is a dream job." Setting his empty glass on an adjacent table, he glanced at the time on his phone, ending the conversation abruptly.

Maybe he thought that his words could rekindle Hanna's hurt, Dan thought. *Seems like a decent guy.*

"I need to get going," Eric said. "It's been good to see you all again, and Hanna, I'm glad that we're OK."

"We're OK," she said. She gave him a friendly peck on the cheek before he walked away.

Dan used the moment to retrieve fresh drinks for himself and Greg. While waiting for them, he thought about the conversation between Eric and Hanna. From past encounters, he knew that they had been referring to Eric's boss, Malcolm Stewart III, the owner of Stewart House Fine Violins. The very prominent London-based dealership had been a family-run operation since its inception and was now being run by the grandson of its founder. The company had a long-standing and prominent reputation in the violin world.

Just as Dan was returning from the bar, Chloé asked Hanna. "So have you bumped into Stewart here yet?"

Hanna's face went sour. "Yes," Hanna said, "I saw him holding court with a handful of hangers-on yesterday, striking poses in his custom-tailored suit in the middle of a convention full of jeans-wearing violin makers. Pompous, self-absorbed jackass." Dan knew that her assessment was shared by many.

"Greg, I'm sure you remember that the head of Stewart's restoration department was one of the early victims of Covid," Hanna continued. "After he died, I interviewed for the position via video conference. We talked several times, and everything seemed very promising. I fully expected him to offer the position to me. But then he just went quiet, and I learned later that he'd promoted Eric Morrison from within."

"I remember reading about Eric getting that job," Greg said, "but I didn't know you'd been up for it, too. Did Malcolm ever tell you why he went in that direction?"

". . . and here it comes," Chloé said.

Hanna tensed. "Oh, yes, I contacted Malcolm as soon as I heard and asked why he'd decided to go with Eric. He just offered a condescending smile and said 'Well, my dear, you're obviously a very talented person, and you could undoubtedly do the work. But I thought that my clientele would be more comfortable having a more, shall we say, *traditional* person overseeing the restoration work on their valuable instruments.' "

"I'm really sorry you had to deal with that, Hanna," Dan told her.

Chloé's analysis was more blunt. "Pig."

Hanna sighed. "And you heard what I said to Eric. I meant it. Somewhere deep down, I want to hate him, but I just can't. He is very talented, he's a nice person, and professionally, he's always been very helpful to me. He's just . . . just . . ."

"Just another straight, middle-aged man who took a job that you should have had?" Chloé suggested.

"Exactly," Hanna said. After a pause, she offered a half-laugh and said, "I hate that I don't hate him."

"I know, I actually kind of like him, too," Chloé conceded. "He is a nice guy, and he has always been a good friend to you. Of course," she added, "I'll always hate Malcolm Stewart."

"Of course," Hanna agreed. Dan watched her face as she seemed to momentarily wallow in her dislike of the arrogant old man. Then her appearance softened as she said, "I'm often pretty cynical. I generally consider myself a nihilist, even. But you know," she said as she turned back to Chloé, "when I feel this beautiful scarf you made wrapping around me, embracing me, I don't worry about the Malcolm Stewarts of the world, and I feel more optimistic and maybe even hopeful. Maybe life actually has real meaning."

"Aw, that's so sweet—and so corny!" Dan teased.

Hanna laughed. "Touché, Reverend."

Greg noticed Bill and Konstantin standing just outside the hotel doors, apparently getting a bit of fresh air. "Oh, hey, I need to see Bill about something. Hanna, Chloé, take care; I'll talk with you later!" He made his way across the lobby. Dan waved goodbye to the two women and followed Greg.

"When are you going to swing by and try the Jackson out?" Bill asked Greg, as soon as he entered the lobby.

"That's exactly what I wanted to ask you. How about tomorrow afternoon?" Greg asked.

"Sure. I'm going to visit some friends, but how about right after I get back—maybe around 2:00?"

"Perfect, we'll see you then!"

CHAPTER 7

ANAHEIM, TUESDAY, 7:50 A.M.

Following his morning walk, Dan quietly showered and left the room again, allowing Greg to sleep a bit longer. He returned to the lobby and settled into a table in the dining area. Before he had even ordered, he saw Bill Sloan approaching, and he motioned for him to share the table. Within a couple of minutes, both men had ordered and were chatting over coffee.

"Bill, we bumped into Hanna Sullenberger last night, and she mentioned she'd be meeting up with you today," Dan said. "What else is on your schedule?"

"It's going to be pretty busy," he said. "Judy and my daughter Jackie will be arriving to attend the luncheon, but even before that, I'm going to get together with Alana Marino to play a duet, and right after, Eric Morrison will swing by to do those tonal adjustments. After the luncheon, Judy and I will visit the friends I mentioned last night, and at some point in the afternoon, Greg is going to stop by.

What's he up to?"

"Well, I know that he wanted to get into the vendors' hall to shop for tone wood, and maybe to buy some bridge blanks. At some point today, he'll hit the antique instrument exhibit, and I'll try to check it out too, as long as I'm not taking a spot from any actual attendees waiting to get in."

They chatted a while longer, but as the server removed their empty plates from the table, Bill said, "Hey, what are you doing right now? If you don't have any specific plans, why don't you come on up to the room? Konstantin will be stopping by, and Hanna will be there a bit, and then you can hear Alana's private performance."

"Honestly, I don't have anything specific planned right now, so sure; that sounds good."

At about quarter to ten, the two men took the elevator up to Bill's floor. Stepping out of the elevator lobby, they could see Hanna Sullenberger and Konstantin Pappas standing in the corridor in front of Bill's room, engaged in a conversation.

"Hey, I hope you weren't waiting here too long," Bill called to them.

"Not at all," Hanna said, "we just got here." Bill opened the door and the four of them stepped inside.

"I want to thank you again for letting me do this," Hanna said. "You're very generous, and I really appreciate it."

"Not a problem at all," Bill said.

Hanna slipped her scarf from around her neck and set it aside as she sat down at the window-side table. "Hanna, I'll just watch you if you don't mind," Dan said as he slipped into the chair opposite her.

Bill retrieved the black case holding the Jackson and set it in front of Hanna. She reached over to it, felt the alligator-skin texture of its exterior, and opened it, each of the three nickel-plated latches offering a gentle pop as they released under the coaxing of her fingers. She lifted the lid to reveal the Jackson, encased in a silk bag and nestled in the form-fitted tan velvet interior. Gently taking the violin by its neck and bottom button through the silk fabric, she eased it out of the case and removed it from the bag. With one hand, she gently spread the bag over a towel padding the tabletop and placed the Jackson on top of it.

"No matter how many times I see it, it's still just as beautiful and exciting to hold as the first time," she said, to no one in particular.

"Here," Bill said. "I brought you this to help." He offered her a pair of headband-mounted magnifying goggles, equipped with high-power supplemental lighting.

"Thank you, Bill; for most of what I'm doing this daylight will be good enough, but they'll definitely be helpful for some detail I'd like to pay particular attention to." She slipped the device around her head and used the knob to adjust the headband for proper fit, then took it off and set it aside. As Dan watched, she began to intently study the instrument. Holding it up in her hands with the belly toward her and the back toward Dan, she slowly turned it in the sunlight. "There, look at the back," she said. He recognized from both Greg's work and his own architectural background that the maple back had been "book-matched": one thick piece of wood had been split, and the two resulting halves flipped open like a book and jointed together with a center seam, causing the resulting single piece to have a pleasant, mirror-like appearance in its texture and grain.

"When that back was first carved, its surface was practically as smooth as glass, but look at it now. Over the years, the grain has moved—'breathed.' The internal strains in the flame pattern in the grain have released, so that now there are subtle ripples in its surface that are visible in the sunlight," she explained. "As I'm working on my own Jackson-based instrument, one of the questions I have to answer is how much of that time-induced rippling I want to recreate. I spent a huge amount of time and effort finding just the right piece of maple with grain characteristics that would make my back look very, very much like the Jackson, but how much of that rippling should I actually carve into my back to replicate its current look? Or should I try to recreate it at all? Should I just let time take its course naturally, as it did with the original? I know a number of makers who have modeled instruments on the Jackson, and some try to replicate its current appearance, while others try to make something consistent with what it must have been like when it first left Stradivari's shop."

Hanna set the violin back down and clipped a macro lens onto the camera on her smartphone and took several photos detailing the purfling—the extremely small, stained strips of wood inset near the outer edges of a violin back and belly. Before meeting Greg, Dan had always assumed this detail on violins was decorative—"violin racing stripes," as it were, painted on just for aesthetics—but now he knew they were actually examples of intricate artisanship that served as edge banding to help prevent the wood from splitting along the grain lines. After taking the pictures, Hanna slipped the headgear on momentarily while she took extremely precise measurements of the distance between the purfling and the outside edge of the belly, especially around the pointed corners at each end of the C-bouts, dutifully jotting down each dimension in a small notebook.

"Dan," Hanna asked, "could you help me by holding it up while I take the same measurements on the back?" Dan was glad to help, but he was extremely nervous about the idea of holding, and possibly dropping, such a rare and valuable thing. He delicately took the violin from Hanna, left hand on the neck, right hand at the end button, uneasily holding it out away from himself.

Bill glanced over and laughed. "Come on, don't be so shy! Hold her with confidence; hold her close, like you would with a beautiful woman!"

"Well, a guy, actually, but I get your point," he laughed, and the tension broke. He was able to hold the Jackson with more confidence and stability while Hanna took her photos and measurements. As she did, Dan looked across the room and saw Konstantin, who was engaged in a text conversation with someone. After few moments, Konstantin said "Bill, I'm sorry I won't be here to see Alana, but I'm afraid I've got to go take care of some business. I'll catch up with you a little later."

"OK. I'll see you in a while," Bill called as his friend headed toward the door.

As arranged, Alana Marino knocked on the door, right at 10:00.

Bill smiled as he ushered her into the room. "Alana, it's great to see you again. Hey, there are some people here I'd like you to meet." Moving toward the table, he continued, "This is Hanna Sullenberger, a great violin maker working out of Paris these days." The two women could hardly have been any more different in physical appearance.

"Hanna, it's wonderful to meet you," Alana said as she offered her hand. "It's always good to meet another woman who has excelled in a profession traditionally dominated by men. So tell me, do you have an instrument in the competition this year?"

"Yes, actually, I do," Hanna replied. "You'll be trying it out soon in your judging, if you haven't already."

"And this is Dan Randolph. He's the husband of Greg Zhu, another great maker in the competition."

Alana smiled warmly. "Oh, I know Dan; I met him and Greg at June's shop in New York. How are you?" she asked, shaking his hand in turn.

"I've been well, thanks," Dan replied. "I hope you've been well, too. Actually, Alana, I saw a big photo of you on the side of a bus while I was out for a walk yesterday, part of an ad for the orchestra."

"Oh, that," she rolled her eyes and laughed. "It's flattering, I guess, but it's also a little embarrassing. I think I look silly in it."

"Oh, come on, silly?" Bill joked, "Alana, you'd turn heads if you showed up at a black-tie affair in a pair of sweatpants."

"Bill," Hanna said, "I actually think I've got all that I needed here. Thank you again, so much, for letting me do this."

"And again," Bill assured her, "it's my pleasure. Just leave the Jackson there on the table; we'll be using it in a minute."

After Hanna's departure, Dan watched as Alana took the Jackson from where it had been resting. She played a few scales, then moved into playing a bit of the opening movement of the Bach Unaccompanied Violin Sonata no. 1 in G Minor. She dug into the opening rolled chord of the piece, immediately moving up through the two-octave span that calls the listener to attention, then slowly, soulfully continued through the piece, effortlessly conjuring melancholy from wood, metal, and horsehair until she felt sufficiently warmed up.

As beautifully as Alana played it, Dan still stifled a smile. He'd mentally predicted it would be the first thing she'd play. *It's the first thing almost everyone plays,* he thought, having heard countless violinists trying out instruments in exhibitions over the years—and with good reason, since the opening of this particular piece gave violinists a good quick sense of an instrument's overall character, tone, and playability.

"I'll bet violin salespeople get as tired of hearing that piece as piano salespeople do when they hear Fur Elise 50 times a day," Dan had once joked to Greg.

"Bill, it sounds wonderful," Alana said as she completed her warm-up.

"It really does, and it's about to sound even better; Eric Morrison will be stopping by in a little while to do some tonal adjustments."

"I absolutely love my own Guadagnini," she said, "but oh, the Jackson is heavenly!" Dan didn't know much about Alana's violin, but he'd seen some of Guadagnini's instruments in the past and knew that he'd been a premier Italian luthier during the latter half of the 18th century.

"Are you ready to give the Bach Double a go?" Bill asked, picking up the Jackson and playing a few scales.

"I've been looking forward to it ever since you suggested the idea," Alana replied, opening the case she'd brought along. Dan noticed that it was an oversized, double case, but at the moment it was only carrying one instrument.

"Do you have another violin besides the Guadagnini?" Dan asked.

"Oh, yes, I do," she replied as she pulled the violin from the case. "I also own a lovely 1675 Jacob Stainer. Authentic instruments from the time period are better suited to playing baroque music, while the tone of the Guadagnini is more appropriate for post-baroque and more modern classical compositions."

Dan loved being privy to the fun, informal performance about to begin, especially of this particular piece, Bach's Concerto for Two Violins in D minor. He'd once heard Bill and Greg play the same piece at their violin makers' workshop in Oberlin, Bill on his del Gesù and Greg on the Jackson.

The violinists began as Dan settled on the loveseat opposite where they were seated. The consummate professional and the gifted amateur began the piece, which was very different from, but every bit as evocative as, the sonata Alana had played earlier. The first movement of this piece was always uplifting to Dan. It was simultaneously energetic and joyful, and Dan loved listening to them move through it. The second movement was a slower, calmer piece that created an overall feeling of rest and contentment. To Dan it had always evoked the image of a person thoughtfully examining their life and being grateful, recognizing that God, or fate, or maybe just blind chance, had been kind to them, that life, even with its challenges, was good. Finally came third movement, an exuberant, almost frenetic piece that placed a high emotional and physical demand on its players and that serves as the pinnacle of the entire concerto—a musical exclamation point that routinely brought audiences to their feet in instinctive applause. It brought Dan to his as well.

"Bravo! Bravo!" he exclaimed as they finished.

"Wow!" Bill added. "That was wonderful; thank you, Alana!"

"Oh no, thank you," she corrected him. "Thank you for the opportunity to play the Jackson, yes, but more importantly, to see you again, my dear friend, and for the opportunity to spend time with a new friend, too," she said, nodding to Dan.

Just then Bill's phone pinged, indicating a text message. He glanced at it and apologized. "Hey folks, I'm sorry to break this up, but it's my daughter Jackie. She's just arrived downstairs to attend the luncheon, and I need to meet her before getting back up here to meet Eric."

"Oh, that's fine, Bill," Alana said. "Just like you, I actually reserved a room here at the hotel for the next few nights to avoid commuting back and forth, and I need to check in. But we've got to do this again, soon."

"Absolutely! Next time at our place."

"Bill, it's been great spending some time together," Dan said. "I'm sure I'll see you later today, but enjoy the luncheon!"

While Dan spent time with Bill, Greg did some serious shopping in the vendors' hall of the convention. The large space was filled with exhibitors' booths selling violin-related materials, accessories, and books. Quickly scanning the room, Greg noticed a vendor he was particularly interested in and walked over to his table.

"Hey, Henri, it's Greg Zhu. Do you remember me?" He reached across the table to shake the hand of a slender young man with dark hair and a mustache.

"Of course. It's good to see you again," the man replied. "Did those chinrest clamps you bought last year work well for you?"

"Like a dream; thanks for recommending them to me. Today, though, I'm looking for some good bridge blanks."

"We have some here." Henri pulled out a large container filled with maple bridge blanks, cut to roughly proper shape. Violin makers begin with these blanks, which they then refine further to get their desired fit, acoustical benefits, and to some extent, aesthetics. The bridge is meticulously positioned between the f-holes of an instrument in a location that maintains the proper developed length of the string from the nut at the top of the neck to the bridge. The bridge keeps the strings the correct height above the instrument's belly, and at the proper tension, and it transmits the vibrations of the strings into the wood of the belly.

"Here, let me make some space for you to sort through them, out of the main aisleway." Henri cleared a bit of tabletop around the corner from the main display table, near the back wall of the booth, where Greg could examine and test the blanks with at least a hint of privacy and quiet.

"Thanks, Henri." Greg pulled out a small digital scale and a pair of calipers from his pocket and set them on the table next to the container of blanks, pulled up an a folding chair, and sat down. He also removed his eyeglasses, replacing them with a higher-magnification pair of reading glasses he'd been carrying in a lapel pocket. Pulling out a blank, he held it up and examined the tightness and other characteristics of its grain. If it was in his parameters, he weighed it. If that checked out, he then he noted its thickness and took measurements of the blank at several critical spots. He carefully ran each one through a list of characteristics that he demanded for all of his bridges.

He had reviewed 25 or 30 blanks, and selected 5, when he heard voices nearby, behind the back wall. In the space behind Henri's booth and the booth fronting on the next aisle over, he saw Alana Marino speaking with a man he didn't recognize. She looked irritated. Their conversation was muted, but Greg thought that he heard Alana tell the man, "I told you I'd take care of it, and I will. You'll have it soon." The man's reply was brusque: "Just remember you've got a lot riding on this. We need to get this done."

Alana started to answer, but just then, Henri set another box of bridge blanks in front of him. "I'll bet you'll find some to your liking in here, too."

"You know, Henri, I think I'll just take these five. I'll probably swing by again during the convention, but for now, I'll settle for these."

Greg moved on to a vendor who was selling spruce and maple tone wood for instrument bellies and backs. He had been there for a little while when he heard his name being called out.

"Greg! Hey, Greg!"

It was Dan. "Hey, honey, how's it going?" Dan filled him in about his morning, then asked, "What have you been up to? Finding any good wood?"

"Yeah, I found a few pieces I think I'll get," Greg said as he showed them to Dan. "I'm pretty sure I'm going to get this piece of maple too." He held it up from its edges with both hands, slowly turning it to see the flames in the grain dancing in the light.

"Nice," Dan said. "I'll bet that will make a really beautiful back."

"Yes, I think so," Greg agreed, and turning it up to its edge he added, "and the end grain is what I'd want for this piece of wood. Now let's check it for stiffness." Dan watched as Greg pinched the piece of wood between his thumb and forefinger about a quarter of its length from the top, allowing it to hang almost like a pendulum. Holding it up to his ear, he knocked on it with his other hand, rapping it with a knuckle about a quarter of its length from the bottom. "For technical acoustical reasons, it's important that I hold it and knock on it at those one-quarter locations. Doing that evokes the wood's fundamental frequency, because those points are—"

"It's okay, no need to explain it any deeper; you're already over my head." Dan tried to stop him as gently as possible, but Greg still shot him a disapproving look. Then he continued.

"Listen," he said. "Do you hear that sound?" He rapped the wood again. "For wood of the same size and thickness, the higher the pitch of that tone, the stiffer the wood is."

"That seems to make sense. I take it that stiffer is better?"

Greg squirmed. He hated categoricals. "Well, assuming the wood's density and all other things are equal, yes. But," he quickly added, "all things are rarely equal, so I need to do a lot of complex analysis. I need to look at—"

Just then, Greg's phone pinged with a text message. Glancing at it, he saw that it was from Bill.

"I'm going to finish here and go meet up with Bill," Greg said.

"OK. I think I'm going to relax and read a bit," Dan said, giving Greg a quick kiss. "Talk with you later."

A couple of minutes later, Greg came around the corner into the palm tree-filtered sunlight of the hotel lobby and saw Bill, sitting in a comfortable chair and chatting with his daughter Jackie, whom Greg had met numerous times.

"Hi Greg, I hope I didn't pull you away from anything important," Bill said. "I thought you might like to say hi to Jackie; she just got here for the luncheon."

"You bet. Hi, Jackie. How are you? It's been a while!"

"Good seeing you again, Greg. I hope you've been well since we met in Oberlin."

The three of them had been casually chatting, catching up with things for about half an hour, when they were interrupted.

"Bill, it's so good to see you again," Phil Goodman said, inserting himself into their conversation. "I've got so much going on with convention logistics, the luncheon, and of course, as usual, volunteering to help with the competition, but I was just coming through the lobby and saw you, and I had to at least stop for a moment to say hi."

Bill smiled politely and nodded. "Hi Phil. You know Greg, I'm sure, and this is my daughter Jackie."

"Yes, Greg Zhu, yes. I've heard good things about your work," Goodman said with a smile. "I've heard some people say that with a few more years of seasoning, your violins might be as good as Anthony Hutchinson's."

Idiot. They're already better, and they have been for years, Greg thought. He maintained decorum, silently shaking Goodman's hand while internally seething.

"Oh, it's actually a good thing to have bumped into you," Goodman said. "I was at a bookseller's display in the vendors' hall, and they told me you'd bought their only copy of the Stauffer Amati monograph. Would it be possible for me to borrow it, just for a day or so? I'd really appreciate it."

After his earlier slight, extending a favor to Goodman was the last thing Greg wanted to do, but out of politeness, he said, "Sure, I can let you look it over for a little while."

"Wonderful, thank you so much!" Goodman immediately turned, physically and emotionally, away from Greg and focused all of his attention on Bill and Jackie.

"It's an absolute pleasure to meet you, Jackie!" Goodman reached to shake her hand. "I assume you're here for the luncheon?"

"Yes, my mother and I will both be here."

"Well, I was part of the luncheon planning committee, and the buffet and program that we've put together is going to be a wonderful tribute," Goodman gushed.

Even while complimenting someone else, you can't avoid self-promotion, Greg noticed.

"Your father is such a great man. I don't think it's an exaggeration to call him a national treasure, an important and beloved part of the violin world." His fawning continued, "I can't think of any single individual who's done more for violins, violin makers, and violinists. It's an honor just to know him, and I'm proud to be able to call him a friend. You must be so proud of him, too."

"Oh, yeah," Jackie replied with a stifled grin. "He's a peach."

After a momentary pause, Goodman's tone changed, and looking at Bill, he tentatively continued. "Bill, I was just curious—by any chance, do you happen to have the Jackson with you? If you do, I'd love to get a look at it, even if just for a few minutes."

Bill's face twitched slightly, and he visibly squirmed in his chair before answering. "Well, yes, I did bring it, but I'd really prefer to keep that under my hat, so please don't mention it to anyone else." He thought for a moment and continued, "We've got some family plans through mid-afternoon, but if you'd like, maybe you could swing by for a few minutes, say around three thirty."

"Oh, thanks so much, Bill; I really appreciate it!" Goodman quickly continued, "Well, listen, I'd better run. As I said, I'm very busy and I've still got a lot to do even before the luncheon, so I won't bother the three of you anymore." Without another word, Goodman flashed a smile that was as artificial as it was broad and strode away.

Once the three were alone again, Bill commented, "You know, there's something about that guy that has always rubbed me the wrong way."

"Is he always like that?" Jackie asked. "Honestly, I feel like I need a shower. Who is he, anyway?"

"He owns a violin shop in Detroit," Bill said. "He went to violin-making school, and while his instruments are good, they aren't really the quality demanded by top-tier professional clientele."

"From what I've gathered," Greg added, "His shop doesn't sell high-end professional instruments, and he doesn't deal in the sale or rental of entry-level violins for individuals or school music programs. He mostly sells to the middle ground—relatively talented amateurs who will never be professional musicians, but who are in the financial position to afford decent intermediate-quality instruments for their personal enjoyment. And that's OK."

"Exactly," Bill said. "He's providing a decent service to an important part of the violin world. We all had to start somewhere. And there are plenty of people who play just for the love of it, who can't afford, or can't justify, the expense of a professional instrument."

"He sells some of the better mass-produced instruments, and progresses up to some handmade ones—his own, and a few other makers at the same level. He also does some minor instrument repair," Greg explained.

"When you factor in the other merchandise—the strings, cases, chinrests, music, and the obligatory smattering of violin-related tchotchkes that his shop sells, I guess he makes a decent living," said Bill. "And to be fair, the time that he dedicates to the VSA is admirable."

"Yes, there's that, I guess," Greg conceded.

Bill paused. "But he still gives me the creeps. He's just such a . . . a . . ."

"Brown-noser?" Jackie suggested, snickering.

"That's a little crass; let's just call him a bootlicker."

"That's hardly much better," Jackie replied. "But yeah, he was laying it on pretty thick."

"As molasses," Bill agreed. "Plus, I just get tired of seeing him everywhere. Every event, every gathering, every social media post, he's front and center. Phil Goodman has never seen a photo op he didn't like."

After a moment, Bill turned to Greg. "What was up with that comment about your violins not being as good as Andrew Hutchinson's?"

"Who knows?" Greg shrugged his shoulders. "I'm sorry, I don't want to sound conceited, but there isn't any question that my violins are better than his, even if he does have better name recognition and gets in the trade magazines all the time. I think Phil just likes Andrew better than me because they're both . . ."

"Publicity whores?" Jackie suggested.

"Well, that's what Dan would call it; I was trying to come up with another term, but basically, yes."

"Listen, I've got to run upstairs and see Eric Morrison. Greg, do you want to tag along?

"Sure, I'd love to!"

"Jackie, will you wait down here to meet your mother?" he asked.

"Sure, I'll just grab a cup of coffee and watch for her. I'll see you in a little bit, Dad."

As Bill and Greg got up and started toward the elevators, Jackie shot after them, "I'll just sit here and bask in the awesome experience of having been in the presence of such greatness."

Bill rolled his eyes. "Smart aleck. Love you, kid—see you in about an hour."

CHAPTER 8

TUESDAY, 11:00 A.M.

Bill tossed his room key onto the desktop, retrieved the Jackson from its case, and cradled it on the table in the same way Hanna had earlier that morning, just in time for Eric Morrison to knock on the door. As Bill ushered him in, he said, "Hey, I really appreciate you doing this Eric; and of course, send me a bill for it when you get a chance."

"Ah, we'll just call this one a professional courtesy. It shouldn't take long, and I'm happy to do it. Besides," he added, "what Malcolm doesn't know won't hurt him." He made his way over to the Jackson. He was briefly puzzled when he saw Greg, but he quickly smiled and extended his hand. "I didn't know you'd be here, too, Greg, but it's good to see you again!"

"I hope you don't mind me looking over your shoulder while you work."

"Are you kidding? Not at all." He moved to the table, set his toolbox on the adjacent windowsill, and carefully looked the violin over. Picking it up, he asked, "Could I borrow a bow for a moment?" Greg retrieved one from the Jackson's case and handed it to Eric, who played through a few scales. Listening intently, he moved through bits of musical compositions. Greg immediately recognized the flowing, majestic Zigeunerweisen, a Roma-inspired piece by Pablo de Sarasate, followed by the broad and powerful Bruch Violin Concerto.

"Well, let's see now," he said as he set the instrument back down. "It really sounds pretty good as is, but I think you and Alana are right, Bill. It needs just a little more response in the bass. I think we could make it even better with a soundpost adjustment and maybe checking the bridge positioning."

One of the most significant variables is the placement of the soundpost—a small friction-fitted dowel inside the instrument that fits snugly between its back and belly, approximately under the right, or treble, foot of the instrument's bridge. The soundpost provides structural support and transmits sound energy between the two surfaces, affecting how they both resonate to create the instrument's tone. It has such an important role in determining tone that it's been referred to as *l'âme*, the French word for "soul." The soundpost must be meticulously cut to provide the right amount of tension, and be placed in just the right location. As with bridge placement, differences of a few tenths of a millimeter can make a huge difference in tone.

"Since I just worked on it a few months ago, I was pretty sure there weren't going to be any serious issues, and it appears I was right," Eric commented. "Probably just a little soundpost adjustment needed due to the change in temperature and humidity." Before he could do that though, he needed to document several existing conditions as reference points: marking the existing position of the bridge feet with small pieces of low-tack tape, measuring the lengths of strings above and below the bridge and their height above the belly. That done, he slightly eased a bit of tension off the strings with the pegs. "Now, let's see about that soundpost," he said. "Greg, it would be great to have another set of hands," Eric said. "Could you grab that little endoscopic flex light from my tool kit and work it into the corpus to get me a little more light?"

"Sure, glad to help." Greg began hunting through Eric's tool kit looking for the light. "Ow, wow, you brought a real complement of tools, pigments, and solvents with you," he commented. "For minor tonal adjustments I'll just pack the essentials into a small bag like a shaving kit." He found the light, flexed its neck, and snaked its LED head down into the corpus through the bass-side f-hole.

"Well, when I'm traveling away from the shop, I like to bring a fuller array of things, since you never really know what you're going to find. It's better to have too many supplies than not enough."

Morrison reached into the tool kit and pulled out a small measuring gauge and a small, disk-shaped inspection mirror—a dental mirror, actually. He carefully slipped the mirror down into the corpus via the treble-side f-hole and positioned it so he could see the soundpost. Then he maneuvered the gauge inside and took extremely precise measurements of the soundpost's exact current location, carefully documenting all the measurements.

"Now, if I want to get improved response in the bass," Eric said, "I'll need to move the soundpost ever so slightly more toward the ribs on the opposite, treble side," giving voice to his internal monologue for the benefit of no one, really. Greg and Bill both already understood that bit of luthier's physics. Eric reached into his tool kit and took out an elongated-S-shaped metal tool designed specifically for setting and adjusting soundposts. Slipping it inside the instrument, he very carefully moved the soundpost an almost imperceptible amount, while Greg adjusted the LED as needed to keep his work illuminated. He alternated snaking the tool through the Jackson's treble-side f-hole and making an adjustment with inserting the mirror and inspecting the adjustment. Then he played the violin to test its tone.

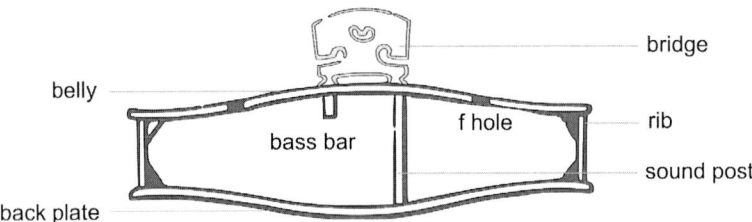

belly

bridge

f hole

rib

bass bar

sound post

back plate

Cross section of a violin

As Morrison continued the tedious process of adjusting, playing, and readjusting, there was a knock at the door. Bill opened it to find Hanna Sullenberger.

"Hi Bill, I'm sorry to bother you," she explained, "but when I was here earlier, I left my scarf, along with a ring I took off to avoid any accidental damage to the Jackson. Could I take a quick look for it?"

"Oh, of course." Sure enough, both the scarf and ring were sitting on the window sill, near Eric Morrison's tool kit.

"Thank goodness," she said. "I feel stupid for leaving them here, but at least I'm glad to know I didn't lose them."

"Not a problem at all. I'll see you downstairs shortly."

At 11:45, Konstantin Pappas knocked on the door to escort Bill downstairs. Eric had just completed his work and was putting his tools back in their case. "Well, Bill," he said, "I think it sounds even better now—just listen." Eric put the instrument back up to his chin and he played a bit of both compositions he'd sampled earlier.

Konstantin exclaimed, "Oh, that sounds wonderful!"

"I agree; it's really remarkable. Thanks so much, Eric!" Bill spoke with Konstantin while Eric put the Jackson back in its case. "It probably sounds odd talking about dinner when we're just about to have lunch, but I know a great Mediterranean restaurant not far from here. Konstantin, let's go there tonight: you, me, Judy, and Jackie." As they discussed the possibility, there was yet another knock on the door.

"Wow, this place is like Grand Central Station," Bill commented.

"Don't worry, I'll get it," Eric said. As the two other men continued planning dinner, Morrison opened the door to find Phil Goodman.

"Hi, Eric," he said. "Hey Bill! I just thought I'd stop by to remind you that it's time to head downstairs. We're all ready to go," Goodman called over to Bill, who was still speaking with Konstantin. "We wouldn't want the man of the hour to miss his own luncheon! And remember, I'd still like to stop by to see the Jackson a little later!"

"OK, thanks. We're on our way down right now," Bill responded, barely looking up or interrupting his conversation with Pappas.

Morrison closed the door and collected his tools from the table. "Bill, I need to drop these off in my room. I'll see you downstairs in a few minutes."

Greg chimed in also, "Bill, I'm going to head down now; I'll see you in a few."

When Dan had left Greg at the vendor's hall, he'd gone back to their room for a book, then back down to the lobby to find a comfortable reading spot. From where he sat, he could actually see Greg, Bill, and Jackie seated together on the opposite side of the large open space. After about an hour, he noticed Bill and Greg leave the lobby, and at the same time he saw a man approaching him. It was Chase Reinhold, a highly respected violin dealer. He and Greg had been friends for years, and by extension, he'd become something of a friend of Dan's, as well. Chase dealt almost exclusively in the highest tier of rare antique violins, not the work of local makers. The last time the two had met before the pandemic, Chase had opened the door just a crack, though, when he'd told Greg that he might consider representing a modern maker or two, given the right circumstances.

"Hi, Dan, I thought that was you," said Chase, sinking into the empty club chair beside Dan's. "How have you been?"

"Pretty good, thanks, hope you've been well, too," Dan said. "By the way, I've really been enjoying the social media posts of all your cooking exploits." Both being foodies was another common bond between Greg and Chase.

"Yeah, that was one of the things that kept me sane during the last two years," he said with a smile. "It doesn't look like you've been eating much; you've slimmed down a lot since the last time I saw you." Glancing at the book in Dan's hands, he asked, "What are you reading?"

"Oh, it's historical fiction based in Louisville in the 1850s, dealing with the rise of anti-immigrant nationalism and the 'Know Nothing' political party. I was just reading a chapter on Louisville's "Bloody Monday"—a riot led by the Know Nothings that rampaged through the city's streets, cutting a swath of death and destruction that actually hit its high-water mark just a few minutes' walk from our house."

"Sounds pretty awful," Chase said sadly.

"It really was," Dan replied. "I can't help but think that the ignorant bigots back then were worked up over German and Irish immigrants. At least those immigrants were white, and ostensibly, straight. They'd have really loved me and Greg."

"Louisville has seen a lot of protest in more recent times too, hasn't it?" Chase asked. "And based on your social media posts, you were right in the middle of it."

"Yes," Dan said thoughtfully. "In 2020, downtown Louisville saw an entire year of continuous protest in response to the police killing of Breonna Taylor, George Floyd, too many others. And yes, I was involved in a lot of it. Sometimes, I was part of a clergy group that stood as a peacekeeping buffer between protestors and counter-protestors. Other times I was present to show clergy support for their cause, as well as to offer spiritual and emotional support. A lot of the protestors were deeply traumatized. Once, a few hundred protestors were taking sanctuary in a downtown church when the police department laid siege to it, and I was part of the negotiating team that got the protestors free passage without arrest."

"I'm guessing none of that was quite what you thought you were signing up for as a pastor," Chase said.

Dan laughed, "That's putting it mildly. You know, one of my pastoral mentors was a man who had been involved in the civil rights protests in the 1960s in the South. He'd even been on the Edmund Pettus Bridge with Dr. King. I never imagined I'd be involved in anything even remotely similar. I guess circumstances, and maybe God, put me in a situation where I became an 'accidental activist.' "

Chase thought for a moment. "Were there ever times when you felt afraid during all that?"

"Honestly, yeah, there were times when I was very scared," Dan answered. "I was scared of the police, whom I saw commit numerous unjustifiable acts of violence and brutality with my own eyes—and of some of the far-right counter-protestors. I was never afraid of the protestors—quite the contrary, actually. There were several times during clashes with police or counter-protestors where some of the protestors actually formed a barrier to protect me from harm, after I'd shown up so many times to help protect them."

"I can't imagine what that must have been like."

The experiences and raw emotions of that year were still fresh in Dan's mind, and he continued. "A lot of people portrayed the protestors as violent thugs, rioters running wild through the streets and tearing the city apart. They weren't. They were protestors, but they weren't rioters. That lie allowed people to dismiss their legitimate grievances. It was a deception allowing them to miss the reality right in front of them."

"In so many circumstances, things aren't what they seem," Chase mused.

"Yes," Dan continued thoughtfully, "the protestors were loud and discomfiting—any protest has to be, to be effective—but they were nonviolent. There was some vandalism, but given the raging emotion of the events that unfolded that year, even that was surprisingly minor."

"A bit of a contrast between that, and 'Bloody Monday,' then," Chase suggested.

"That's exactly what I was thinking. Kind of ironic, isn't it?" Dan said. "I've told critics of the protests to always remember that the worst violence and vandalism in the city's history was perpetrated by racist, anti-immigrant white nationalists 165 years earlier—true violent thugs who burned countless building to the ground and who killed every immigrant in sight, while they swarmed through many of the very same streets that were filled with the nonviolent protestors of 2020.

"I'm sorry, I can get a bit passionate and carried away when talking about those experiences," Dan apologized.

"No problem," Chase said. "Now I know a little bit more about Louisville—and I know a little bit more about 'the accidental activist,' too," he chuckled. "Hey, I've got a question for you," Chase said, changing the subject. "It's actually for Greg, but I'm not sure how he'd receive it, and I'd like to run it past you first."

Dan was intrigued. "Sure, what's on your mind?"

"I'm thinking about asking Greg if he'd be interested in me carrying his instruments in my shop. He's really at the top of his game now. Too many makers get so wrapped up in copying antique instruments that they never allow their own artistry to show through. He's really mastered the ability to meld the masters' work with his own vocabulary in a way that's very successful. And while I've seen some makers antique their instruments to the point that they look beat to hell, Greg's antiquing is much more subtle and graceful. What's more, I've seen that he can produce instruments of great, unique beauty, but that also have an uncanny consistency in workmanship from one instrument to the next—a real plus from a dealer's standpoint. I'd love to be his dealer. Do you think he'd be open to that?"

Dan half-stifled a smile. Before leaving Louisville, he had encouraged Greg to open that precise line of discussion with Chase while at the convention. He'd watched from the periphery as the two had danced around the possibility of having a business relationship for years, and he'd suggested to Greg that the timing might be right. Covid had reset so many of life's assumptions; maybe this would be one of them.

"Well Chase, you know that Greg has immense respect for your dealership and for you personally. I won't speak for him—God knows I've gotten in trouble that way too many times, and I'll never do it again—but if you're receptive to carrying more than top-end antique instruments, I'm pretty sure he'd be receptive to working with you."

"I'm glad to hear that, and I appreciate your thoughts. I'll talk with him later today."

"Great! Just one thing," Dan cautioned. "Don't tell Greg we talked. If he knew that we did, and if he mistakenly thought that I'd made any commitment to you on his behalf, the whole idea would go ass over teakettle."

Chase got up from his seat. "We never spoke," he intoned soberly, holding up his hand as if swearing an oath. Then, breaking out in a smile, he asked, "Drinks with the two of you at the bar this evening?"

"Of course!" Dan smiled back. Dan went back to reading, but watched when Bill and Konstantin walked across the lobby to the entrance to the luncheon. Numerous people stopped them to say hello to Bill and wish him well. Eric Morrison and Phil Goodman were standing nearby, engaged in a conversation, but when they saw Bill, they both smiled, waved, and went over to join the others and talk with him. While they were talking, Dan saw Greg hustling through the lobby. He offered a quick wave to Dan, stopped to say something briefly to Bill, and headed into the hall just ahead of him and Konstantin.

Later Greg told Dan about the luncheon: he had been seated at the same table as Bill, Judy, Jackie, and Konstantin Pappas. Dinnerware clinking, water glasses being refilled, subdued talk and occasional laughter, people coming and going from the room—all of it served as the cantus firmus for the speeches offered from the lectern, all offering tribute to Bill. As the hour-long affair drew to a close, Greg texted: *Hey, we just wrapped up. Do you want to stop in and say hi to Bill and Judy?*

Dan was still sitting in the same spot, just across the lobby from the banquet hall. With the actual event over, Dan felt less like an intruder, and he slipped into the room to say a quick hello. Eric Morrison, Konstantin, and a number of others were gathered around Bill.

After a few minutes, Eric excused himself. "Phil Goodman asked if I could lower the bridge on a violin he's got here, to make it easier on the fingers for a potential customer of his, and of course," he rolled his eyes, "with all the extra tools I brought, I didn't include a bridge jack, so I'll have to unstring it."

Greg laughed. "Never seems to fail, the tool you need is the one you left at home."

"Yep," Eric agreed. "In any case, I'll talk with you all later."

"Yes, we need to get going, too," Bill said. "We're running over to see some friends in Anaheim Hills, but we should be back by 3:00 or so. Greg, do you want to stop by and play the Jackson a bit then?"

"Sure, that's perfect timing," Greg replied.

"Oh shoot," Bill said, "I left my car keys up in the room; I'll need to go up and get them."

"No, don't bother," Greg offered, glad to help. "I'll run up and get them for you. Just give me your room key, and I'll be right back. You and Judy just relax."

"Great, thanks!" Bill said. He reached into his pants pocket. "Shoot! With everything going on in my room this morning, I must have walked out and left my card on the dresser. Oh, wait," he said, reaching into his jacket pocket. "They gave me two cards when I checked in; the other one is still in my other pocket." He handed Greg the card.

"Listen, when you get up there, the keys should be sitting right on the desk; you can't miss them." Greg took the key card and in a few minutes, he was back downstairs with the keys, and Bill and Judy were on their way.

Dan and Greg stopped in the lobby for a small gelato, even though Greg had already had dessert with lunch. Chase Reinhold was sitting by himself at a nearby table, so the two of them joined him. A few minutes later, Alana Marino strode confidently across the lobby, approaching them with a broad smile.

"It doesn't matter what the setting is," Chase said. "She just owns whatever room she's in, doesn't she?"

"So how are my three favorite people in the world?" she asked as she neared.

"Well, I don't know how they're doing, but the three of us are doing all right," Chase joked in return. "And we're doing even better now that you're here." Alana laughed.

"Alana, I meant to ask you when we met in New York," Dan began. "You're originally from Reggio Calabria, right?"

"Yes, that's right. Why do you ask?"

"That's actually the same city that my mother's family is from," he replied. "After coming through Ellis Island in the early 1900s, my Italian great-grandfather settled in southwestern Pennsylvania and became a coal miner."

"Really? How wonderful! You probably know that there was a terrible earthquake in Reggio Calabria around that time, and a lot of people came to America following it. Several members of my own family—three brothers—came to America," Alana said. "One of them was a coal miner in Pennsylvania, too. Maybe he knew your great-grandfather," she joked. "Another one of them became a shoemaker in a little town not far from Syracuse, and the third one owned a tavern in Detroit."

"Fascinating," Dan said. "I've never been to Reggio Calabria, but I'd like to visit it someday."

"It's gorgeous," she said. "The coast is stunning, and the history, the museums—well, my friend, if you do ever go, let me know and I'll make arrangements with my family to show you around and have you over for dinner."

"Alana," Chase asked, "what are you up to now?"

"Oh, it's time to start the tone judging for the competition," she said. "I was headed there just now but had to stop and say hello. Ciao!" And with that, the force of nature that was Alana Marino was gone.

"She's really something," Greg said. "I hope she likes my violin."

"Wouldn't it be something if our ancestors actually did know one another, back in the day?" Dan asked.

Chase paused before speaking. "Well, I do know one thing that she didn't say about her family. She left out one of those brothers who came to America; there were actually four."

"Four?" Greg asked.

"Yes. The one that she didn't mention was Francesco—'Little Frankie'—Marino; he was a real heavy-hitter in Philadelphia organized crime, and his family is still deeply involved in it. I can understand why she wouldn't have wanted to mention him."

"Speaking as someone with Italian heritage myself," Dan said, "it's annoying when someone just assumes if you're Italian, you've got some connection to organized crime. I can only imagine how a person like Alana would feel, not being part of all that but knowing that at least for her, a part of that ugly stereotype is true."

"Yeah," Chase agreed. "I've got to run. Greg, I told your husband that we'd meet at the bar for drinks this evening."

"That's good," Greg said. "I already checked with them and found out that they have a really nice selection of zero-proof cocktails that I'll be able to choose from. See you then!"

Greg turned to Dan. "Let's take some time to go through Ping Yi's antique instrument exhibit, but first, Phil Goodman asked to borrow the Amati book I bought, and I need to take it up to his room. I'll be quick; why don't you meet me up at the exhibit in about 15 minutes?"

"Sounds good; see you then," Dan said.

Greg quickly retrieved the book from their room and made his way to Phil Goodman's room in the opposite tower. He knocked on the door, which was opened by Eric Morrison.

"Oh, hi, Eric," Greg said. "Is Phil around?"

"No, he's downstairs doing some convention-related work. I'm doing that bridge lowering I mentioned downstairs," he said, nodding over to the unstrung violin sitting on the table by the windows.

"I was just dropping this book off for him; he said he wanted to borrow it for a couple of days. I'll set it here on the dresser," Greg said. "Dan and I are going to spend some time at the antique instrument exhibit now. Are you planning to see it?"

"Yeah, I'll get there later today or tomorrow."

"OK, well, see you around!"

A few minutes later, Greg met up with Dan at the entrance to Ping Yi's antique instrument exhibit, where a handful of others were patiently waiting for their turn to be admitted. Several rows of tables with white linen tablecloths filled the quiet, softly lit room, each table holding two instruments. In one corner, a uniformed security guard sat at a desk, trying not to look bored. Greg and Dan took the next hour or so examining a couple dozen beautiful 17th and 18th century instruments by master luthiers of the Guarneri family dynasty.

At 3:30, Greg got a text message from Bill: *Hey Greg, we're back. Why don't you and Dan swing by so you can play the Jackson now?* Greg replied to the text, and a few minutes later he and Dan had arrived at Bill's room.

"Come on in," Bill said, opening the door.

"Did you have a good visit with your friends?" Greg asked.

"Oh, yeah," Bill said. "It had been a while since we'd seen them, and it was good to catch up. But now, let's have some fun." Bill held up a violin he'd pulled from a case. "Judy brought the del Gesù from home; let's play a duet. Do you still remember the Vivaldi Opus 3, no. 11 that we played at Oberlin a few years ago? I've got the music."

"I might be a little rusty at first, but I think it will come back to me once I get started," Greg answered.

"Well, here, take the del Gesù for a minute, and I'll fetch the Jackson." He passed the violin to Greg and walked across the room to retrieve the Jackson's case. He set it on the bed next to where Greg was sitting and opened the case.

The Jackson was gone.

Two folded hotel hand towels occupied the cavity where the violin belonged. Bill was puzzled. "What is this? Where is it?" He was beginning to panic; his gaze darted around the room. "It isn't on the table . . . not on the dresser . . . it isn't anywhere in this room. Why isn't it in the case? Where is it?" Bill grabbed his head, as reality set in. "What's happened to it? Where is it?! It's gone. It's gone, gone, gone!!!"

Greg and Dan drew alongside Bill, alternating their attention between the case and their friend. Bill seemed to actually be having trouble breathing, and they tried to calm him down as he started to moan, "How could this happen? Who could have done this?" Greg held Bill by the shoulders trying to calm him.

"Bill, we need to call the police and hotel security," Dan said. "And we need to do it right now. Let's get them involved as quickly as we can."

Greg got Bill seated on the edge of the bed and started talking him through some deep breathing to keep him from hyperventilating. His breathing began to even out, but he was still clearly upset. "Why, why, why didn't I take the case with me when I left? I always carry it with me; I never just leave it in a hotel room. I must have been distracted by all that was going on with the luncheon, then forgetting my car keys, and everything else. How could I have done that?"

"It's OK, Bill," Dan said calmly. "Everything is going to be all right." It was more a prayer than a statement. He quickly got on his phone and contacted both the Anaheim police and the hotel's security staff.

When Bill was finally calm enough, he called Judy and Jackie to let them know what had happened. As he spoke on the phone, Greg's mind returned to his own experiences earlier in the week. *I remember the panic I felt when I thought I'd lost my violin, and it isn't anything like the Jackson. I can't even imagine how he feels right now. We've got to help him as much as we possibly can.*

CHAPTER 9

TUESDAY, 3:45 P.M.

Bill sat in a chair at the table in his room, still wearing his sweater and hat, his hands clutching and twisting at the handle of his cane. A cup of coffee someone had gotten him sat in front of him. Side by side, Dan and Greg remained next to Bill, to offer moral support. Two hotel security guards talked and took notes nearby. Before long, there was a rap on the hotel door, which had been propped open. Three men walked in: a plainclothes detective, gruff-looking, stocky, somewhere in his early to mid-40s, and two uniformed police officers.

"Mr. Sloan, I'm Detective Jim Kavanaugh with the Anaheim Police Department." The man handed Bill a business card and sat opposite him at the table. "I understand that you're the owner of the missing violin. Can you tell me what happened?" Over the next half hour, Bill recounted the morning's activities in detail.

"So, let's summarize. This violin was in your possession, at least within view to you, pretty much the entire morning before you came down to your luncheon."

"Yes."

"And once it was put away, you left it alone in the room and you went downstairs."

"Right."

"Can you tell me everyone that you're aware of that was in your room today, other than yourself?"

Bill ran through the short list for the detective: Konstantin Pappas, Hanna Sullenberger, Alana Marino, Eric Morrison, Phil Goodman, and finally, Greg. Greg and Dan had stepped back a bit to give the detective some room, and Bill had nodded toward Greg as he mentioned his name. Kavanaugh looked over at Greg, then quickly at Dan, too, who had his arm around Greg's waist. The detective's stare was cold, penetrating—invasive. Under that gaze, Greg felt as if he'd just been physically violated.

Turning his attention back to Bill, Kavanaugh asked, "As far as you know, this Mr. Zhu was the last person in the room with your violin?"

"Well yes, but—"

"And was there anyone other than those six individuals who knew that this violin was here today?"

"No, I really don't think so."

"All right, well, we'll talk to these people and do a bit of investigation. I'll be back in touch with you soon."

"Is that all?" Bill asked.

"For now, yes, sir."

"You aren't going to call in a search party, or cordon off the hotel and check things going in or out to see if someone's trying to get it off-site?"

"Well, no, Mr. Sloan, that really isn't the way these things work. I know that's what happens in movies and TV; you see police cruisers surrounding the building and dozens of officers swarming the place. But in the real world, we just don't have the manpower to do those kinds of things. To be very honest—and I hope this doesn't offend you—if you hadn't told us the value of your violin when you called us, we'd have just directed you to fill out a form online and we'd have come out to talk with you when we were able to. I mean, we'll examine the room, and I'm sure we'll look for fingerprints, but there isn't really a whole lot more that we can do along those lines. We'll continue investigating a few different angles, and I'm sure I'll have some more questions for you, but first I'm going to talk with everyone you've mentioned who knew it was here." As he said that, he glanced coldly at Greg.

"You can talk with anyone you want," Bill said, "but you really need to take control here! The Jackson might still be in the building.

You need to lock it down and search the place!"

The detective looked down at the carpet and scratched his forehead for a moment, apparently considering his response. "Mr. Sloan, I know that you're upset, and we're going to do everything in our power to recover your stolen violin. But the truth of the matter, as I told you, is that we just don't have the personnel to lock down a 300-room hotel, and I'm not even really sure how we'd go about searching every guestroom. You'd need a search warrant for every room, and you aren't going to get one of those without probable cause that the person in that room is an actual, viable suspect in the theft. Plus, I'm very confident that the violin was taken out of the building within minutes of it being taken. I know you're frustrated, but that really isn't something we can do."

"What about getting more people involved?" Bill asked. "Isn't this something that the FBI or someone would get involved in?"

Kavanaugh bristled and cut Bill off. "Mr. Sloan, there's no need for that, at least not for now. Let us do our job, and we'll keep you informed as things progress. Trust us, you're in good hands." Within a few minutes, the detective left the room while speaking to the uniformed officers.

Greg was unimpressed, and he could see that Bill clearly wasn't satisfied with the detective's assurances. Despite his gentle appearance, this was a man with powerful connections. Bill and

Judy socialized and were on a first-name basis with highly placed officials at every level and branch of government, and he wasn't going to forgo any of those connections that might help retrieve the Jackson.

"This guy's bad news," Bill said. "I think he's in way over his head here, and I'm not going to sit around and lose the Jackson because of him."

"What can you do, Bill?" Greg asked.

"I've got a few connections. The most amazing thing—true story—there's a guy I performed surgery on a few years back, really nice guy. In one of our appointments, we started talking music. He told me that he played the guitar and liked Country & Western music, and I told him I played the violin. He was really nervous about the surgery, so to help calm his nerves, we made arrangements to play a little bit of music together in Pre-Op. His wife brought his guitar in that morning, and you know what we played? The Tennessee Waltz. He played the guitar and sang, and I played the Jackson. It was fun, and it helped to put him at ease. Well, that and a good dose of Valium," he said, smiling. "Anyway, after the surgery, we ended up becoming friends. It turns out he's a bigshot in the Justice Department. I'm going to call him and ask him to contact the governor, who's also a good friend of ours. If they both call the Anaheim police chief, I don't think it's going to take much arm-twisting to get the FBI involved. I actually suspect he's going to welcome the help."

"Kavanaugh might be a basically competent detective for more run-of-the-mill things," Dan offered, "but you need more help than he can provide."

"Obviously," Bill said.

"Of course," Dan added, "Kavanaugh is going to blow a gasket when he gets word of it."

"Obviously," Bill said as he sipped his coffee.

CHAPTER 10

TUESDAY, 4:30 P.M.

Detective Jim Kavanaugh offered a businesslike greeting to Dan and Greg and instructed them to have a seat directly across from him at a table in the main lobby of the hotel. Once seated, he immediately began jotting on a legal pad. The routine activity and sounds all around them in the lobby seemed amplified by the increasingly awkward silence at the table as Kavanaugh continued writing for what seemed like an inordinate amount of time. He was obviously aware of, but completely ignoring, their presence. *A BS theatrical power play*, Dan thought. *He's just trying to unnerve Greg, and I suppose me too, and to show us who's in charge before he starts in.*

Eventually, Kavanaugh looked up from his notepad and began speaking as if there had been no gap in their communication.

"So, Mr. Zhu, I understand that you're a good friend of Mr. Sloan. How long have you two known each other?"

"Oh, probably 20 years or so," Greg answered, going on to explain the nature of their friendship in some detail.

"And Mr. Sloan had told you that his Stradivarius violin would be on-site with him?"

"Yes, he told me a few weeks ago, and he invited me to stop by and play it."

"Did you tell anyone else that it would be here, either then or since you've been here?"

"No, no one."

"Well, that's really not true, is it?" he asked pointedly. He looked at Dan, who at the moment was holding Greg's hand. "I'm sure that you told your . . . friend? Partner?"

" 'Husband' works just fine," Dan said dryly.

"No, I didn't need to tell him, since he was standing right beside me when Bill told me on a video call—so no, I wasn't lying to you, detective," Greg said.

The detective stared at the two for a moment. After a pause, he continued, speaking to Dan, "And you, Mister . . . Zhu?"

"Randolph."

"OK, so Mr. Randolph," Kavanaugh said, "are you part of the convention, too? Are you a violin maker?"

"No, I'm just here to support my husband. I'm a Presbyterian minister."

Kavanaugh's face appeared surprised and puzzled as his eyebrows arched. "A minister?" he asked. "They allow that?"

"I assume you mean being gay, and married," Dan replied, "and yes, they allow that."

"Hmm. Presbyterians," he said simply. Dan thought that he noticed the detective's head shaking slightly as he jotted into his notepad before turning back to Greg and continuing.

"For the record, Mr. Zhu, where are you from?" Kavanaugh asked Greg.

"We live in Louisville, Kentucky," Greg answered.

"No, I mean, where are you *from*?" the detective prodded.

Greg knew exactly what the detective meant—people of visibly Asian heritage got this question repeatedly—but he obviously didn't feel like answering the detective's real question, at least not without making him work for it.

"Well, legally, I'm from Canada. I'm a Canadian citizen, and after moving from rural western Ontario I lived in Toronto for 30 years before I moved to Louisville to marry Dan."

Kavanaugh winced momentarily at the word "marry" but continued to press his original question. "No, I mean before that— originally. Where are your people from?"

There it was. Your people.

"Detective Kavanaugh," Greg replied pointedly, "I was born in

Hong Kong to Chinese and Taiwanese parents. I spent the next four years of my life living with my grandparents in Taiwan while my mother continued her doctoral studies in Canada, before I joined her there. Now, I'm a permanent resident of the United States, living in Louisville. So you see, the answer to your question is complex. Your question is too simplistic, and I'm sorry, but it's also completely irrelevant to the Jackson Strad having been stolen."

"So, you're Chinese," Kavanaugh said.

"Chinese and Taiwanese," Greg corrected tersely.

"Same thing, isn't it? In any case, I'm glad that you're here legally," Kavanaugh said. "I assume you're planning on actually becoming an American at some point?"

"I've been an American since I was four. If you're asking if I'm considering becoming a US citizen, I don't know. I love this country, but honestly, I'm proud to be a Canadian, where we're at least as free as you all, plus we have really good, universal healthcare."

"And poutine." Dan was ever the smart aleck.

Kavanaugh pursed his lips. After a momentary pause, he continued, this time with a more relevant line of questioning. "Can you tell me about your day today, what you did and when?"

Dan chuckled, knowing what was about to happen. Greg proceeded to offer the detective a comprehensive rundown of his day since getting out of bed, to a level of detail that few other people could have and that almost seemed to annoy the detective as he feverishly jotted notes while simultaneously trying to study Greg's face and body language. *Well, you asked for it*, Dan thought.

"And I understand that you attended Mr. Sloan's luncheon at noon, correct?"

"Right, I got there just before noon, and just a few minutes before Bill arrived."

"Did he arrive with anyone else?"

"Yes, he must have met his wife, Judy, and his daughter Jackie in the lobby. They all came in together, and Konstantin Pappas, another violin maker, came in with him, too. We all sat together at the same table."

"OK. And were you there for the whole time? Did you ever leave the room during the luncheon?"

"No, I was there the whole time."

"No, that's not really true," Kavanaugh interjected. "At the end of the reception, you left, and you actually went to Bill Sloan's room, didn't you? Bill Sloan actually even gave you his room key, didn't he?" Kavanaugh carefully studied Greg's reaction.

"No, what I said was exactly true," Greg replied. "As you said, that was after the reception. You asked me if I left any time *during* the reception." Once again, Greg's linguistic precision visibly annoyed the detective, which in this case was surely Greg's intention.

"All right. So the violin was out of its case and visible to several people in Sloan's room, right up until the luncheon started, and then you were in that room, the room it was taken from, right after the reception. As far as I can tell, you were actually the last person to be in the room before Sloan came back and you all discovered the violin was missing."

Kavanaugh wrapped up his questions around 5:30. Dan and Greg decided they needed to get some fresh air afterward, so they walked up the palm tree–lined boulevard to a quiet little Italian restaurant. They were led through the pleasant, tastefully furnished restaurant, through the bar with its large stone fireplace—*seems out of place in Anaheim, but it's attractive, I guess*, thought Dan— and into the large, dimly lit dining room, where they were seated in a booth along one wall. Two glass walls allowed a view of a broad dining patio surrounded by palm trees and accented with warm, welcoming lighting. In one corner of the room, a jazz trio was performing, the piano, double bass, and drums adding to the relaxing atmosphere.

"What can we get you to drink this evening?" the server asked.

"A Pinot Grigio for me, please," said Dan.

Greg added, "I'd like to try your Sumo Citrus Ginger mocktail please, and be sure to go strong on the ginger." They ordered a bruschetta appetizer.

"Well, that was pretty horrible," Greg said as they relaxed and scanned the dinner menu.

"Yeah," Dan said. "It doesn't take much reading between the lines to know that Jim Kavanaugh is an idiot."

"That isn't very nice," Greg replied. "I'd just say he's homophobic, xenophobic, and ignorant of Asian culture."

Dan shrugged. "Potayto, potahto."

The server broke the flow of their conversation as he placed their drinks on the table and took their dinner order. After he disappeared again, Dan asked, "So is the mocktail gingery enough?"

"It can never be gingery enough."

Their shared appetizer arrived shortly thereafter, and as they were enjoying it, Greg said, "Look, right over at that table: that's Alana."

It was indeed Alana sitting there, as glamorous as usual. She couldn't see the two of them from her angle, but across the table from her was an equally well-dressed man about her own age—tall, muscular, with the same dark hair, olive skin, and interestingly, the same unusual, piercing blue eyes.

"Yes, it is," Dan answered. "I wonder who the guy is? He's kind of good looking, in a rough kind of way."

"I don't know, but I saw them together earlier," Greg said under his breath. "Look at them. They could practically be brother and sister."

"Almost," Dan agreed. Watching the two, and especially Alana's body language, it seemed clear that she was agitated about something and not enjoying the conversation. Due to their close proximity, it was hard for Dan and Greg *not* to hear bits of their conversation around the ebb and flow of the restaurant's background noise.

"I told you this morning, you'd have it soon, and you will. I'll get it to you; just let me enjoy it two more days for myself," Alana said.

The man sneered. "Don't push me, Alana. You just remember, you've got a lot at stake here—a lot. You owe me."

Dan and Greg looked at each other. Intrigued, they were now actively trying to eavesdrop, but the server returned to clear away their dinner plates and take their dessert orders. Moments later, their attention returned to trying to overhear the conversation at Alana's table.

"You hold onto it for two more days—just two more days—but that's it. If I don't get it then, things come crashing down for you."

To Dan and Greg's disappointment, the trio picked that exact moment to return from their break, opening their set with the Bill Evans classic "Waltz for Debby," filling the room with strains of the best jazz—with the worst timing.

It turned out to not make much difference. Alana snatched the napkin from her lap and forcefully tossed it down onto the table. It wasn't quite a slam, but it wasn't far from it. She said something under her breath that neither Dan nor Greg could make out, but they could tell from her tone that it was malevolent. She stood and strode from the dining room, oblivious to Dan and Greg's presence.

"Woah, I wonder what that was all about," Dan finally said.

"I don't know," Greg said, shaking his head, "but I'm glad we didn't accidentally step into the middle of it by walking over to say hello."

They appreciated the jazz much more while they were enjoying dessert and coffee.

"Now that we've got some time to think about it," said Dan, "what do you suppose happened to the Jackson? And who could have taken it?"

"Well, you heard Bill give Kavanaugh the list of people who knew it would be here. I'm sure the police will focus on them first, and that's probably a good place to start."

"Yes, you're probably right," Dan agreed as he sipped his coffee. "Unfortunately, that places you on the list of potential suspects, and by extension, me too, even though I guess we really only count as one combined suspect."

"Yeah. Unfortunately it makes me a prime suspect," Greg said. "I saw the way Kavanaugh homed in on me right after he questioned Bill. I don't think that was just because we happened to be standing nearby."

"Nope," Dan said. "And let's face it, it wasn't lost on Kavanaugh that when you went up to get Bill's car keys, it made you the last known person in the room before it disappeared."

"Yes," Greg admitted. "If I were Kavanaugh, I'd probably start my investigation with me, too. And I hate to say it, but the biases he seems to have will probably color the way he sees me as a suspect, and how he directs the rest of his investigation. I worry that he won't seriously look in any other direction."

"Once law enforcement has an idea in mind, it's often hard to get them to change directions," Dan said.

Greg nodded. "Occam's razor, you know: the simplest explanation, the one right in front of your face, is usually the right explanation."

"Except for when it isn't." Dan paused. "Just for the record, let's think about who could have really done this—maybe saving your bacon in the process. To begin with, we know all the people who knew the Jackson was going to be there."

"Right." Greg recapped: "There's me, Konstantin, Eric, Hanna, and Alana who knew beforehand. And then, Phil Goodman thought that maybe Bill would bring it, and Bill confirmed it to him. In total, that's six of us."

"And of course, we can immediately rule you out; we know you didn't steal it. Wait—you didn't, did you?" Dan teased.

"Jerk," Greg lobbed back. "So really, taking me out of the mix, that leaves five people who knew it was here and who, in theory, would be the prime suspects."

"Heh," Dan chuckled. "You know what that makes them?"

"No, what?"

"The Jackson Five," Dan said, offering a broad, ornery grin before sipping his coffee.

"Oh, I can't believe I didn't see that one coming," Greg groaned, shaking his head. He took a sip of his own coffee. "I just hope that Bill is successful in getting the FBI involved."

"I'm sure he will be. Let's head back; it's just about time to meet Chase Reinhold at the hotel bar."

The two of them walked back to the hotel, hand in hand, enjoying the evening and each other's company. Dan was a head taller than Greg, with completely white hair; Greg's was still mostly jet black.

"I forgot to mention," Greg said, "I was talking to Chase earlier today, and I've got some news about him—but that can wait 'till we get there."

Dan tried to look surprised and intrigued.

A few minutes later, they passed through the large, glass entry doors of the hotel and walked across the lobby to the bar, where they saw Chase Reinhold standing with several others.

"I recognize Eric, Phil Goodman, and Malcolm Stewart," Dan

said, "but who's the other guy Chase is talking with?"

"Oh, that's Edwin Olivetti, a really talented violinist," Greg said. "He's a tone judge in the competition." While Dan got their drinks— an Old Fashioned and another ginger-rich mocktail—Greg joined the others. Chase and Olivetti were just wrapping up a conversation about the merits of various brands of Cuban cigars, which both men were fond of. The conversation shifted when Greg came over. When Dan joined them with the drinks, Chase spoke up.

"I've got an announcement to make. After years of discussing the possibility, I'm going to start carrying Greg's violins in my shop."

"That's the news I was going to tell you!" Greg beamed at Dan.

"What?" Edwin exclaimed. "You, Mister Antique Instruments, now starting to carry a modern maker? Quick, alert the media!"

"That's fantastic news!" Dan said. "And yeah, really surprising!" he said, offering a conspiratorial wink to Chase when Greg wasn't looking.

"Well at least there's one good thing to come out of the day," Goodman said. "But man, the rest of the day sure has been horrible."

"That's putting it mildly," Reinhold agreed. "And I just realized that I'm sitting here with three prime suspects. Maybe I shouldn't be seen with you all," he joked, "or the police will start to think I'm an accomplice."

"Well, I'm not really worried about it. I mean, I'm sure that they'll eliminate all of us pretty quickly," Goodman said.

Malcolm Stewart had been standing by the bar quietly until then. Always impeccably dressed, Malcolm was in his mid-60s, tall and gaunt, with a slightly bulbous nose and long, snow-white hair, combed back. He chose this moment to enter the conversation almost as theatrically as if he'd stepped onstage. "Of course, no one here had anything to do with the theft. It is a horrible tragedy, though," he continued. "I just can't tell you what it's meant to me, personally, over the years that I've been entrusted with caring for the Jackson. Of course, my shop services a number of other rare, 'golden period' instruments, but none of them has meant as much to me as being able to tell people that the Jackson—the unparalleled gem of the music world, a very piece of history itself—is cared for by me, Malcolm Stewart. Oh, yes, of course, and by my staff as well," he quickly added, in what seemed to be a pro forma footnote.

Dan noticed Eric's discomfort with both his employer's self-aggrandizing dramatics and the patronizing dismissal of his staff.

"In any case," he said, "the whole sordid question remains: if none of us stole it, who did?"

"There's another of the prime suspects over there," Eric said, gesturing across the room to where Hanna Sullenberger sat alone, sipping a drink. "I'm sure she wasn't involved either."

"No," Stewart agreed haltingly as he leaned on the bar, "probably not. Although," he said with a melodramatic shoulder shrug and flipping his palm upward, "I do know that she's a very troubled, sometimes even hostile, person. Maybe some of that anti-social hostility boiled up and led her to try something drastic."

"Malcolm, I suppose you might be a bit hostile too if you were in her shoes," Edwin answered. "I know her work, and she doesn't get half the credit, or half the pay, that she deserves, just because she's a woman trying to make it in what's always been a man's world."

"But Edwin, that's precisely my point," Stewart objected. "Yes, I know that she's quite talented—probably more talented than she gets credit for, even—but I'm suggesting that's largely her own fault. You're right, Edwin, this is a professional world that has always been, and frankly will remain, a man's domain. Whether that's a good or a bad thing is almost irrelevant; if you're a woman trying to succeed in such a world, you'd better do what it takes to make yourself accepted in it. If one wants to be taken seriously in this industry, by its employers and its clientele, that means having the right, upbeat personality. And I'm sorry, but yes, it also means paying attention to one's appearance."

The others in the group were stunned into silence at Stewart's comments until Edwin Olivetti countered, "Things change. People change. Frankly, attitudes about appearance and aesthetics change. I just don't think the world you're describing exists anymore, and if it does, it's on its deathbed. The world has moved on." Looking over at Hanna, he added, "I know she's an immensely talented luthier; I've played her instruments. And frankly, as far as appearance, I find her quite attractive. I don't see anything that would keep me from working with her or hiring her."

Completely ignoring Olivetti, and the others too, for that matter, Stewart continued his soliloquy. "You know, I actually interviewed her for the job Morrison has now, but I knew from the moment I saw her that no one who looked like that would ever work for me. Oh, I chatted several times with her just to be polite, but really, from that first moment the die was cast. I didn't care how talented she might be."

When Stewart finally stopped speaking, Chase said, "Malcolm, you do realize this is 2022, not 1922, right?"

"Joke all you want, my friend," Stewart said, "but really, just look at her over there, with that severe haircut—I refuse to call it a hair style—the heavy boots, the dark clothes, the complete absence of femininity. And for mercy's sake, those piercings! I mean, just what kind of message is she trying to convey with all of that?"

"How about this?" A voice spoke from behind the group— Chloé Lavigne's. "Maybe, just maybe," she said, walking around and coming to within a foot of Stewart's face, "what she's trying to say is that she doesn't really need you, or your permission, or your acceptance. That she's going to live on her own terms, without needing to worry about what you, or any other man, thinks about them. That you may win a battle here or there, but in the end, she's going to beat you at your own game—or at least, what used to be your game." She reached over to the bar, picked up Stewart's glass, and turned it upside-down, dousing Stewart's shoes with 12-year-old single malt. "And trust me, she's going to do it—we're going to do it—without changing our clothes, or our hair, or our makeup, and without growing a penis, just to please you." Without another word, she turned and walked over to meet her wife.

"Well of all the nerve!" Steward sputtered, while the others barely concealed laughter. "Morrison, don't just stand there; make yourself useful. Go fetch me another drink, and be quick about it."

Eric delivered the drink to Stewart, who stood nursing humiliation in his replacement Scotch.

"Well, it's probably time for me to call it a night," Olivetti said, excusing himself. "I still have a lot of fiddles to play and score tomorrow."

"That goes for me too," Goodman said, "since I'm scheduled to be your scribe." Scribes assisted the judges by recording their assessments. "Folks, we'll see you tomorrow."

A moment later, Stewart was patting his shoes dry with a cocktail napkin. "You see, that's what I mean, right over there," he said defensively, gesturing toward Alana Marino, who was across the lobby engaged in a pleasant conversation with several men. "There's a perfect example of a woman who is clearly talented and professional, but who also knows that isn't enough by itself. Appearance, personality, amiability, going with the flow, is every bit as important to one's success. She knows that to get ahead, you have to play the game."

Eric Morrison was doing a poor job at hiding his agitation at Stewart's comments, finally blurting out "Well, I think I've had enough for one night. You gentlemen have a good night."

"Yes, Morrison, I suppose you're right," Stewart added. "It is getting late. I'm calling it a night as well; I'll see you all in the morning." The two of them left the bar, Morrison headed toward his room in the east tower, Stewart to his in the west tower.

"It looks like Alana has recovered from her incident at dinner," Dan said, looking over at her. He and Greg filled Chase in on what they'd seen earlier.

"That's very interesting," Chase said. "You remember what I told you earlier, about the criminal side of her family? There's more to that." The three of them moved to a high-topped bar table and sat around it.

"It turns out that when Alana was trying to get into a top musical conservatory here in the States, she really wanted to go to the Curtis

Institute," Chase said. "She knew her relatives were crooked, but also that they were very well-connected. She apparently reached out to some of them to see if they could use their influence to get her in."

"You're kidding!" Greg said in disbelief.

"How do you know this, Chase?" Dan asked.

"I'm very good friends with Harrison Ellis, who was the president of the institute at the time, and Martin Mayfield, who was the dean of admissions. One night a number of years ago, after we'd all had more bourbon than I care to admit, they told me the whole story. They'd gotten a visit from Anthony Marino, one of Alana's distant cousins, and he'd made a heavy-handed 'suggestion' that they admit her."

"That's incredible," Dan muttered, shaking his head. "She got into the Curtis because of arm-twisting."

Chase began to add, "And here's the thing—"

"And what are you three talking about this late?" Alana Marino crossed the lobby and interrupted him at just that moment. Her smile fading, she continued, "I can only imagine, given everything that's happened today."

"It's certainly been one for the record books," Chase said, changing gears quickly. "But you know, you're right about it being late; I suppose I should get up to my room."

"Same here," Dan chimed in. "Folks, we'll see you all tomorrow, no doubt."

Later that evening, Dan sat up thinking about the day. Greg had drifted into a deep, relaxing sleep almost as soon as his head hit the pillow. Dan envied how he could be fully alert one moment and snoring the next. *Where is all this going to lead?* Dan wondered. Surely, it wouldn't take Kavanaugh too long to recognize that Greg wasn't the thief, would it? *Will the police find out who took the Jackson and get it back to Bill safely? Who could have stolen it?* At some point in the middle of all the scenarios running through his mind, exhaustion finally overcame curiosity, and he fell asleep as soundly and restfully as Greg.

CHAPTER 11

WEDNESDAY, 7:00 A.M.

"Good morning, sexy man." Greg stirred, still half asleep, and looked at Dan standing across the room.

"Sorry, I was trying to get up and out the door for my walk without waking you," Dan half-whispered. In the mottled daylight filtering through the partially drawn curtains, Dan was standing in front of the full-length mirror on the wall, silently studying his naked body. Yes, he was 62 now. Yes, he had gray hair and some wrinkles. His youthful good looks had faded years ago. Still, the body he saw wasn't a bad one. Especially with the weight loss, it had aged reasonably well, and even given the parts that had sagged or wrinkled a bit, he was at peace with it.

"Nice view," Greg commented. "What are you thinking?"

"Oh, I was just thinking about how many years I spent dealing with extreme self-consciousness, body shame, and sex shame, from social norms when I was a kid, and especially in my teens when the fundamentalists started beating their theology into my brain. It took me decades to get over that, to be comfortable in my own skin, and to develop a body-positive, sex-positive philosophy—and theology, for that matter."

"Well, from my standpoint, I'd say you've arrived, and I'm glad you did," Greg teased.

Dan chuckled, then thought for a moment. "I was just remembering something from when I was, I don't know, maybe 13 years old. I joined the junior high school wrestling team, which made my dad so proud because he'd been a wrestler when he was younger. But after my very first match, I quit the team. I know it disappointed my dad, who thought I'd quit just because I was beaten my first time on the mat, or because I didn't want to push myself and become good at the sport. But that wasn't why I quit at all. I actually liked the sport, and I wanted to work out and practice. I knew that over time, I could become pretty good at it."

"So why did you quit then?"

"Honestly? I was embarrassed beyond words that everyone could see the shape of my adolescent junk telegraphing through the flimsy spandex singlet."

Greg knew that his husband was sharing something important, but he couldn't help giggling a little before Dan continued.

"I still remember my face burning with embarrassment when

I stepped out onto the mat, imagining, as only a self-conscious adolescent could, that the eyes of everyone in the whole gymnasium were focused on my crotch."

At this, Greg laughed openly. "We do tend to think the whole world is focused on us when we're teenagers, don't we?"

Dan thought for a moment before adding, "I remember being so embarrassed about that, and too embarrassed to talk about my body to my own father to ever tell him why I really quit. I've regretted that ever since. I felt so bad disappointing him."

"I wouldn't worry. I think you've done plenty to redeem yourself in your dad's eyes, no matter how much he might have been disappointed back then."

"I hope you're right. Funny. No matter how old we get, we always want to have our parents' approval to some degree."

"Yes. I still do, too," Greg agreed. "Well, for what it's worth, I wouldn't worry about your short-lived wrestling career and your 'wardrobe malfunction.' The reality is that most people don't notice what's right in front of their faces, even when they're actually looking. I'm pretty certain that no one was paying any attention at all to the lump in your uniform."

"No one?" Dan asked, with feigned disappointment.

"Well, I'd have noticed if I'd been there," Greg offered in mock consolation.

Dan smiled. "Well anyway," he said as he slipped on a T-shirt and shorts. "Time to get going. I'll see you in a little while."

Just after nine, near the end of his walk, Dan approached a small camera shop along the route. As he got closer, he saw Malcolm Stewart and Konstantin Pappas walk out, talking together. At one point, Dan could see that they were engaged in a serious conversation, and Pappas, who almost always had an easygoing smile on his face, was visibly upset. As he drew closer to them, Pappas shook his head. "No, the price is the price and I'm not changing it," he said. "If you want it, let me know; otherwise, I'll sell it to someone else."

Wanting to avoid the awkwardness of walking through a heated discussion, Dan called out a little louder than usual and acted as if he hadn't heard anything. "Hey guys, how's it going?" The men turned toward him, and Konstantin's face immediately shifted to his happy expression. Stewart offered Dan a polite nod and what passed as a smile for him. It appeared that he'd regained his composure after his humiliation the night before.

"Good morning," Konstantin said. "Getting some fresh air to start your day?"

"Yes, but it's time to get back and get cleaned up," Dan replied.

"I was happy to find this camera shop so close to the hotel," Konstantin said. "Malcolm and I are both photography buffs."

"Yes," Stewart chimed in. "While we were inside, Konstantin

mentioned a particular lens that he no longer needed, and I was suggesting that I might be interested in buying it."

"Ah, well, don't let me interrupt you. I hope to see you around later," Dan said as he walked away, leaving the two to their conversation.

A short while later, Dan and Greg were enjoying breakfast when Bill Sloan stopped by and joined them.

"Any luck with getting the FBI involved?" Greg asked.

"Yes," Bill said, "I heard back from my Department of Justice friend late last night, and he said there would be someone from the FBI here today."

"Well, that's a relief," Dan said. "I feel much more confident now."

A server stopped by their table to clear their plates.

"Is there anything else you'd like?" she asked while refreshing their drinks.

"No thanks; that's all," said Greg. "Everything was delicious."

The server left the check on the table. Dan scanned the lobby and saw Alana Marino and Edwin Olivetti chatting as they walked toward the competition hall, Phil Goodman following close behind Olivetti. As his eyes tracked them, he also noticed Jim Kavanaugh sitting at a table not far away, apparently interviewing Hanna Sullenberger.

"Look at them over there," Dan said. "I wonder how that's going."

He sipped his freshly topped-off coffee. "It looks like Kavanaugh is studying her the same way he did you," he said to Greg, "and with what looks to be similar displeasure."

"Maybe it's just the nature of the job," Greg offered.

"Maybe."

Just then, they saw a man approach Hanna and the detective. He was tall, with short, dark hair and that effortless, slender build that only the young can have. He was wearing a well-tailored charcoal-gray suit, accessorized with an uninspiring, diagonally striped necktie that screamed public servant. *Given the rest of him,* Dan thought, *even that looks good.*

Kavanaugh stood up, and the two men started speaking. They were too far away for Dan to hear what was being said, but it didn't matter, since just then Kavanaugh pointed across the lobby toward them, and with a quick word to Hanna, the two men came over to the table.

"Hello, Dr. Sloan?" the man asked, holding out one hand and setting a business card in front of Bill with the other. "I'm Special Agent Luis Romero, with the FBI Art Crimes team. The Anaheim police chief has requested that the FBI assist his department, given our past experience with similar cases of rare musical instrument theft, and I'll be the agent on the case."

Kavanaugh was clearly unhappy with Romero's presence, and

before Bill could say anything, he jumped into the conversation.

"Thanks, amigo, but I didn't ask for anyone's help, here. We've got things under control."

Without any visible emotion, Romero replied, "That might be true, but for whatever reason, your chief has asked for the bureau's assistance. I'm just going where they told me to. If you have a problem with it, detective, you'll need take it up with the chief, not me." Then Romero softened a bit and added, "In any case, just so there's no mistake, you're still in charge of the investigation. We're just here to provide support, not to take over." Dan saw the tension in Kavanaugh's body ease a bit.

Romero continued with a disarming smile. "Look, Detective Kavanaugh, the truth is I don't have any say whether I'm here or not, and honestly, neither do you; that's all stuff above our pay grade. But think about it—I really do have specific experience with this kind of crime and criminals—you know, academic, behind-the-scenes, lab-type stuff—and you have tons of field experience. Maybe I can learn practical field technique from you, and with my specialized expertise feeding into that, you could end up looking like a national hero when you solve this case."

There you go, play to his vanity, Dan thought.

Kavanaugh's resistance eased. "Yeah, I suppose you could offer us some assistance. Of course, you'll need to get yourself up to speed with what we already know," he said. "I'll email our case notes so you can get caught up."

"Sounds good," said Romero. "But if it's OK with you, I'd like to sit down and get a feel for things from Dr. Sloan even before that."

"Sure, that should be fine," Kavanaugh said. "I'm going to go finish my questioning of Hanna Sullenberger over there." He walked back across the room.

"Do you have some time right now, Dr. Sloan?"

"Absolutely, let's talk right now!" Bill replied. Romero sat down at the table and ordered a coffee.

"By the way," he said, "This is Greg Zhu and his husband Dan Randolph, good friends of mine. Is it OK if they stay?"

"Of course. To be honest, Kavanaugh's office already sent the case files over, and I scanned them quickly before I got here. Mr. Zhu, Reverend Randolph, it looks like I'll be talking with both of you soon, anyway."

"Listen, I'm so glad you're here," Bill told him. "If we're going to get my violin back, we're going to need your help. I think that Kavanaugh character is in way over his head."

Romero looked down, a faint smile showing on his face. "Well, I want you to know that we've handled very similar cases in the past, and the Art Crimes team can use our expertise here, too." The agent's coffee arrived, and he paused to thank the server.

"One way or another, Dr. Sloan, rest assured that you've got the best possible resources working on your case—and we're still less than 24 hours since your violin went missing. I know you've already gone over yesterday's events with Detective Kavanaugh, but it would help me get up to speed if I could hear about them from you." He added cream to his cup and stirred, listening intently as Bill proceeded to describe the previous day's events.

"So you see, Agent Romero," Bill said after a long back-and-forth with the agent, "it's true that Greg here was the last person known to have been in the room before the Jackson went missing. I know that Kavanaugh suspects him of being the thief, and I know he's at least got to do due diligence in following that lead to some extent. But I'm telling you that I've known Greg for years. He's the most honest person I've ever met. He's like family to me, and I know he didn't take the Jackson." Greg blushed and looked down as Dan put a hand on his shoulder.

"Honestly," Bill continued, "I can't imagine that *anyone* on Detective Kavanaugh's shortlist of suspects had anything to do with it." A small group of people walked by just then. One of them called out to Bill, and he smiled and waved. After they'd passed, he continued, lowering his voice a bit. "The only one of them I might ever suspect would be Phil Goodman, and I don't think he's got enough brains to figure out how to do it."

Dan chuckled. That was probably the only time he'd ever heard Bill insult anyone.

"Listen, Luis—may I call you that?" Bill asked. "Before we go any further: Kavanaugh wouldn't go along with the idea of a deep search of the hotel yesterday. He said he thought the violin would have been taken out of the building as soon as it was stolen. What do you think?"

"Of course you can call me Luis. And actually, Detective Kavanaugh has a point. Doing a deep search of all the public and back-of-house areas is relatively easy, but it would be pretty much impossible to do a blanket search of all the hotel rooms, from a legal standpoint."

Bill's shoulders drooped. "I know that Kavanaugh thinks it's long gone, but do you think it could still be here?"

The agent thought for a moment. "That depends on what kind of theft it was."

"What do you mean?" Dan asked.

"Art crimes like this are typically one of four basic types," he explained. "You could call the first 'theft on spec': the item is stolen to sell on the black market. That can often be high risk, with relatively low reward. Since everyone knows the item was stolen, the buyer can't ever let anyone know that they have it, and for most collectors, that's half the joy of owning it. That makes the item worth less, so the thief usually ends up making pennies on the dollar."

"Makes sense," Bill nodded. Shifting in his chair and leaning his cane on the edge of the table, he asked, "What's the second type?"

Luis took another sip of coffee before continuing. "You can think of this type as 'theft for hire': someone pays a thief to steal a particular item, for a predetermined price. That means the thief doesn't need to find a buyer, but again, since the buyer can't let anyone know they have the item, the thief is still only going to get a fraction of the item's actual value."

The conversation at the table paused as a busload of vacationers unloaded into the large lobby. Their guide, wearing a vibrant floral-print shirt and black mouse ears for easy visibility, herded them up and led them all past the restaurant seating toward the registration desk.

After the lobby returned to relative calm, Dan asked, "So what's the third type?"

"That's undoubtedly the rarest," Luis said, "and maybe the most fascinating. That's a crime of passion; maybe you could call that 'theft for love.' The thief doesn't want to sell the item for profit; they want to keep it to enjoy, or in the case of a rare musical instrument, to play."

"Like the theft of the Totenberg Strad back in the 1980s," Greg chimed in.

"Exactly like the Totenberg," Luis nodded. "I was actually involved with that case when it finally resurfaced in 2015; it was my first experience dealing with a rare musical instrument, in fact." The server returned to drop the check for the agent's coffee, but Bill snatched it before it even hit the table. The agent continued without missing a beat. "But probably the most famous example of this type would be—"

"The Gibson Strad!" Greg exclaimed a little more loudly than needed, causing people at several other tables to turn in their direction to see what was happening.

"Absolutely," Luis agreed.

Greg explained for Dan's benefit. "A violinist stole the Gibson from a dressing room in Carnegie Hall in 1936. He ended up disguising it by smearing black shoe polish all over it so everyone would think it was just an old, run-of-the-mill violin, and he ended up playing it all over the place for almost 50 years."

"It was a simple deception to be sure, crude, even," Luis added. "But it worked well enough. The Strad was hiding in plain sight all that time."

"Right," Greg nodded. "No one ever discovered it. It wasn't until the thief confessed to the theft on his deathbed that it was recovered. Once it was, an expert restoration team removed the shoe polish very carefully without damaging Stradivari's original varnish, and now it's as beautiful as ever. It's an amazing story."

"Historically," Luis said, "these kinds of thefts can have the most, I don't know, 'romantic' back stories, and they can often go unsolved for years because the thief isn't interested in letting anyone, not even a potential buyer, know that they have the stolen item."

Dan leaned back and stretched his legs out, alongside the table. "I could see how that would be rare," he said. "So, what's the fourth type?"

Luis drained his cup. "The fourth type is the least romantic, but it's also the simplest and most common: 'theft for ransom.' The thief doesn't have to find a buyer for the item; they basically just sell it back to its actual owner."

"A violin-napping," said Bill.

"Like with the Lipinski Strad," Greg said.

"Yes. I worked that case also," Luis said.

Bill tipped his hat back and rubbed his forehead. "Based on your past experience, you must be one of the most qualified people in the country to be working this case."

Luis modestly sidestepped Bill's compliment. "So, doubling back to where the violin might be right now: if the Jackson was stolen for ransom, or stolen on spec, or preordered, it would likely have left the building immediately. On the other hand, if we're dealing with an obsessed musician thief, it could still be on-site. And that might very well be the case, given the number of violin lovers who are here for the convention. Maybe one of them has that kind of obsession."

"When you think about it," Dan said, "if it were someone here for the convention, they wouldn't want to leave with it right away, because that could arouse suspicion."

"Exactly," Luis agreed. "So you can see, we'll have to consider both scenarios—on-site or off-site—as we try to track down the Jackson. Considering the off-site possibility, we'll get a list of all registered convention attendees and cross-reference hotel records, both here and in surrounding hotels, to see who's checked out since the Jackson went missing.

"Oh wow," Bill said dejectedly, "that's going to be like looking for a needle in a haystack."

"It won't be too bad," Luis said, "just some simple name-searching to find commonality across a handful of lists, and then doing at least some initial research to see if the people who turn up on the list had any opportunity to be an actual suspect. Ultimately, I suspect it will be a fairly small number of people who will justify more than a quick look. But it's still an important task, and we'll have people starting it probably within a couple of hours."

Across the lobby, Hanna Sullenberger stood up from the table where she'd been speaking with Jim Kavanaugh and was now walking toward the elevators. Kavanaugh continued jotting down notes.

"What other avenues do you think you'll be taking at the same time?" Bill asked.

"Well, we're going to be taking a hard look at the six people you mentioned, even though you don't suspect any of them. And yes, Mr. Zhu, since you were the last known person in the room with the violin, you are an obvious suspect."

Greg grudgingly nodded his head.

"In reality though, I'm sure that there were actually more than just those six people who knew the Jackson was here. You're evidence of that, Reverend Randolph."

Dan always felt awkward with the formality of the title "Reverend Randolph," but this time it caught his ear for a different reason. Since his vocation hadn't come up in conversation earlier, it was evidence that Agent Romero had already familiarized himself with the case, and the people involved, before he'd even arrived.

"Any one of the six, or Dr. Sloan, even other members of your own family, could have casually mentioned it to someone else. You just never know."

"Oh, wow," Greg said as he noticed the time. "I've got a seminar to get to."

Dan stood and stretched. "And I think I'm going to read a bit more of my book," he said. "Greg, after your seminar, let's grab some lunch and then make a quick side trip to the House of Seasonings and take care of Chet's request.

"Is there anything else you need from me?" Bill grasped his cane and stood up.

"No, nothing right now," Luis said. "But if it's all right, I'd like to meet with all three of you this afternoon. I'm going to be reviewing hotel security video from yesterday, and it might be helpful if you could watch it with me. Maybe one of you will notice something unusual that I might miss."

Greg was the first to speak. "Sure. I'd be free right around 2:00 this afternoon. Would that work?"

"That's actually perfect," Luis said. Bill quickly agreed to the time as well, and Dan chuckled, "Hey, I'm just along for the ride, so my schedule is open."

"All right then, we'll get together here in the lobby at 2:00," the agent said, "and then we'll go into the hotel's security room to review the video."

Bill and Greg were starting to leave when Luis said, "Actually, Reverend Randolph, would you have some time to talk one-on-one right now?"

Dan was surprised but replied, "Sure, no problem at all; my book can wait." He and the agent found a couple of comfortable club chairs in a quieter part of the hotel lobby.

"I understand you're a Presbyterian minister," Luis began.

"That's right," Dan answered. "In fact, I was going to say that your last name actually reminds me of one of my great heroes, Archbishop Oscar Romero. His life and his commitment to liberation theology have been a major influence in my own life and ministry."

The agent nodded his head knowingly. "Yes, the good Archbishop from El Salvador. A truly great man in a truly corrupt institution. I'm sorry; I hope that doesn't offend."

"Trust me, that doesn't offend me at all," Dan assured him. "Given your last name, is it correct to assume you are, or were, Roman Catholic yourself?"

"I was," he said. "But that was a long time ago. I just disagree with too much in the Church, or maybe it's more accurate to say that it disagrees with too much of me."

The comment triggered Dan's pastoral ears, and he wanted to dig deeper. In this setting, though, he simply said, "I can relate. The bureaucracy, the theological pretzel-twisting, the politics and turf wars. It's sickening." He shifted in his seat and leaned forward, continuing. "And if you're gay, there's a whole other layer of anger at the Church, considering how much it's harmed folks like us. Some days I feel like a traitor just for wearing a clerical collar." Luis looked even more intently at him.

Relaxing back into his seat again, Dan concluded. "All of that garbage smothers the real point of it all—that God loves us all, and that we need to love and care for each other. That's what it all comes down to."

The soft bubbling of a nearby fountain was the only sound as both men sat momentarily without speaking. Finally, Luis broke the silence, saying, "So, about the violin theft: I'm going to tell you that while it's obviously too early to rule anything out completely, and while I'm still going to talk with your husband, I really don't see him—or by extension, you—as likely suspects here."

"Not that I want to change your mind about that, but I have to ask, why not?"

"A part of it is intuition: your words, your body language, the way you interact with Bill Sloan, and even with each other. You don't seem to be talking and acting in a way that a guilty person might. Mostly, though, it's logic. Greg being the last person in that room before the violin was discovered to be missing wasn't anything that was planned; it was pure chance. No one could have made Bill forget his keys, or guarantee that they would be the one to retrieve them for him and gain access to his room. And while it's theoretically possible that this was a spontaneous crime of opportunity, it's extremely unlikely, to my mind. I honestly think this theft was planned well in advance. I'm confident that the video we see this afternoon will show your husband walking out of Bill's room empty-handed."

CHAPTER 12

WEDNESDAY, 2:00 P.M.

"I don't like this," Kavanaugh said to Luis Romero. "We definitely need to see that security video, but I don't like that my prime suspect at the moment—and his 'husband,' " he said, rolling his eyes, "—are going to be right there watching it. I wish you'd have asked me about that before you invited them."

"I thought that they might see something that we wouldn't, based on their familiarity with the violin world," Romero responded. "At the same time, we'll be able to watch their reactions as we review the video together—also why I interviewed them together—to see if they get nervous or worried that we might see something they don't want us to see."

Kavanaugh didn't respond to the comment. "For the record, Romero, I'm not an idiot. I know when someone is trying to play me, like with that whole 'Oh, I could learn so much from a veteran field guy like you' crap. Just knock it off. I don't like you being here, period. But you are right: if I can use you and the FBI as a tool to help me solve this case, and yeah, be a hero for saving the big, fancy violin, then fine. *Tómalo con calma.* You just stay in your lane, and remember who's in charge here."

"Detective, of course you're in charge," Romero said. "And I was serious earlier; I wasn't trying to play you. Yes, I have a fair amount of field experience, but I think that ultimately I can learn something from you—from anyone who's been a detective for a long time," he said. "But detective," he continued, "that's the second time you've spoken to me in Spanish. I actually do speak Spanish fairly well, but really, you can stick with English."

"Oh," Kavanaugh said sarcastically, "I thought you might appreciate it if I spoke a little bit in your native tongue."

"I'm from Pittsburgh."

"Whatever."

Romero did, in fact, think of a few Spanish words appropriate to the moment, but he chose to keep them to himself—for civility's sake, and because he saw Bill Sloan approaching.

"Good afternoon, gentlemen," Bill greeted them, just as Dan and Greg joined the small group coming from the opposite direction.

"Well, are we ready to do this?" Bill asked.

"I think so," Luis answered. "Detective?"

"This way," Kavanaugh answered. He led the small group around the rear of the registration desk where they were met by a professionally dressed woman.

"Gentlemen, I'm Amanda Wilhelm, the general manager. Please follow me to our security office." She led them around the corner and into a sparsely furnished, windowless room about 20 feet square. Its plain, off-white walls were dotted with a few pieces of inexpensive, framed hotel art, a whiteboard with various notes scribbled on it, and a bulletin board covered with the obligatory legal notices that employers are required to post. A built-in countertop at desk height ran the full width of one wall. Several pedestals of desk drawers and racks containing video archiving equipment sat below, forming three distinct workstations for staffers. A large monitor was mounted on the wall above each of the workstations, each one displaying multiple incoming video images from security cameras, the images changing several times per minute in a preset rotation of the many cameras installed throughout the facility. A middle-aged man in gray slacks, white shirt, and a navy blazer sat at one of the stations working at a separate computer as he periodically scanned the security camera feed.

"This is Elliott Cherson, our technical operations manager," Wilhelm said, introducing them to a young man in his late 20s or early 30s who had walked over as they entered.

"Hi. I hope I can help you.," Cherson said. He began to extend his hand to greet Romero, but Kavanaugh intercepted it and announced, "I'm Detective Jim Kavanaugh, from the Anaheim Police Department. I'm leading the investigation here."

"Yes," Romero quickly said, before introducing himself. "Thank you for your help. I think we'd like to take a look at any video that you have of the 10th floor of the west tower, in the corridor where Dr. Sloan's guestroom is, from yesterday morning. Right, detective?"

"Exactly," Kavanaugh said. "Let's see what you've got."

"Sure, that shouldn't be any problem," Cherson offered. "We have cameras covering both ends of all guestroom corridors, and we keep our video archived on a month-long loop, so we should be able to pull the video up." He sat down at one of the vacant workstations while the others pulled up chairs and sat around him. Within a minute or so, Cherson had called up the video in question. "Okay, so what time do you want to begin?"

"Let's start the review at about 8:00 yesterday morning, when Bill left his room to go downstairs for breakfast with Mr. Pappas," the agent said. "Detective, I know that the violin was obviously still there at that time, but I was thinking that if we watched the video from earlier on, we might pick up something important. Does that make sense, or should we just start looking later in the morning?"

Kavanaugh thought for a moment. "No, actually I was thinking the exact same thing," he said. "Let's start watching from there."

Cherson dutifully cued up the video to the time requested. As expected, the video, while far from high-resolution, clearly showed two men easily recognizable as Bill and Konstantin leaving Bill's room to go downstairs for breakfast. Cherson fast-forwarded through the dead spaces, switching back to real time whenever something was visible. Eventually, and without seeing anything suspicious in the interim, the video showed Hanna Sullenberger coming down the corridor from the opposite direction, arriving at Bill's door, and knocking. When there was no answer, she stepped back and leaned back against the wall, retrieved her phone, seemed to be sending and reviewing text messages. A minute or two later, Konstantin came down the hall from the direction of the elevator lobby and joined her. The time stamp on the video indicated that just four minutes later, Bill and Dan came into view from the same direction Konstantin had, and the four of them entered the room.

"Well, so far so good," Bill said. "Now the next thing we should see is Konstantin leaving and going back to his room down on the ninth floor." Almost on cue, the video monitor showed exactly that, as Konstantin walked out of Bill's room and headed down the corridor, moving toward the camera before disappearing below it as he headed toward the elevator lobby, just behind the camera location.

"The next thing we should see," Bill said, "is Alana showing up at about 10:00."

But just then, the video jiggled, as if the camera had been bumped as it scanned the empty corridor. A moment later, and for just a moment, part of a gloved hand could be seen holding an aerosol can of something, spraying the camera lens with a translucent film that allowed the camera to still pick up some shape and movement, but no real detail at all. For all practical purposes, the camera was recording a fog bank.

"Dammit!" Kavanaugh uttered as the video continued to play. The others remained silent, at least for a moment, though they shared Kavanaugh's emotion.

"What did we just see?" he continued. "I was really hoping we'd get something meaningful out of this video. How could this happen, Cherson? I mean, wouldn't one of your security people have seen someone do that, and go investigate? Or at least, wouldn't they have seen that the camera had been obscured?"

"Actually, probably not, " Cherson said as he continued to watch the gauzy screen. "Everyone imagines security operations like ours as being what they see in the movies—a whole bank of people staring at monitors 24/7, like the fate of the world depended on it. But we're a hotel. Our video is more of a tool to go back and see something that's already happened, not to see something and stop it real time."

"Don't you have anyone just assigned to watch these feeds live?" Luis asked.

"I'll step in here," Amanda Wilhelm said, somewhat defensively. "No, we really don't. This is a very large facility, and we keep our security people scattered throughout the property most of the time. It's our corporate policy to minimize the security staff spending a lot of time here in the center, and even when they are in here, they're usually just catching up on paperwork until they can get back out on their rounds. Overall, we've found that deployment of our security staff keeps our property more secure."

"Until it doesn't," Kavanaugh commented.

As the group stared in frustration at the paused image from the corridor camera, Cherson reset the monitor from highlighting the one feed to its typical multiple display. "It's more complicated than that, though. Just look at what you see here yourselves. Each one of these monitors normally shows 18 different views at any given moment," he continued. "Not only that, but each camera view only appears on-screen for 10 seconds before rotating to feeds from other cameras around the property. Even if someone was stationed here full time, unless the camera was feeding to screen at just the right moment, or if they weren't looking at the right spot on the right screen at the exact right time, they'd have missed it."

As Cherson thought about the situation, he said, almost to

himself, "Probably the smartest thing this person did was to not black the camera out entirely, but to allow it to still capture light, if not actual detail. Someone sitting at the monitor would immediately notice a black spot on the multi-view, but they could easily miss one that was just fuzzed out of focus. I hate to admit it, but at least in terms of being caught in real time, the odds are actually pretty good that they'd get away with what they did."

After a moment, Romero said, "Well, let's see at least one thing that might be helpful. For all anyone knows, the camera itself is still clouded over. Can you call that camera up for a moment on one of your monitors?"

Cherson moved over to the other empty station, entered a few commands, and the real-time view of the camera appeared on the screen, offering a clear view of the corridor.

"OK. Whoever obscured the camera obviously cleaned it off, putting it back online. Can we fast forward the video to see when it was cleaned off?"

After a few minutes, Cherson found a spot where the camera momentarily blacked out, showing motion as if it were being wiped with a rag, and a moment later, the view was unobstructed. The time stamp on the recording indicated that it had been cleaned off at 2:20.

"Well," Romero said, "at least we got one valuable piece of

information here. We may not have seen who was coming and going from the room, but based on when the camera was cleaned, we can be pretty certain that the violin was removed from the room sometime before 2:20. That's helpful."

"Hold on," Kavanaugh said. "No one caught it going on real time, and this camera didn't pick up who the person was. But what about another camera, from a different angle? Maybe we can see who it was by looking at the video of the elevator lobby, just before this."

"Good point," said Cherson. "Let's take a look." He called up the footage from the camera covering the elevator lobby on that floor, but as soon as he saw it his shoulders drooped.

"Problem," he muttered. "The cameras that cover that corridor and the elevator lobby are basically mounted back-to-back, suspended from the ceiling. Based on the angles that the cameras are directed, there's a blind spot—a wedge of space below them that neither one picks up. Unfortunately, one of the three elevators and the lobby space in front of it are within that blind spot."

Luis instructed Cherson: "Run the video anyway; maybe we'll see someone using one of the elevators we can see." He fast-forwarded through the 15 minutes of the coverage before the corridor camera was sprayed, but the only person seen using the two visible elevators was Konstantin, after he left Bill's room. The video showed him standing in the lobby, then moving toward one of the visible elevators as the door opened, but then he hesitated. Two people got off the elevator and walked down the opposite corridor, away from Bill's side of the tower.

"Look, he's gesturing and saying something to whoever's in the elevator," Greg said. "It looks to me like the elevator must be going up, not down, so he's waiting for another elevator."

In fact, the video did show the elevator doors close a moment later, without Konstantin getting on, and after another moment of standing in the lobby, he walked over, and into the area not visible to the camera—presumably to the elevator, which must have been going down. Other than Konstantin, and the couple that had gotten off the rising elevator, no other people showed up during the entire 15-minute time span.

"Pappas was in that blind spot for some time, and at about the right time. He could have been the one spraying the camera lens," Kavanaugh said.

"At the same time," Luis replied, "anyone else could have come up to the floor using that particular elevator, too."

Frustrated, Kavanaugh slumped in his chair. "The video gives us a pretty good confirmation that the violin was stolen sometime between 10:00 and 2:20. But that's about it."

"Let's see if we can learn anything else from other video," Luis interjected. "Let's scan footage from other areas of the hotel to see if we notice anything out of the ordinary, focusing on the video from the banquet room where Dr. Sloan's luncheon took place."

"It sounds like you're going to be a while," Amanda Wilhelm said, pulling out her phone. "Let me order some complimentary refreshments for you to enjoy while you work." After getting back off the phone, she excused herself from the group. "I've got to get on to other things now, but if you need anything else, just let me know."

"All right then, let's start with video from the luncheon first," Luis suggested.

"The luncheon took place in a hall that's subdividable into two smaller rooms using movable partitions, Cherson explained. "Each of the two smaller spaces is equipped with a single camera, and there's additional video coverage that picks up the main entries into and out of them. We'll have access to video from four different angles. Can I suggest setting up two stations to review the video, with each one having enlarged views of the video from inside the room, and the coverage of the entry door to that same room? Detective Kavanaugh, you could review the video at one station, and Agent Romero, you could review the other."

"We'd cover more ground in the same amount of time that way," Luis said. "Yes, let's set things up that way."

Just as Cherson had the two stations cued up, the door behind them opened and a server pushed in a cart filled with coffee, tea, some cut fruit, and a platter of pastries.

"Here you go, gentlemen," the server said cheerily, "compliments of Ms. Wilhelm. I'll check back with you in a while; please let me know if there's anything else you need."

Kavanaugh walked over to the cart and picked up a cheese Danish. "What we really needed from Ms. Wilhelm was for her to properly staff her security operation, but it's too late for that," he muttered.

Kavanaugh's comment hung in the air while the server retreated from the room.

For some time following, the group reviewed the video that Cherson had called up, with Bill reviewing alongside Kavanaugh and Greg and Dan joining Luis. Reviewing them, the group could easily see that of the primary suspects, all were present at the function, and all of them except Eric Morrison and Alana Marino had left it at one point or another during the hour.

"I'm not sure what that tells us," Kavanaugh said during a break. "Any one of them could still have taken the violin, even the ones that never left the banquet hall, since they could have taken it afterward, when you went out to visit with your friends, Mr. Sloan."

Bill nodded. Romero agreed. "That's true," he said, sampling some grapes from the cart, "but let's overlay some of this information. For example, let's compare who left the banquet hall at a certain time, and then look at video from the elevator banks to see if any of them went up to the 10th floor of the west tower during that time. That might move someone up on the list of suspects. If they aren't seen going up to that floor at all, it would tend to eliminate them from serious suspicion. Do you agree?"

"That makes sense," Kavanaugh said. "Cherson, can you set that up?"

"Already working on it," Cherson said over his shoulder.

An hour or so later, the server returned, cleaned up, and removed the refreshment cart. The group had just finished the video review.

"OK, so from what we've seen," Luis said, "it appears that for whatever reasons, every single one of the primary suspects ended up on the west tower 10th floor at various times."

"So, the video doesn't rule anyone out," Kavanaugh said.

"Not at this point," Romero agreed. "But it's late now; let's call it a day. Mr. Cherson, would you please get me copies of all the video we've looked at today—the corridors, the elevator lobbies, the stairways, the banquet hall, and the main lobby? I'd like to review them in detail."

"Sure, no problem," Cherson answered. "I'll have one of the people on our second shift copy all of them, and you should have them by tomorrow morning."

CHAPTER 13

WEDNESDAY, 6:00 P.M.

"See you in about an hour and a half?" Greg asked Dan. Despite the drama of the Jackson's theft, the VSA convention activities continued, largely uninterrupted. The competition judging went on through the evening and would wrap up by noon the following day, with the judges' results to be tallied shortly thereafter, so the awards could be personalized in time for the banquet on Thursday. Greg still had one official convention event to attend this evening, and he and Dan planned to meet for dinner immediately afterward.

"Sure," Dan said, "I'll see you when you get out of your seminar. In fact, I was going to walk up the street to that bar we saw yesterday; why don't you just meet me there whenever you're done?"

"Sounds good, see you then," Greg said, kissing Dan and heading to the seminar.

After the seminar, Greg heard Hanna call from across the hotel lobby. She and Chloé walked over to join him.

"Hey, I'm just walking up the street to meet Dan and then go to dinner."

"Mind if we tag along, at least to the bar?" Hanna asked. "Chloé, let's go have a drink. I need to stretch my legs a little after sitting through that seminar."

As the three of them stepped out into the warm evening breeze, Greg said, "Wow, Chloé, you really put Malcolm Stewart in his place last night. I couldn't believe you did that, but it was absolutely hilarious!"

"He had it coming," Chloé said, "and the fact that he gave me an opportunity to do that with an audience made it even better. Ever since Hanna told me she wanted to come this year, I knew I was going to end up seeing that idiot, and one way or another, I knew I wanted to cause him some pain where it hurt most—his ego."

"Well, you definitely succeeded," Greg affirmed.

"Nobody screws with my wife," she said coolly.

Changing tone, she asked, "Are they making any progress about who stole the Jackson?"

"Who knows? Not that I'm aware of, anyway," Hanna replied. "You know the police detective interviewed me this morning. He definitely considers me a suspect. I could tell he didn't like me, and I saw him actually squirm when I mentioned having a wife. I have to admit, once I realized I could push his buttons, I did it some, just for sport."

Chloé snickered. "That's one of the things I love about you."

"Well, he is a bit of a fool," Hanna said. "I know he's just doing his job, but really, he was wasting valuable time talking with me when he could have been going down other paths to find the real thief."

"Now that I agree with," Greg said.

"Oh, I don't know, I wouldn't put it past you to have stolen it just to have for yourself," Chloé teased. "You seem obsessed with that violin. Sometimes I think you love it more than me. Plus, stealing the Jackson would put an end to Stewart's bragging rights. Maybe you did have something to do with this. You do have a dark side."

"And that's another thing that you love about me," Hanna said in a conspiratorial tone. "You really do know me well—sometimes, better than you realize."

An hour later, Hanna and Chloé had left the bar and returned to the hotel, while Dan and Greg remained. Dan wasn't a completely obnoxious bourbon snob, but when he'd arrived at the bar earlier that evening, he'd been disappointed by the fairly small selection available. Without any really noteworthy option to drink neat, he settled for an Old Fashioned made with a middle-of-the-pack bourbon. *Maybe you're more of a bourbon snob than you're willing to admit*, he thought to himself. He was halfway through his second one, sitting alone at the bar since Greg had slipped away to talk with a friend at a neighboring table.

"Hey, Reverend Randolph!" Dan turned and was surprised to see Luis Romero sitting halfway down the bar. Dan smiled and waved him over.

"Hi Luis, how are you? What brings you here? Oh, and for the record: my parishioners call me Dan; you can, too."

Luis smiled. "All right, Dan. Actually, I just left the hotel a little while ago and thought I'd clear my head in some 'neutral territory' as it were, before I head home."

"I get that," Dan said. "Your glass is almost empty; buy you another?"

"Sure, I guess so. Thanks." Luis sat on the padded barstool next to Dan. "Vodka tonic," he called out to the bartender, who was wiping down the glass-topped bar in front of them.

"So, Luis, how exactly did you come to be an FBI agent?"

"Well, for me, it was easy; it was sort of the family business," he said. "My father was an FBI agent, and it always seemed natural for me to follow in his footsteps. I joined the bureau as soon as I could."

"It must have been very helpful learning the ropes when your father had been through it, too."

"Absolutely. In some ways, he had it tougher than me, though. Back then, the FBI was still very much an Anglo men's club."

"And now?"

Luis smiled. "Well, it's gotten better, at least. J. Edgar Hoover has been dead for a lot longer now." The bartender placed his drink in front of him, and he paused to take a sip. "Sure, I've had to deal with racism, and other things, too, but my dad's advice was very helpful."

"What did he tell you?" Dan asked.

Luis thought for a second before summarizing. "A lot of technical ins and outs of bureau life that have been helpful. But most importantly, based his own experiences as a Latino agent, he told me that it would be harder for me, and I was going to have to deal with people who rejected me just based on who I was, whether that was my race, my age, or whatever. But he'd tell me, 'Just let them see what they want to see, let them hear what they want to hear, let them say what they want to say. Just keep up the deception and keep stroking their egos while you work twice as hard, and twice as smart, and you run rings around them.' "

Dan took another sip of his Old Fashioned, nodded thoughtfully, and said, "Sounds like pretty good advice. If you don't mind my saying so, I sense that you're doing some of that while working with Detective Kavanaugh."

Luis looked down. "Oh, I've had to deal with far worse than him—but yeah, a little."

"I probably shouldn't ask you how your investigation is going," Dan said, "since in the movies, the person who asks the most questions usually ends up being the actual criminal," he chuckled.

"There is some truth to that," Luis nodded. "So, tell me, just why did you steal the violin, anyway?"

Dan looked up at the bartender. "Tonic water with a twist of lime, please. Luis, another?"

"Actually, I'll have the same thing, please."

Looking back at Luis, Dan continued as seriously as he could muster, "Oh, for resale, obviously. I don't play the violin myself, and you know, we clergy have so many contacts in the international black market."

Luis smiled. "I suppose I really should look in a different direction."

"As far as the investigation goes," he continued, "Detective Kavanaugh's office and ours spent most of the day putting together personal profiles on all the people closest to the theft, and I spent the last bit of the day starting in on those, in addition to my own interview notes and Kavanaugh's.

"Anything of interest pop up?"

"A few things—yellow flags, at least, if not outright red ones." The bartender set the two drinks in front of them. "As I told you earlier, these crimes come in different types, and so do the motives. The thief might be in a financial bind and see this as a solution. They might be seeking revenge for something, or want to prove some twisted point. Of course, there are the crimes of passion and obsession we discussed earlier. Most times, it's strictly to make a buck, plain and simple."

"Well, wherever the investigation goes, I really do hope you get to the bottom of this thing, and soon. I'd hate to see Bill lose the Jackson."

Luis sipped his tonic. "You asked how I became an FBI agent. So tell me, what's it like being a gay minister?"

Dan arched his eyebrows. "That's as complicated a story as your own must be," he said, "but a few thoughts. I've actually been blessed in a way. Attitudes have changed so much in many parts of the Church, and as you've said, while there's still much room for improvement, things are much better. My own denomination has accepted ordained gay folk for 10 years now. I can be out, married to a man, perform same-sex marriages, talk about my relationship openly, just have a relatively normal life. And I can do all of that while serving God as pastor to a truly remarkable, loving congregation, without secrets, without pretense, authentically—as authentically as straight clergy, anyway: "Just As I Am, Without One Plea." That's something that we couldn't even dream of just a generation ago. Yes," Dan said, "I'm blessed."

"I'm sensing that there's a 'but' somewhere in there."

"Yes," Dan said, "and a big one. I still get my share of hatred and rejection, both inside the Church and in society in general. Every so often, our congregation still gets emails or social media comments about having a gay pastor and telling us we're all going to hell. Obviously, a lot of the Church still rejects me outright." He paused for another sip of tonic.

"Maybe the worst part is that some days, I feel like a man without a country. A lot of Christians reject me because I'm gay, and a lot of gays reject me because I'm Christian, and part of an institution that's hurt so many of us—me included. That can be exhausting and demoralizing. In spite of that, I still feel that I'm doing what God wants me to be doing. I mean, God knew I was gay—God created me gay—long before calling me into the ministry. So if anyone has a problem with it, they can take it up with God, not me."

"Are you talking shop again?" Greg scolded. He was standing directly behind them. "Hi Agent Romero, it's good to see you again."

Romero tipped his glass to Greg. "Please call me Luis."

"Hey, sorry, didn't see you slip in," Dan said as he reached around Greg's waist and pulled him closer. "No, that's all I had to say on the subject for now. Sermon over, I promise."

Greg shook his head, smiling as he rolled his eyes. "You can get awfully preachy and wordy at times."

"Occupational hazard. You know what it means when a preacher looks at their watch? Absolutely nothing," he joked.

"Except for right now," Greg said. "We've got to get some dinner."

"That's very true," Dan agreed. "And on that note, Luis, we'll leave you to your tonic and lime. Have a good remainder of the evening."

He and Greg stepped back out into the warmth of the evening. "Hey," Dan said, "would you be in the mood to mix it up a bit for dinner?"

"Why, what are you thinking?"

"I saw a street about a block away that was lined with trucks selling all kinds of different foods. How about we just graze from truck to truck trying out some things and enjoying the outdoors, instead of sitting inside another restaurant?"

"Yeah, I'm up for it. Let's do it!"

A short while later they'd reached their destination. They strolled up and down the street surveying the various offerings. "I can't believe it!" Greg said. "There's a truck selling Stinky Tofu! We need to get some!"

Dan buried his head in his hands. "Oh, God. I thought I smelled something awful; I just assumed someone's sewer had backed up."

"I don't care what you think, I'm getting an order." They walked over to the truck, and Greg placed his order.

"I'll just have the *takoyaki*, please," Dan told the woman in the truck window. "I honestly don't know how you can eat that," he muttered as they sat down at a picnic table with their orders.

"Hey, I don't trash-talk your *pierogies*," Greg said.

"My *pierogies* don't smell like toe jam."

"I'll grant you, it is an acquired taste," Greg admitted.

"But why would anyone want to acquire it?"

Greg just smiled.

"Oh, by the way," Dan said, "I forgot to tell you earlier, but I had an interesting experience today during my walk." He filled Greg in on his encounter that morning with Konstantin and Malcolm Stewart.

"You aren't suggesting that it had something to do with the Jackson?" Greg asked.

"I don't know; it was just odd. Based on what I heard, it could have been something perfectly innocent. What caught my attention was their reactions, their body language—the vibe of it all. It seemed like they were acting guilty, evasive—worried that I'd heard something I shouldn't have. It felt weird."

Greg shook his head. "Well, weird or not, I'm positive it doesn't have anything to do with the Jackson. First of all, there's no way in the world that Konstantin would ever steal anything, much less anything from Bill. They're practically like brothers."

Dan nodded.

"Beyond that, I can't imagine two people any more different than Konstantin and Malcolm Stewart. I know from previous conversations that Konstantin doesn't like Malcolm, and really, can you blame him? Even in some parallel universe, it would just be unthinkable that the two of them would partner up in something like this."

"I'm sure you're right," Dan said. "It was probably something innocent. As I said, it was just weird. Not as weird as Stinky Tofu, but still pretty weird."

"Jerk."

Dan smiled. "So what do you think? Time to move on to another truck?"

"Sure," Greg said. "I picked the last one; now it's your turn." They wandered down the street until Dan exclaimed, "Ah, now you're talking: Italian street food!" This time, Dan ordered *gorgonzola arancini*, while Greg got an order of *panzerotti*. This time, they continued walking while they ate, enjoying the night.

"Hey, gentlemen." It was Phil Goodman. "Looks like you've found something good to eat."

"Hi, Phil. How are you this evening?" Greg asked.

The heavenly aroma of Mexican *elotes* breathed from an adjacent street, and Phil fell in beside them. "Oh, I'm fine, thanks," he said. "You know, I've always wanted to ask you why you made pretty much exclusively Amati-based instruments."

Greg explained the reasons for his preference.

"I guess it just seems odd, since most players prefer a Strad pattern to an Amati."

Greg's face darkened. "I don't really think it's true."

For whatever reason—maybe simple meanness—Goodman seemed intentionally trying to get under Greg's skin. He pushed further: "But you know that people say that Amati violins are sweet and subtle, but the tone of a Strad model will carry above the rest of the orchestra."

"No!" Greg countered strenuously. "There are great and mediocre Strads, and great and mediocre Amatis. Every instrument, regardless of its pattern, stands on its own." Greg was passionate on this point. "You know as well as I do that Stradivari was a mere mortal like the rest of us. He had good days and bad days. Out of the 500-odd Strads surviving, some are masterpieces, and some are completely unremarkable. The unremarkable ones still fetch high prices, but only because they're Strads, not because they're superior musical instruments."

Goodman didn't seem convinced. "But why specialize in using a particular design when potential customers—justifiably or not—seem to want another design? Why limit your potential market—your potential profitability—that way?"

Greg's face was red. "That's just never really been true. The reality is that the subtleties between a Strad and an Amati design might stand out to you or me, but most violinists wouldn't even notice, let alone care about, the differences. What they care about is: 'How does it sound?' 'How does it feel?' and 'Can it do what I want it to do?' And on those points, I'm happy to have my instruments compared to those of any pattern, made by anyone." Looking pointedly at Goodman, he repeated, "Anyone."

"Well, maybe you're right," Goodman said—his exit strategy for the conversation he'd started. "In any case, I'm starving. I think I'm going to try some of the tacos from that truck over there. I'll talk with you gentlemen later!"

"I hate that guy," Greg muttered.

"He's an ass. He was clearly trying to needle you," Dan agreed. He paused to take his last bite of *arancini*, before adding, "On the other hand, he may have a point."

Greg looked cautiously at Dan. "What do you mean?"

"Well, if—I'm just saying if—he's right, that for whatever reason, potential buyers automatically, maybe even subconsciously, lean first toward Strad-pattern violins, wouldn't it maybe be a good idea to make, maybe not all, but at least some that are Strad pattern?"

"Well, that's just illogical," Greg said. "As I told him, it isn't true. Amatis are often better sounding than Strads."

"I'm not disputing that," Dan said. "But in the violin world, like everywhere else, sometimes the perception becomes the reality."

Greg bristled. "I'm not going to change to accommodate something that isn't true."

"I'm not saying to change. I'm just wondering if you could supplement what you normally do, to appeal to that specific portion of your market."

"If they feel that way, I'm not interested in them as customers, anyway. If anything, I need to keep doing what I think is right, to show those people how mistaken they are."

"But you aren't going to educate everyone, no matter how good your instruments are. Wouldn't it be a good business decision to diversify a bit? I mean, when I was an architect—"

"Stop." Greg's face was red again, and his hand extended out in front of him as a barrier between them. "I don't care about what you did when you were an architect. This is different."

"Yes," Dan pushed, "parts of it are different, but parts of it follow the same principles, and—"

"Just stop it!" Greg shouted. "You don't really understand anything about this, and I wish you'd keep your nose out of it! I'm going to do it the way I want to do it, no matter what Phil Goodman thinks, and no matter what you think!"

"You don't give a damn about anything I think!" Dan yelled back. "So many times I see you doing the exact opposite of what you should do, and I'll say something about it to try to protect you, to try to help you, and it just gets thrown back into my face. I swear to God, I'm never going to say anything to you about your business ever again!"

Dan paused for a breath. "It just—it just—oh, I give up. The hell with it."

"Yeah." Greg muttered, "The hell with it."

CHAPTER 14

THURSDAY, 6:30 A.M.

When Dan's alarm sounded that morning, he discovered himself jammed as close as possible to his side of the bed, and Greg as far away as possible on the opposite side. The tension between them was palpable. Dan crawled out of bed and got dressed for his walk, this time not paying much attention to being quiet, still mad from the night before. Greg opened his eyes momentarily; they were still filled with anger and hurt. He rolled away rather than deal with Dan as he finished getting dressed.

When Dan returned about an hour and a half later, Greg was up. They remained silent until Dan said, "I'm going down for breakfast. Do you want to come, too?" Greg didn't say anything but headed toward the door, and the two of them made their way to the lobby.

At their table, they only spoke to place their orders. "Breakfast number 4, scrambled, wheat toast, and a black coffee," Dan muttered.

"Breakfast number 3, blueberry syrup, home fries. Coffee;

double double," Greg said.

The server, clearly sensing the tension at the table, acknowledged the order and made a quiet retreat. The order arrived and the two ate in silence.

A few minutes into their meal, the server tripped on a floor mat, falling forward and crashing into their table, sending an entire order flying—and landing all over Greg. Dan instinctively jumped up and started wiping Greg, scooping bits of food off his clothing and patting his face dry with a napkin.

"Oh my gosh, are you all right? Are you OK?" he asked, panicked. "You didn't get burned by anything, did you?"

"I'm fine; I'm fine," Greg assured him. Once it was clear that he was messy but otherwise all right, the two of them sat back down.

"Thank you," Greg said quietly.

"You're welcome."

They quickly returned to their room, where Greg washed off and got a fresh change of clothes. The silence was broken, and they were able to resume at least something resembling normal discourse as they sat side by side on the edge of their bed.

"Honey, I'm sorry," Dan finally said. "I know I overstepped my bounds. I just get carried away sometimes. It all comes out of my wanting the best for you, but I know that no matter what my intentions are, sometimes I cross a line—like last night. I'm sorry."

Greg looked into Dan's eyes for the first time that morning. He responded carefully and thoughtfully. "I know that you meant well. I know that you always mean well. And I know that you do have some experience from your time in the business world that can be helpful sometimes. But the world you were in isn't the exact same as the world I'm in. There are differences. This is my world. And I need to navigate my world in the way I think is best. I have to follow my instincts, express my art, and conduct my business, my way."

Dan sat, listening as he looked at Greg. He felt horrible, not only for having overstepped and upset Greg, but also knowing that this wasn't the first time they'd clashed over this same subject.

"And just as I wouldn't have ever told you how to design a building, and I won't ever tell you how to write a sermon, I have to decide—by myself—how I'm going to make my violins." He paused before continuing. "You can—and you do—help me in my work in a lot of ways, you really do," he said. "But they are always going to be my violins."

"You're absolutely right," Dan answered. "I'm glad I can help you in the ways that I can. I'm not going to insult your intelligence by promising I'll never make this same mistake again," he said, "because we both know that at some point, I will. But I will try, and I promise that most of the time, I'll succeed. Honey, I really am sorry."

Greg looked at Dan with a remnant of hurt, but mostly love in his eyes. "You're right; it's unavoidable. We will have this same argument again. But I know that your words come from you caring about me, and I know that you're trying. That isn't perfect, but it's something. In any case, it's time to move forward."

After a few moments, Dan changed the topic. "The time here is going by quickly. So tell me, putting aside the situation with the Jackson—and, well, this—how are you feeling about the convention and competition?"

Greg relaxed into what Dan could only consider a contented, whole-body smile. "I don't know how else to put it other than to say that it's been soul-restoring. So many of the people here are like family to me, and my spirit seems like it had just atrophied, not being able to get together with them—working, discussing, sharing, socializing. I've needed this so bad."

"I can tell," Dan said. "You've basically been glowing the whole week. Plus," he added, "You've been able to settle on a dealership arrangement with Chase, which will put your instruments in another major market. You have every reason to feel good." He paused, and then asked, "And now that the competition judging is almost over, how do you feel about your chances for some recognition this time around?"

Greg didn't answer immediately. He carefully thought about the question and finally answered, "Well, to start with, I'm always very honored and grateful that I have the opportunity to collaborate with, and at the same time compete with, so many incredibly talented makers. As far as my chances for an award this year, we'll just have to see. But however all that comes out, I am really very happy with the way this particular violin—the first Vieuxtemps Amati—came out."

"I'm glad to hear you say that," Dan said, and he reached over to grab Greg's hand. Smiling, he asked, "Now that you aren't covered in hash browns and maple syrup, what would you like to do?"

"I've got a short seminar to get to right now, but after that, Bill asked a handful of friends from the Oberlin workshop to join him for a mini-reunion down in the lobby. You're welcome to join us, if you want."

"I think I'm going to stay here in the room and read while you're in your seminar," Dan said. "But when you get back, we can go down together."

CHAPTER 15

THURSDAY, 6:30 A.M.

Luis woke up without need of an alarm, quietly rolling out of bed and slipping into the bathroom to prepare for the day. After working his way through his normal morning routine, he tried to get dressed as quietly as possible, but as he was putting on his pants, his belt slipped from his fingers and clanked on the hardwood floor.

"Dammit!" he whispered.

"It's OK. I'm awake anyway," his husband, Josh, mumbled from under the sheets. "Sometimes I like to pretend I'm asleep while you're getting ready for work, just to see you struggle to be quiet."

Luis rolled his eyes. "*Pendejo.*"

Josh snorted. "I love your ability to swear bilingually."

"I guess I'm just a man of many talents. Well, sorry about the noise anyway."

"You were up late last night reading," Josh said. " 'The Case of the Missing Violin,' I presume?"

"Yeah, and I'll be with that Detective Kavanaugh a lot of the day. We'll go over all the stuff I was reading and taking notes on last night. A couple of things caught my attention in the background research that our office pulled up on the initial suspects, and I think we're going to need to dig into them further. We'll be going through even more video from the hotel to see if we can find anything else that might be helpful."

Josh rolled his eyes. "Sounds like fun."

Luis sighed. "Yeah. I am not looking forward to spending the whole day with Jim Kavanaugh. That guy is a real piece of work."

"Piece of work?" Josh toyed with him.

"Piece of something," Luis grumbled.

"Well, whatever he's a piece of," Josh assured him, "I know you'll solve the case, with help from him or without it. When it comes to famous violin thefts, you're the man. Own it."

"Well," Luis said, "whether I'm the man or not, I'm going to be late if I don't get going. I'll see you this evening." He gave Josh a peck on the cheek and headed out.

About an hour after Luis left home, he and Kavanaugh grabbed some coffee and set up shop in a meeting room on the second floor of the Anaheim Police Department's sprawling brick headquarters.

"So have you reviewed all the files we sent you?" Kavanaugh asked.

Luis answered, "Yes, I've gone over them in detail. I had a few questions and thoughts, but let's look at the video first." He connected his laptop to a large monitor and opened one of the video files. "We know that the primary camera was obscured from 10:00 until 2:20, so it's safe to assume that the theft took place between those times, and no later. We also know that the camera was obscured just before Alana Marino showed up at Sloan's room."

"Yeah," Kavanaugh agreed. "I will say, before seeing any of the video, I originally thought the queer Asian guy was the most likely suspect. But the more I learn about him, the less likely I think he's our guy. The timing of the camera tampering makes me suspect Marino more. You saw in her file that even though she looks like she's living high on the hog, she's really almost broke. That's hardly rare here in LA, but it's still some motivation to steal something worth millions of dollars if you get a chance to. Plus the fact that she's connected to the Philadelphia Marino crime family."

Luis cringed internally. He had heard Alana Marino perform multiple times and was aware of her reputation in the music world. To put it mildly, he was impressed by her. Still, he admitted, "Her financial situation did come as a surprise. I'd have thought she'd be doing very well for herself, and I didn't realize before now that she had any connection to the Marino crime family. It's a relatively common last name, after all."

He sipped his coffee before continuing. "The bureau has been tracking the Marino organization for a long time, and we know they've been involved in international smuggling for years. If Alana Marino actually were the thief, and if she were working with them, they'd definitely have the connections to sell the violin on the black market, for a good price, and even to get it out of the country if need be."

Luis was calling up video of the hotel lobby when Kavanaugh's phone rang.

"Hang on, I have to take this call." He pushed himself away from the table, walked to the other side of the room and dropped into an armchair. Luis wasn't trying to listen to Kavanaugh's call, but it was hard not to.

"Hey honey, what's up?" It was quickly clear that the detective was talking with his wife. Luis noticed an immediate and substantial shift in Kavanaugh's demeanor. "Again? Well, what did the principal say?"

As the conversation continued, Luis was able to discern that Kavanaugh and his wife were discussing their son, who was having recurring problems with some other boys bullying him at school.

"Is he there right now? Let me talk with him," Kavanaugh said to his wife.

Surprisingly, he wasn't adopting the stereotypical tough guy, suck-it-up attitude toward the boy's difficulties. In the conversation with both his wife and son, Luis noticed that the hardened detective was genuinely compassionate, thoughtful—tender, even. *Actually human*, Luis thought.

It reminded him of something from his past. "Even Hitler loved his dog," his father would sometimes say—meaning that everyone is multi-dimensional, complex, and often enough, even contradictory. Just when you think you have a person figured out, the elder Romero told his son, they do something completely contrary to your perception. He always remembered his father's phrase, and his point: we can easily deceive ourselves into thinking the wrong thing about anyone, good or bad, if we reduce them to something simplistic, binary.

A few minutes later the phone call was over. "All right let's get back to work," Kavanaugh said gruffly. Luis noticed that he immediately slipped back into his more familiar persona.

"We're going to need to dig a little deeper into Marino—her background, her alibi, everything." He sat back down at the table next to Luis, who had pulled up video from the hotel lobby. "I'll tell you what, though—even if she was the thief, wow, can she fill out a dress."

Ah well, Luis thought. *Even Hitler loved his dog. And a racist, homophobic, misogynistic bigot can have his moment, too.* But apparently, only a moment.

Sidestepping Kavanaugh's last comment, Luis said, "Let's recap what she told us. When you first sat down with her, she told you that she'd gotten up Tuesday morning, around 7:00, and was doing her tone judging from about 8:00 until about 9:45 or so, when she said she took a break to go to Dr. Sloan's room to play the Jackson."

"Right," Kavanaugh agreed. "We also know, based on what she told us (and confirmed by the registration desk), at 11:00 she checked into a room on the ninth floor of the hotel, the floor just below Sloan's. We know that she was at Sloan's luncheon from noon until just a few minutes after one, when it wrapped up. So she's unaccounted for between 11:30 and noon."

"Wait, something isn't right with that," Luis said thoughtfully. Opening a folder on his laptop and scanning a particular file, he said, "Right, I thought I remembered something like this. When I was talking with Greg Zhu, he said that he saw her having a heated conversation with a man in the vendors' hall, probably around 8:30."

"So she wasn't being completely honest about what she did that morning," Kavanaugh noted.

"Right. Of course, we know that the Jackson was still in Dr. Sloan's room much later on, so her not being where she said she was doesn't carve out time when she could have stolen it, but it does prompt questions about why she wasn't being completely honest."

Luis' heart sank even before he'd completed the sentence. "And who was she was talking with?" It was the first time he'd put the possibility of Alana being the thief into words.

"Based on the rundown I got from Zhu, he and a group of people were talking with her in the elevator lobby for around 15 minutes at around 1:30. But any time after that, until 2:20 when the security camera in the 10th floor corridor went back online, she would have been free to get into the room and take the violin," Kavanaugh said. "Assuming she could find a way to actually get into the locked room."

"There are relatively easy ways to clone a magnetic key card and to create a duplicate card or even turn your phone into a viable substitute key," Luis admitted. "If anyone had access at any time to Dr. Sloan's room key, and a bit of know-how, they could have duplicated it."

"And," Kavanaugh added, "Sloan told us that when she was in his room, she had a violin case that would hold two violins, but it was only carrying one, so she'd have had a place to stow the Jackson and get it out of the hotel."

"OK, let's hold that thought for a moment," Luis suggested, "and look at some of the video the hotel provided us."

They sat reviewing video footage for quite some time. At first, they focused on video from the ninth-floor corridor, just below

Bill Sloan's floor. Konstantin Pappas and a number of other violin makers had rooms on this floor, and cross-referencing other video, the two of them verified the comings and goings of their primary suspects. Several times, the ninth-floor video picked up Konstantin coming and going to his room, often avoiding the wait for an elevator to get to Bill's room by using the stair tower at the far end of the hall. Right around 11:00, the video captured Alana Marino checking into her room, as she'd told them she had. At one point, shortly before noon, Phil Goodman used the same stair tower to enter the corridor.

"Ah, this is right after we determined he'd stopped at Sloan's room to call him down to the reception," Kavanaugh noted.

"He must be giving similar notifications to others. You can see him knocking on doors as he makes his way down the hallway before he disappears under the camera angle," Luis replied.

Next, they turned their attention to video from other parts of the hotel from the past several days. Around 6:00 Tuesday evening, Alana Marino had been sitting at a table talking with a man about her own age, dressed in expensive-looking business-casual wear. It was clear from the video that she wasn't enjoying herself.

"Hey, there she is!" Kavanaugh exclaimed, pointing at her on the screen. They watched Alana talking with the man for about 15 minutes, in what appeared to be tense conversation. Then she and the man got up and left the hotel together.

"Wait a minute," Luis said. "Let's rewind this a bit and focus on the man." Using the touchpad on his laptop, he quickly click-dragged a window framing the violinist and the man and zoomed in.

"Do you know who that is? That's Anthony Marino. He's well known by the bureau as a mid-level operative in the Marino crime family. Clearly not the brains of the operation, but he's still a fairly important player."

"I wonder if that's the same guy Zhu saw her with that morning, and then at dinner a little after this video," Kavanaugh muttered.

"It will be easy enough to show him screen captures to see if he can identify him," Luis said. "I'm going to log into the bureau's files and see if there's anything on him that might be important for us." He sat at the laptop for several minutes, reading through notes on Alana's cousin. Kavanaugh waited impatiently as Luis read from the file, getting up from the table and walking over to the seating area where he'd taken the phone call. He refilled his coffee mug and selected a donut from a box he'd brought into the office with him. He returned to the table, impatiently drumming his fingers on the tabletop.

"Ah, that's interesting," Luis finally said, breaking the silence. He turned and looked at Kavanaugh, noticing the donut in his hand.

"Don't you say a damned word," Kavanaugh warned. He was

a living law enforcement cliché. "What did you find out about Marino?"

"It seems that Anthony Marino has gotten himself upside-down with a few other mobsters—apparently skimming from the profits he owed them, holding out on payouts he'd promised—and now they're hammering him hard to square up."

"No kidding?"

"Yeah, it seems word on the street is that Marino needs a lot of money, and fast, or someone's going to find his body floating in the Schuylkill River."

"It sounds like these two Marinos both have serious money problems. Maybe they decided to team up to steal this violin."

"It is at least a possibility," Luis admitted. Trying to stroke Kavanaugh's ego, he asked, "What do you think we should do, detective? Should we take a break here and follow up on this at the hotel?"

Kavanaugh stretched back in his chair. "Well, yeah, I think that's exactly what we should do. Let's get over there right away and see if we can talk with Alana Marino, and maybe even find out where her cousin might be."

They pulled out of the gated parking area about 10:00, and in just under 15 minutes, they arrived at the hotel. As they approached the glass entry doors, Luis asked, as innocently as he could, "What do you think, detective? You think maybe we should review video from this morning to see what Marino might be up to?"

Kavanaugh oozed satisfaction. "Yeah, I want to make sure she's still here, and I want to see video from around her room to see who's come and gone this morning. You check on where she is right now, and I'll track down the security guy."

Dan and Greg were sitting in the lobby with Bill Sloan and several other convention attendees, and Greg was laughing loudly.

Kavanaugh grunted when he noticed them. "I know it's old fashioned, and it isn't politically correct to say it—this is just between us—but I've never really been able to be comfortable around gay guys. They're just different. It just isn't natural, you know?"

"Oh, I don't know," Luis countered. "I guarantee you that you've worked with gay people your whole life."

"Oh, sure," Kavanaugh agreed, "I've worked with gay guys, and some of them were pretty good at their jobs. But still, it's weird."

"Detective, you've undoubtedly been good friends with gay people, and probably even had gay people in your own family. You just didn't know it, because they weren't different from anyone else."

"Nah, I always know. I can spot a gay guy a mile away."

Ignoring the irony, Luis looked across the lobby again, and just then saw Dan instinctively reach over to hold Greg's hand. Suddenly, he wanted to be done with this day, done with Kavanaugh, and home with Josh. But that was hours away.

They learned that Alana Marino was still checked into the hotel and wasn't scheduled to leave until the next morning. Phil Goodman approached them as they spoke to the front desk clerk. "I'm sorry," he said. "I don't mean to interrupt, but did I hear you say you were looking for Alana Marino?"

"Yes," Kavanaugh said. "Do you know where she is?"

"Actually, I do," he replied. "She and the other tone judges are in the competition hall right now, finishing up their work before the awards banquet. Did you want me to get her for you?"

"No," Luis said, as long as we know she's here in the building, it's fine. She can finish up what she's doing, but we'll need to see her shortly."

"I'll go tell her that you're here and want to talk with her when she's finished." Goodman strode across the lobby.

Luis turned to Kavanaugh. "In the meantime," he said, "let's find Elliott Cherson and look at some video." Within a few minutes, they were in the security room, where Cherson had pulled up video feeds of the ninth-floor east corridor and the hotel lobby.

"OK, there's Alana Marino leaving her room this morning," Kavanaugh said.

"And here we see her a few minutes later going through the lobby and entering the competition hall," Luis noted as he watched on a separate screen. "Now I can see her leaving the competition hall and coming back through the lobby, right at 9:00 this morning."

Kavanaugh leaned in closer to his screen. "Yeah, here she is coming back down the hall, and she goes back to her room."

"Let's keep watching her room to see when she comes back out." They didn't have to wait long to see something important, but it wasn't Alana leaving her room.

"Hey, check this out!" Kavanaugh said. Luis slid over to watch the screen. "Rewind this a little, Cherson." The footage showed Anthony Marino leaving a room just a few doors away from Alana's. He moved to her door and knocked. A moment later, Alana opened the door and the two talked for a moment or two. Then, she disappeared back into the room.

"Now what's going on?" Kavanaugh wondered. He barely got the words out before Alana reappeared at the door, holding a violin case, which she handed to Anthony Marino. The two exchanged a few more words before he returned to his room. Alana stepped back into hers, but within just a few minutes she left and went back downstairs.

Luis leaned back in his chair, rubbing his forehead.

Kavanaugh broke the silence. "What's going on? What just happened there?"

Cherson looked up and said, "Whatever it was, we've run through all the recorded video. What you're watching on that camera now is live—real time." He'd hardly spoken the words when the camera feed showed Anthony Marino leave his room and head toward the elevator lobby, a carry-on suitcase in one hand, the violin case in another.

"Looks like he's leaving right now," Luis said. Forgetting or disregarding his previous efforts to defer to Kavanaugh's leadership, he ordered, "Quick! Out to the lobby! Cherson, get Alana Marino from that competition hall and bring her to us right away, whether she's done judging or not." Leaping from his chair, he said grimly, "It's time to get to the bottom of this."

He and Kavanaugh sprinted back out to the lobby. Quickly scanning from the east tower elevators outward, they saw that Anthony Marino had already almost reached the main doors and was about to exit the building.

"Marino! Stop!" Kavanaugh shouted, attracting the attention of many in the crowded lobby. Surprised, Anthony Marino turned toward Kavanaugh's voice and stopped.

"Anaheim Police!" the detective bellowed. He strode over and waved his badge in the man's face. "Hand over that violin, Marino!" By this time, Dan, Greg, and Bill had made their way over to the scene that was unfolding.

Dan noticed that while Jim Kavanaugh wasn't short, Anthony Marino towered over him. His demeanor suggested that he wasn't easily intimidated by a badge—or anything else, for that matter.

Quickly regaining his composure, Marino smiled at the detective and casually moved to a seating group. "OK, OK. Take it easy. I don't know what you're getting all worked up about." He set the violin case on a table and opened it. He picked up the violin and handed it over to Luis. Luis gave the violin an odd look.

"Wait," Luis said. "This isn't right."

Before he could say anything else, Bill Sloan moved forward from the crowd. "I don't know what's going on here, but that isn't my violin!"

"No, it isn't," said a voice behind them. It was Alana Marino. "It's mine."

Slowly drawing a deep breath, she shot her criminal cousin a determined look and added, "And I want it back."

CHAPTER 16

THURSDAY, 10:30 A.M.

"I feel like such an idiot." Alana Marino sat with Luis Romero and Jim Kavanaugh. Over the course of 15 minutes, she laid out the basic details of the blackmail she'd been subjected to, and the reason behind it. "That man has been milking me dry for something stupid I did a long time ago."

"Yes, we know. We didn't know why, but we know from your financial records that you'd been sending him pretty much everything you had," Kavanaugh confirmed.

"He'd been coming down on me harder and harder lately. Apparently, he was under some financial pressures of his own, but the reality is, other than my Guadagnini violin, the only other asset I had that I hadn't already liquidated was my Jacob Stainer."

"And he was demanding that," Kavanaugh said.

"I think he realized that there just wasn't much more he could get out of me, so he agreed when I offered to give him the Stainer as payment in full, as it were. And I agreed to give it to him while I was here this week."

She opened the case in front of her and brought the Stainer out, holding it up and turning it in the light. "Do you know, in Stainer's own time, his instruments were more sought after, and much more expensive, than Strads. Now, Strads are worth multiple millions, while a Stainer is 'only' worth maybe half a million. It doesn't make sense; there's no logical reason for that based on actual quality of the instruments. It just shows the value of reputation, the power of public "buzz"—which is exactly why I tried so hard to protect my own. In any case, whatever Anthony was going to get out of selling the violin, I imagine he saw the writing on the wall. He'd gotten just about all he was going to get out of me, so he'd settle for this one final score."

"Well, for better or worse, it's over now," Kavanaugh told her. "Based on what you've told us, I'm sure that we'll be able put together a paper trail of your financial dealings that will keep Anthony Marino behind bars for a long time."

Luis sensed actual compassion on Kavanaugh's part. "And you get to keep your violin," he added. "All in all, not a bad outcome."

"No," Alana agreed, "that's not a bad outcome. The bad part will be the damage to my reputation once the truth about me comes out.

But you know what?" she asked, shaking her head. "At this point, I don't even care. The blackmail is over, I'm out from under that, and whatever else happens, happens. I'll just rebuild my career, my life, one step at a time."

Luis felt sorry for her. As talented and as beloved as she was worldwide, she'd been brought to near financial ruin by blackmail. Still, he was very relieved to learn that in this case, appearances had been deceiving. She hadn't been involved with the theft of the Jackson. At the same time, he recognized that they'd been down a rabbit hole and were no closer to finding the Jackson.

After their conversation with Alana, Luis and Kavanaugh returned to the police station conference room where their day had begun.

"OK, so let's review where we are," Kavanaugh said. We know that the violin had to be stolen sometime between 10 and a little after 2:00. In all likelihood, it was probably taken by one of the six people who knew in advance that it was going to be on-site. It looks like Marino isn't the thief, and in all likelihood, we can rule out Zhu, as well. I'm not completely sure yet, but at this point I'm doubtful that Pappas had anything to do with it, either."

"Really, why?" Based on his own research, Luis was leaning in the same direction, but he asked anyway.

"Well first, our file on him shows him to be clean as a whistle.

No financial problems, no business or personal drama, and just like with Zhu, his friendship with Sloan is genuine. It just doesn't seem likely that he'd do this."

Luis nodded. "I agree." He walked over to the window and stared down into the parking lot below them. "You know, there's one person we haven't really considered yet."

"Who?" Kavanaugh asked.

"Bill Sloan himself. I mean, at the bureau, we've dealt with a lot of supposedly stolen items that just ended up being attempted insurance fraud. And no matter what that violin is actually worth, you can guarantee it's insured for far more."

"You have a point," Kavanaugh agreed. "We've dealt with a lot of cases that ended up being insurance fraud, too."

"For example, maybe Sloan just took the violin with him when he left to visit his friends, who might even be accomplices in the fraud." Luis turned back from the window and looked at Kavanaugh. "To be honest, I don't think that happened. I don't think Dr. Sloan had anything to do with it at all; his grief and worry were too real."

"And," Kavanaugh added, "if he was trying to get away with fraud, he wouldn't have worked so hard and pulled so many strings to get the FBI in on the case."

Luis looked at Kavanaugh, saying nothing.

"I told you before, Romero, I'm not an idiot. And you're right," he continued. "For due diligence, we need to look carefully at Sloan as a possible suspect, even though neither of us think he's involved."

"Yes," Luis finally said. "Tomorrow. It's been a long day, and I'm going to go home and have some dinner and relax a bit."

"Yeah, same here," Kavanaugh concurred. "You know what? I still don't think I needed your help on this case, but you aren't a bad guy. I like working with you." Noticing the wedding band on Luis's finger, he added, "We'll get to the bottom of this. But for now, go home, have your wife fix you a nice hot meal, and check in with me tomorrow."

Luis was already halfway out the door. *Yeah, you can spot us a mile away.*

CHAPTER 17

THURSDAY, 3:30 P.M.

"This has definitely been an interesting afternoon," Chase Reinhold said to no one in particular. He, Dan, Greg, Konstantin, and Eric Morrison sat in the hotel lobby watching people cross the space on their way to some of the last scheduled activities of the convention.

"That's putting it mildly," Dan agreed. "We were sitting right here when all hell broke loose."

Sipping an iced latte, Eric Morrison said, "It's really something, isn't it? Since they didn't find the Jackson right away, I wonder if they ever will. Every day that goes by increases the chance that they won't."

Dan and Greg nodded their heads in agreement.

"One thing's certain," Chase said, "no matter what else happens, the Jackson theft and the whole Marino business is definitely going to put a damper on the awards dinner tonight."

"I'm sure it will," Eric agreed. "Unfortunately, whatever its mood, I'm afraid I'm going to miss it. My flight leaves while the dinner is taking place, so I'm going to need to get to the airport in just a short while."

"Oh, that's a shame," Greg said. "We'll miss you there. Dan and I will be sitting with Bill, and I'm sure that he'd planned on you sharing the table with us."

Eric shrugged his shoulders. "Yes, I'd have definitely enjoyed that, but I've got to get back for an appointment with a major client. You know, business is business. I hope that I see you all again soon, much sooner than it's been this time around," he said with his typical warm, friendly smile. "I've got just a few last things to take care of, then I'm on my way." He got up and waved them all goodbye.

Alana Marino walked slowly through the lobby, absent-mindedly, almost aimlessly, but in the general direction of the remaining men.

"Alana!" Greg called over to her, getting her attention. "Please, come join us." Looking a bit forlorn and not at all like her usual self, Alana approached them and sat down at an open spot on the sofa, her red dress offering a sophisticated counterpoint to its tan, leather upholstery.

As she was sitting down, Dan looked across the lobby and noticed Phil Goodman walking from the elevators to a door just around the corner from the registration desk, a few yards further away than the door to the security room. It looked like he was carrying something bundled up in a hotel towel, and when Goodman reached the door, he nervously glanced around, passed the bundle from his right hand to his left, opened the door, and went inside.

Chase was the first to speak to Alana, his voice filled with compassion. "Alana, what on earth was happening earlier? Who was that man, and what was he doing with your Stainer?"

Alana sat silently, motionless, mentally, and seemingly physically, weighed down with an exhaustion that had been building for more than a year. Finally, she told them all the details that she'd explained to Detective Kavanaugh earlier.

"And there you have it," she said. "Yes, I've had a wonderful career, and yes, I have innate talent, but many other people do too—probably even more—and in order to get ahead of them I got into bed with criminal members of my extended family. I got preferential treatment, and an unfair start to my career. Once this all comes out, my professional life will be ruined."

Dan, Greg, and Eric sat, not knowing what to say but expressing shock and condolences. In the background, Phil Goodman was just coming back through the door he'd entered earlier, scanning around him as he'd done before, but now his hands were empty. Something about Goodman's actions struck Dan as suspicious.

Chase Reinhold looked down at the coffee table in front of him.

After a moment, he broke his silence. "Alana, I'm so very sorry that you've gone through all of this. I know it must have been awful. To be honest, I don't know what the future will bring for you, but I know that you're going to be just fine." He paused for a moment before continuing. "And I know something else, too."

Alana looked over at him, her face filled with puzzlement and doubt.

"I've known the story about your cousin trying to strongarm the Curtis to accept you for some time now, due to my friendship with the people involved. But what you don't know is that those same people confided in me that the whole idea that your cousin had to intervene to get you in was laughable. In fact, they'd already decided to accept you to the conservatory days earlier, based entirely on your own talent. It had nothing to do with him. In fact, they told him that when he first came to them. He's known that all along."

Chase leaned forward and looked intently at her. "You see, Alana, your career is based on your own talent, and nothing more. You aren't a fraud. You have nothing to be ashamed of—and nothing to punished for."

The group could almost see the years of heavy guilt fall from Alana's shoulders.

"I know that I'll never get restitution for everything I've paid Anthony Marino in the past," she said. "But at least I was able to hold onto both of my precious violins. I'm sure I'll slowly but surely climb out of the financial hole I'm in right now. But more importantly, I'll be able to look at myself in a mirror without feeling like a fraud, without feeling like the self-confidence that I try to project to others is just a deception."

Alana walked over to Chase, bent down, and gave him a gentle kiss on the cheek. "Thank you, dear friend," she said with a warm smile. "You've given me the greatest gift possible." Pausing a moment, she said, "I'll see you at the banquet in a few hours," and quietly walked away.

"That's beautiful, heartwarming. Such wonderful news for her," Konstantin said, a sparkle in his eye. That sparkle clouded as he continued, "It makes me feel better after my experience the other day."

Greg looked concerned for his friend. "What happened, Konstantin?"

"Oh, it has to do with Malcolm Stewart," he said. "I've sold a number of violins through his shop over the years. Obviously, his shop is well known to top professional violinists, so my instruments get in front of a lot of potential customers. But Malcolm and I were out the other day at a local camera shop, and while we were talking, he told me he was increasing the sales commission he wanted to charge for carrying my instruments in their shop—by 50 percent, actually—and at the same time, he demanded that his be the exclusive shop to carry my instruments in all of England."

Greg sat back, stunned. "That's a pretty gutsy move on his part."

"Very gutsy," Konstantin replied. "He already charges a higher commission than most other dealers, and now he wants even more. He's hounded me about it several times this week."

"What kind of rationale did he offer for it?" Dan asked.

"Oh, you know, the usual puffery," Konstantin said dismissively waving his hand. "He has such a big reputation, they're the ultimate dealership in all the UK, and on and on. I'm sure that you're all familiar with Malcolm's standard spiel."

"Yes, we've all heard it ad nauseam," Chase agreed, rolling his eyes.

Konstantin shook his head and continued. "In addition, he said it would increase my reputation to continue being able to say that a dealership as prestigious as his carries my instruments."

Chase asked, "What did you tell him?"

"I told him that he was being ridiculous. Only I used different words," he chuckled. "I told him that my reputation is already solid and could stand on its own, with or without him. Most of my customers are referrals by word of mouth—violinist to violinist—regardless of the dealership. And once they try my instruments, that's what sells them, not the name over the front door."

And not because it looks like a Strad instead of an Amati, Dan thought, reminded of his earlier argument with Greg.

"I told him that his shop was fine—excellent, even—and under Eric Morrison's leadership, their repair and restoration work is some of the best in the world, if not the best. But there were certainly other shops out there with reputations just as good, who charge more realistic commissions. I assured him that within the next several days or weeks, I'd be moving my instruments to one of them. I actually walked away, leaving him standing on the sidewalk by himself."

"Good for you!" Greg said. "It makes me wish that I had a London dealer that I could refer you to."

"If you did, my friend, that is precisely where I would go," Konstantin said.

Chase interjected, "Well, I certainly know some London dealers who are excellent—smaller, but every bit as good as Malcolm's shop, with at least as good a reputation, probably better, with violinists and violin makers, both. If you like, I can make introductions. And Greg, if you ever wanted to have a dealer in London, I'd do the same thing for you, too."

"Ah, so you see," Konstantin said, "it does turn out to be a good situation. Thank you, Chase, I'd like that very much!"

"Now," he added more somberly, "let's hope that there's a good resolution for the Jackson, too."

The group went their separate ways a few moments later, but Dan pulled Greg aside from the others and told him about what he'd seen Phil Goodman doing earlier. "I know he's busy and has his hands in a lot of things around the convention. Still, something just didn't seem right about it. You want to do a little snooping?"

"Why not?" Greg said. "Let's do it."

They walked to the door that Goodman had passed through—a metal door with no window, no sign. Dan tentatively tried the door, and he was happy to find that it was unlocked. "Let's find out where Phil Goodman was going," he said.

Behind the door, they found a wide, unadorned corridor with heavily scuffed vinyl bumper rails attached to the sidewalls and a sole exit at the end. It was essentially a long vestibule to the space beyond. Reaching the end of the hall, they found themselves in a large, unfinished maintenance area that included two loading docks opening to the outside, as well as a third bay that housed a large trash compactor and dumpster.

"So what was Phil Goodman doing in here?" Greg asked. "And what did he leave behind?"

"Whatever it was, it's got to be in here somewhere. I wonder if—" Dan's voice trailed off as he looked toward the trash compactor sitting down in the recessed dock, where a janitorial staffer was dumping a cart of trash from the upper floors into the hopper.

Once he emptied the cart, he stepped over to the controls to start the compactor plunger, but Dan yelled, "Wait! Wait a minute!" The man looked at Dan curiously and stopped. "We need to look at something in there first!"

They pulled back the doors that opened into the hopper and peered inside. There was just enough light to make out a mass of cardboard, empty shampoo bottles, used tissues, and other miscellaneous trash. Dan and Greg leaned over with their hands on their bent knees, scanning through the mound of debris below them.

"Look! There!" Dan shouted, pointing to a white towel nearly buried in what had been dumped on it. "I'll bet that's what Goodman brought in here."

Greg looked at Dan, not saying a word but speaking volumes. *Just standing this close to a hopper filled with guestroom trash must make Greg's germophobic skin crawl.*

"Well, crap," Dan muttered. "I guess I'm going dumpster diving. Give me a hand down in there," he said to both Greg and the janitor, who by this time had walked over to them. Each of them grabbed an arm, and they carefully eased Dan down into the cavity. He made his way through the disgusting pile, pushing it aside with his arms as his shoes sloshed through the dumpster gravy underfoot. Once in arm's reach of the towel, he pulled it and its contents out of the pile, holding it up over his head as he waded back to the front edge of the hopper.

"Here, take this," he said. The janitor grabbed it and set it on the floor nearby. "Now help me get up out of here!" The janitor took Dan by the arms, pulling while Dan tried to get a footing in some of the trash to climb his way up and out. He was eventually able to flop over the edge of the opening and wriggle the rest of the way out.

Dan brushed himself off and scuffed the bottom of his shoes on the concrete floor to scrape leftover debris from the soles. "Let's take a look at this," Dan said picking the bundle up off the floor. He pulled the towel back, revealing a violin—or part of one. Otherwise complete, it was devoid of any strings, pegs, tailpiece, or bridge.

"This doesn't make any sense," Greg said as he carefully retrieved the violin from Dan's grasp. They walked to a nearby workbench, and Greg set it down. He pulled out his phone, and using the flashlight app, he peeked inside the left f-hole of the corpus.

"I can't believe it!" he said. "Look inside." Greg held the phone at the right angle while still keeping his distance from his smelly husband. Inside, glued to the violin's belly, Dan could see the maker's label:

Eric Morrison
London
Faciebat Anno 2022

"This is Eric's competition violin, or part of it," Greg said. "I definitely recognize it; he showed it to me before he turned it in at the competition hall. What's it doing here?"

"Why would Goodman have had it?" Dan wondered. "And why on earth would he dump it into the trash?"

"Where's the rest of it?" Greg wondered.

"Whatever's going on here, it's unusual enough that we should call Luis Romero."

"You do that," Greg said, "but before he gets here, you really need to go shower and change your clothes!"

CHAPTER 18

THURSDAY, 5:00 P.M.

Luis contacted Jim Kavanaugh immediately after getting Dan's call, and the two of them arrived in the hotel security office within 15 or 20 minutes. Greg and Dan were waiting for them, Dan now freshly showered and wearing a clean outfit. Eric's violin was on the counter in front of them.

"Just look at this," Greg said unwrapping the violin.

"I don't get it," Kavanaugh said, shaking his head. "First Sloan's Stradivarius is stolen. Then there's the drama with Alana Marino and her violin. And now this business with Morrison's. What exactly is going on here?"

"And," Dan asked, "does this have anything to do with the Jackson's theft?"

"One way or another, we need to have a conversation with Phil Goodman," Luis said, "and right now." He seemed done with continuously deferring to Jim Kavanaugh's ego. He rewrapped Morrison's violin in the towel and handed it to Kavanaugh, instructing him, "Take this out to your car for safekeeping. Then meet me back here. We're going to find Goodman." Kavanaugh sensed the change in dynamic between him and Luis, but he let it go, at least for the moment.

"We're looking for Phil Goodman," Luis said to the volunteer at the entry to the competition hall. "Is he inside?"

"Yes," the staffer confirmed, "but only authorized personnel are permitted inside."

The FBI agent's credentials superseded the otherwise tight security that the VSA had established, and they quickly entered the room. The large space was filled with row after row of long, rectangular tables, covered with white tablecloths. Each table displayed violins, violas, and bows, each in their respective sections of the warmly lit room. Cellos and double basses occupied a part of the room that was free of tables. With the awards banquet beginning in just a few hours, there were relatively few people inside the space, so they easily spotted Goodman.

"Mr. Goodman, I need some help," Luis began as they approached.

"Well, all right, whatever I can do," he replied. "But please make it quick; I'm in the middle of a lot of things right now."

"Could you please take us to Eric Morrison's violin?" Luis asked.

"Well, it isn't that easy," Goodman said. "These instruments are all numbered and have all identifying information covered."

"Yes," Luis countered, "but you have access to the submissions and the numbers each competitor has been assigned. I'm sure you could look it up easily enough, especially now that all of the judging is complete."

Goodman hesitated, but only for a moment. "I guess that's true," he offered. "Let me look that up." Dan, Greg, and Luis followed him across the room, back toward the entry and out to the registration table, still set up just outside. Goodman retrieved the proper entry number and led the three to the location where Eric's violin should have been.

"I don't understand. . . . Where is the violin?" Goodman asked with a manufactured look of surprise. "Wait, let me check something." He led them back to the registration table computer. He dutifully checked the records again, and pointing to a spot on the screen, he said, "Aha, here we are: Eric Morrison has already retrieved his violin from the competition hall. Another volunteer must have checked him out. It says that we returned his entry to him at 4:45." Goodman glanced at his phone. "It's just about 5:15 now; looks like you missed him by half an hour."

Greg said, "Eric did tell us earlier this afternoon that he was going to be leaving before the banquet began."

"Mr. Goodman, I need to tell you that these two gentlemen saw you—and I'm sure that security video will confirm it as well—taking something wrapped up in a towel into the trash room around the corner right at 4:00, and that you left the room with empty hands. They found Eric Morrison's competition violin wrapped in a towel and tossed into the compactor. That was just before 4:30. So Mr. Goodman, it isn't possible that Eric Morrison retrieved it from this room at 4:45. You obviously aren't being honest with us. Do you want to back up and try again?"

"That can't be!" Goodman protested. "Yes, I was in the trash room, but I was just throwing out trash, not a violin!"

"Let's talk more in the security office," Luis said. "I'm sure that we can clear this up by looking at video of the lobby, and especially of the trash room."

"I'm telling you, I have no idea what you're talking about," Goodman protested. "Eric Morrison signed his violin out; whatever was in the compactor must have been another one that he made, and someone dumped."

"All these competition instruments have been photographed in detail," Greg said. "It will be easy enough to tell if it's Eric's competition instrument or not, and I can tell you from having seen it myself, I already know that it is."

Phil Goodman was uncharacteristically quiet as the four of them walked down the corridor. Nearing the lobby, though, he panicked and shoved Luis in the chest, catching him off guard and knocking him backward, off his feet. Dan and Greg stood stunned.

"Hey! Stop! Stop!" Romero yelled, leaping off the floor to pursued Goodman. By that time, Goodman was running toward the exit. Luis was in much better shape and was closing the gap between them, but Goodman was still out of range. But Jim Kavanaugh was waiting for them in the lobby.

"Kavanaugh, stop him—stop Goodman!" Luis yelled.

Goodman was running right toward him, and Kavanaugh instinctively tackled him, both men crashing in a pile onto the granite floor. Everyone in the lobby turned toward the excitement unfolding for the second time that day.

Kavanaugh stood up, rubbing the hip he'd landed on, although he'd mostly landed on Goodman. Goodman propped himself up, moaning, and remained seated on the floor. Blood ran from his nose, which had hit the granite hard. As curious hotel guests looked down at them from the interior faux-balconies, Kavanaugh and Luis lifted Goodman and guided him to a small seating area among the interior palm trees—the same seating area where Dan had spoken with Chase Reinhold earlier in the week.

"Here," Luis said, handing Goodman a handful of tissues to wipe the blood from his face. "Now, why don't you tell us what's going on?"

Goodman cleaned himself up as best as he could, wadding some tissue into a nostril to stop the blood flow. Leaning back into the seat, he spoke for the first time since he'd been peeled off the floor.

"Look, I told you," he said, as best as he could. "I was just throwing some trash away. I didn't have Morrison's violin with me, and I definitely don't know how it ended up in the trash. I'm telling you, Eric signed his violin out at 4:45."

"Or," Kavanaugh suggested, "you just entered that into the computer when he really hadn't."

They placed Goodman in a small room while they spoke with Elliot Cherson.

"Cherson," Kavanaugh asked, "could you show us video from the lobby around the entry to the trash area, and any footage you have from the loading dock and trash area, from right around 4:00?" Cherson quickly retrieved those views, and the five of them gathered around the screen.

"Look, here he is!" Greg pointed to the screen. Phil Goodman had appeared coming down the corridor, carrying the bundle. Looking around, he quickly opened the door to the loading dock and trash area.

"That isn't very helpful," Dan noted with some frustration.

"Let's take a look at the video from inside the loading dock area itself," Luis suggested. "Maybe we'll be able to see more there."

Unfortunately, the camera angle in that area didn't offer any more clarity regarding what Goodman was tossing into the hopper.

Kavanaugh was clearly frustrated. "That gave us absolutely nothing."

"Maybe not nothing," Luis said. "It isn't quite clear to me yet, but I've got a couple of thoughts. As stupid as it might sound, the first video shows us that he didn't just materialize out of thin air at the entry door. What I mean is that it shows us what direction he was coming from."

Dan understood his point. "And if we know what direction he was coming from, maybe there's other video that might confirm that he's holding a violin."

"Exactly," Luis confirmed. "The video shows us that he isn't coming from the direction of the competition hall, but rather, the opposite direction."

"Well, that's almost half the hotel," Kavanaugh said.

"Yes," Luis said, "but let's look at one place in particular. Mr. Cherson, let's look at the video from the elevator lobby, shortly before Goodman showed up at the loading dock door."

"There he is," Greg said. Goodman was getting off an elevator with his bundle. "I'll bet he's coming downstairs from his room."

"Let's test that theory," Luis said. "Let's take a look at video from the ninth floor, both the corridor and elevator lobby video, just before this." Cherson navigated to those feeds and called them up in separate windows on the screen. Within minutes, they saw Goodman leaving his room with the bundle already in his hands.

"So he had Morrison's violin upstairs. It wasn't in the competition hall," Kavanaugh stated.

"Assuming we're correct that it's the violin wrapped up inside." Luis nodded. The video showed Goodman coming down the corridor toward the elevator lobby before he disappeared under the camera angle. A moment later, he appeared in the video recorded in the elevator lobby. The group offered a collective sigh of relief that Goodman had waited for an elevator that was within camera range. He reached forward to push the elevator call button, and as he did, the towel in his other had shifted, slipping down and partially exposing what was underneath.

"There!" Luis almost shouted. "Zoom in on that!"

A second later, Cherson had zoomed in on the view, where it was obvious to everyone that what they were looking at was the neck and scroll of a violin.

"Gotcha!" Kavanaugh said decisively.

"Yes, we do," Luis said, "and I'm sure that he's going to become more talkative about that very soon. But there's something else that's been running through my head."

"What's that?" Kavanaugh asked

"It isn't so much a matter of what we've seen, but what we haven't." He thought for a moment. "What I mean is that we haven't seen or heard anything about Eric Morrison trying to retrieve his violin and it not being there for him." Thinking for a moment, he continued. "Before anything else, let's do a double-check on that point."

They made their way down the hall to the competition hall, where they spoke to a woman seated behind the registration table. "Oh, yes," she confirmed, "I entered that on the computer myself. I remember he had a violin strapped over his shoulder. He was here less than an hour ago."

After returning to the security room, the conversation continued. "So apparently, Goodman wasn't faking that point. At 4:45, Eric really did retrieve his violin," Dan said.

Thinking for a moment, Greg added, "Well, he couldn't have done that, since his violin is sitting right here. But he retrieved *some* violin."

"And presumably," Dan added, "a violin that he would have thought was his. But if he did, it must have been a dead ringer for his."

"I can't imagine him not realizing it was a different violin," Greg said. "Let's face it, there are few more discerning eyes in the violin world than his."

"Unless . . ." Luis trailed off. Suddenly, he jumped out of his chair and ran out toward the front desk, calling over his shoulder, "Unless he walked away with a different violin because that's exactly what he'd planned on doing."

CHAPTER 19

TUESDAY, 7:30 A.M.

This is it. Today is the day it's all been leading up to. Eric Morrison lay in bed, wanting to sleep just a bit longer but too heavily engaged in his thoughts to do so. Grudgingly accepting the futility of the effort, he pushed the covers aside and rolled out of bed. After a quick shower and shave, he made a cup of coffee and sat at the small table in his room. Looking out at the sun-drenched courtyard below, he thought about how he'd come to this moment. It really all came down to his employer.

Malcolm Stewart was an insufferable ass. Narcissistic, egomaniacal, he never missed an opportunity for self-promotion or self-enrichment. He sadistically put the screws to people just to see if he could get away with it—and inexplicably, he almost always did. He overcharged customers at every opportunity, and he treated luthiers abusively, too, sitting on payouts for sold instruments for months sometimes, floating their cash as long as possible. He was an example of a particularly frustrating type of person: clearly, even proudly, loathsome, and able to spin that to his advantage.

Eric remembered when Stewart finally offered him his current position—a promotion in title, but without additional compensation. "Don't worry," he'd said. "You just keep dazzling me, and show me I can trust you, and eventually, I'll pay you more. In the meantime, enjoy the prestige that comes with being able to tell people you're my head of restoration and repair."

Anyone, no matter how good, will snap if pushed beyond a certain threshold, and Eric discovered his that day. In that moment, he swore that he would find a way to make up for all the emotional abuse he'd endured, and in a way that hurt his sociopathic employer at the same time.

Shortly after that, air travel had resumed after the pandemic lockdown, and Bill Sloan had flown to London with the Jackson for some routine care.

"Oh, Bill, my dear friend, it's so wonderful to see you again after so much time!" Stewart gushed as he welcomed Bill into the shop. He continued in the same vein. "I can't tell you how many customers we've had who say they use our shop because they heard that we are the official caretakers of the Jackson. You are absolutely our favorite customer!"

Bill had looked down and shaken his head at the excessive flattery.

This time, it isn't just flattery, though; it's true, Eric had thought. *We have a steady stream of top-level clientele, but probably a third of our long-term business comes from people who respect the fact that we take care of that one instrument. To have that connection taken from Malcolm would hurt both his ego and his balance sheet.*

That was the precise moment his plan began.

Sometime when it's in here, I should just figure out a way to steal the damned thing. I'd make a mint selling it, and it would cause a scandal for Malcolm.

It was one of those thoughts that pop into a person's head unbidden, without it passing through applied filters of reason or morality. Eric had been angry at Stewart and embarrassed at even having such a thought. But no thought, no matter how highly or lowly pedigreed, can ever be fully forgotten. Stoked by years of mistreatment, this one kept returning to his consciousness over the following week, and each time it resurfaced it seemed to make a bit more sense.

At first, his conscience battled the idea. Beyond the fact that it was morally wrong, not to mention illegal, he couldn't conceive of hurting Bill Sloan. Over the years, the two had become fast friends, something that Malcolm Stewart's efforts had failed to prevent. As the idea resurfaced over time, though, Eric's thoughts shifted.

The Jackson is insured for far more than its current estimated market value, so even though Bill would suffer emotionally, he wouldn't actually suffer financially.

It was sufficient rationalization to fuel Eric's hurt and anger, and to allow him to continue imagining how he might actually do it.

He finally decided that the best way to steal the violin—and in a way that pointed less directly at himself—would be to steal it somewhere away from the shop. As the world emerged from the pandemic, his plan began to take shape. The first in-person VSA gathering since before the lockdown would take place in Los Angeles. Morrison knew that he probably wouldn't even need to coax Bill to be there and to have the Jackson in tow. Even if he did have to ask him, Bill would readily agree to the idea.

Being intimately familiar with every square centimeter of the instrument after maintaining it for years, Eric would make a new violin for this year's competition. It would be a new instrument crafted as an homage to the Jackson, following the dimensions, style, varnish color, and wear patterns of the original instrument, and it would feature a very similar seamed back and book-matched flame pattern in the quartered maple. But there would be differences, too. The tailpiece and pegs would be different from the deep, warm brown ones on the Jackson. The Jackson's tailpiece featured a very distinctive bas relief carving of a seated man playing a vielle, a stringed instrument from the medieval period, and its pegs featured finely carved rosettes at the tips. Eric's fittings would be devoid of those artistic flourishes, and instead of the deep brown wood of the originals, his fittings would be crafted of African Blackwood, a species closely resembling ebony. While the corpus would look very much like the Jackson, Eric would make sure to include a few obvious differences in the antiquing, including some minor scratches and distressing to its finish that didn't exist on the original and adding faux "dirt" in places where the Jackson had none. While Eric's violin would be an impeccable work of artisanship bearing a striking resemblance to its inspiration, no knowledgeable person in the violin world would confuse it for the actual Jackson.

Which is exactly what I'll need, he'd thought.

He would enter the violin into the competition, get it accepted into the highly restricted competition hall and inspected nearly under a magnifying glass by multiple violin experts. He would then have to gain access to the Jackson and steal it—obviously a difficult task, but not impossible, given his professional and personal relationship with Bill Sloan.

At some point after his copy had been examined by the judges, Eric would need to find a way to slip it out of the competition hall. Then, with both the actual Jackson and his copy in hand, he would remove the Jackson's fittings and replace them with his own, add just a bit of wax-based faux dirt to make it look more like his copy, and get it slipped back into the competition hall in place of his own. The expert judges would see his instrument before the switch and identify it as a respectful homage to the Jackson—implicitly and expertly confirming that it wasn't the original.

Once it's there, it will be hiding in plain sight—a needle in a haystack. And afterward, I'll find a place to dispose of my copy, retrieve the Jackson from the competition hall, and walk out the front door with it.

There were obvious challenges to his plan, not the least of which was how to get his violin out of the competition hall and replace it with the Jackson. After considering multiple options, Eric recognized that he was going to need help to pull it off—help from someone who had unfettered access to the competition hall throughout the convention. He found just the right person in Phil Goodman. The two men could hardly have been more different, but from a logistical standpoint, their odd coupling made sense. Eric had the technical skill needed, and sufficiently high ethics to avoid suspicion, but no access to the competition hall. Goodman, on the other hand, had a sufficiently low ethical bar to be part of a scheme like this and access to the competition hall, but insufficient skill to craft a Jackson-like instrument of the quality needed for the plan to work.

Even now, it gnaws at my gut to work with someone like Goodman, Eric thought. *But he's a necessary evil. I need him in order to accomplish my goal.*

Eric finished his coffee and sat in the stillness for a moment. *Now, it's all come together,* he thought. *You've worked for almost a year to bring this all together. There's no turning back, now. Today is the day.*

He took the elevator down to the hotel lobby. Needing to calm his nerves, he stepped out into the sun-drenched morning and walked up Katella Boulevard to a casual restaurant featuring traditional breakfast fare. As he sat eating comfort food, his thoughts wandered to his wife and children. What would they think of him if they ever found out what he was about to do?

It would tear them apart if they ever found out the truth. But they'd paid a big emotional price over the years that he'd suffered under Malcolm's thumb, too, and they'd be better off.

Eric wasn't an ostentatious man. He wasn't planning any lavish changes to his lifestyle after the Jackson had been successfully sold. Yes, he'd treat his family to a bit more of the finer things in life, but never enough to elicit suspicion about where the money was coming from.

The money would obviously be nice, but sticking it to Malcolm Stewart was far more important.

After returning from breakfast, Eric stopped to chitchat with a few people in the lobby, but he wasn't really paying much attention to what they were saying. Instead, his mind was rehearsing the next few hours, as he'd done countless times before. Just before 10:00, he made his way to the elevator lobby on the 10th floor, taking care to wait for the elevator in the security cameras' blind spot. He waited until no one was in the lobby or adjacent corridor, pulled a small wooden side chair from the lobby, just under the mounted security camera, and stepped up, onto the chair while staying behind the camera's view. Next he pulled out a sample-sized aerosol can of hair spray, and coated the lens with its contents. He'd experimented with several types of spray while planning the theft. This product worked well and easily blended into the contents of his own toiletries without arousing notice.

It's so simple, he thought, but sometimes the simplest solutions really are the best.

Once the lens was disabled, Eric returned the chair to its place before anyone saw him. He returned to the main lobby, then took another elevator—one visible to security cameras—to return to his own room until just before 11:00, when he gathered up his luthier's tools and headed to Bill Sloan's room to perform the tonal adjustments Bill had requested.

It was perfect that he'd asked. It eliminated the need to offer.

His adjustments complete, Eric stood and sampled the Jackson. It was truly remarkable. Its rich, warm tone had the ability to cut above the rest of an orchestra. It was almost effortless for a violinist to get exactly what they wanted out of the instrument. *If any musical instrument had an actual soul, it would be this one,* he thought. That soul seemed to become perfectly attuned to the soul and the desire of the person playing it.

"Here, Bill, try it for yourself," he said, handing Bill the instrument.

After playing it, Bill handed the violin back to Eric. "Beautiful— just beautiful!" he affirmed. Within minutes, as Morrison and Goodman had planned in advance, Goodman knocked on the door.

"Hey Bill! I just thought I'd stop by to remind you that it's time to head downstairs. We're all ready to go. We wouldn't want the man of the hour to miss his own luncheon! And remember, I'd still like to stop by to see the Jackson a little later!"

"OK, thanks. We're on our way down right now."

The fact that Bill had hardly acknowledged Goodman's presence in that moment made things even easier than Eric had hoped. Using his body to block anyone's view, Morrison stealthily handed Goodman the Jackson, wrapped in a hotel bath towel, which Goodman quickly took back to his own room. Meanwhile, as Bill, Greg, and Konstantin talked, Morrison discreetly took two of the hotel's hand towels, placed them in the Jackson's case, and quickly but casually closed and fastened the lid. Having worked on the Jackson for years, Morrison knew the Jackson's weight to the gram, and while the hand towels weren't exactly the same weight, they were close enough. The weight, something just less than a pound, would provide sufficient deception that the Jackson was safely inside, at least for the short time he needed.

CHAPTER 20

TUESDAY, 11:50 A.M.

"Here," Phil Goodman said, handing Morrison a keycard to his hotel room. They were standing in an alcove just outside the luncheon. "I put the Jackson in your case and set it inside the closet."

Eric had been nervous about revealing his plan to Goodman. It isn't easy inviting someone into a criminal conspiracy, and he knew that if Goodman said no, the whole plan would be dead. But whether it was strictly due to the percentage of profit Eric had promised or for other reasons, Goodman had agreed almost immediately.

"OK," Eric said. "As soon as this is over, you have got to get into the competition hall, slip my violin out, and get it up to your room, where I'll be waiting. It will take me about an hour to replace the fittings and disguise the Jackson. Come back to the room at 2:15 sharp, and I'll be done. Then get it into the competition hall without anyone noticing."

"I can do that pretty easily," Goodman said. "At some point in the next couple of days, after the initial activity after the theft tapers a little bit, I'll get rid of your violin in the trash."

It bothered Eric that the plan included destroying his own violin, but they couldn't end up with one violin too many, and it seemed a relatively small price to pay in order to gain the Jackson.

"Once you get the Jackson out of the room, I'll wait until no one is in the corridor and use a bit of window cleaner to get the hair spray off the security camera lens and get back to the convention, making sure lots of people see me."

"All of the artisanship judging took place yesterday and this morning, and just to be sure, I scheduled the judges to look at your violin early this morning," Goodman said. "They've been done with it for hours and will be paying attention to other things, so it shouldn't be too hard for me to slip your violin out and the Jackson in."

Eric was struck by the ease that Goodman had in discussing the scheme without even a trace of conscience or moral misgiving. In that sense, he envied him. His moral wrestling showed on his face, and Goodman offered him reassurance.

"Relax, you've thought out every detail of this plan for a long time now, and it's a good one. It's going to all go very smoothly, and any ethical problems you're feeling right now are going to disappear as soon as you've made the handoff to the buyer and you're sitting on that plane back to London."

Eric's twinges of conscience subsided as he realized that Goodman was probably right. After all the planning, this really was going to work.

After the luncheon, Eric left as quickly as he could. Briefly returning to his own room to retrieve his tool kit, he made his way to Goodman's room where the Jackson was waiting. He pulled the case out of the closet and set the Jackson on a towel on the tabletop. Within a few minutes, he heard a quiet tap at the door. He verified through the peephole that it was Goodman and opened the door. Goodman quickly stepped inside.

"Did you have any trouble getting it out of the hall?" Eric asked.

"Not really. There were a few people hanging around the side door I was planning on slipping out of, and I had to wait until they moved on, but otherwise everything went just fine," Goodman handed Eric a black case holding his own competition violin.

"Good, I'll take it from here. Just be back here at 2:15; I want to get this into the hall as soon as possible, before it's missed." Goodman left the room, heading for the main lobby and the convention activities.

Eric took his violin out of the case and set it on another towel, side by side with the Jackson. He took just a moment to appreciate the quality of his own work. Looking past the obvious, superficial differences that he'd intentionally made, the two instruments were strikingly similar.

You did really good work on this, he thought to himself. *But no time to think about that now. Let's get to it.*

Eric worked quickly but didn't rush. In a matter of minutes, he had removed the strings, bridge, pegs, tailpiece, and end button from his own violin. Then he moved to the Jackson. First, he applied small strips of gentle-adhesive tape to meticulously mark the positions of the feet of its bridge, which was being held in place by the tension of the strings spanning the top. He knew that bridge placement plays a critical role in determining the tone of an instrument, that variations of a tenth of a millimeter could have a profound effect on the instrument's sound, so he wanted to be sure to mark its actual location before removing it. Next, he gently eased the tension on the strings, a little bit at a time, moving repeatedly from string to string until the tension was fully removed from the bridge, which he carefully removed and placed aside. He then removed the strings from the pegs and tailpiece. He rolled up the strings, wrapped up the fittings and bridge in a piece of velvet, and gently tied it closed with a string. He placed the velvet package inside his own violin case. Then he turned his attention to the Jackson.

Eric knew the precise measurements of the original Stradivarius label inside the instrument, and he had made one of his own—a duplicate of the one inside his competition instrument—that was just slightly larger than the one in the Jackson. Using tools made for just this operation, Morrison carefully placed his label over the original, confident that the gentle-release adhesive backing on the paper he'd printed the label on would prevent any damage to the original label below when it was eventually removed.

It was just after Eric had done that when there was a knock on the door.

Is that Goodman again? What does he want? I told him not to come back until 2:15; he's too early.

Eric walked to the door again and looked through the peephole, seeing not Goodman, but Greg. *Damn. What could he want?*

"Oh, hi, Eric, is Phil around?"

Moments later, after Greg had left the book that he'd agreed to lend to Phil, Eric was back to work on the Jackson.

Well, that could have been a disaster. Thank God he didn't look too hard at the violin sitting over here, he thought, *or he'd have recognized it immediately.*

Following the unexpected interruption, he installed his own fittings, strings, and bridge to the Jackson and made the necessary tonal adjustments. Finally, he carefully added some of the wax pigments in a few places to make the Jackson more closely resemble the appearance of his own violin. *Not as drastic as covering it in shoe polish like the Huberman,* he thought, *but it will do the job. And these little bits of wax pigments just sitting on top of the varnish surface will come off much easier.*

Even working as quickly as he'd dared, he was just finishing up when Goodman knocked on the door at 2:15.

"How does it look?" he asked Eric.

"Actually, not bad," he answered with a bit of guilty pride, but pride nonetheless. "When you look at the two side by side like this, you definitely see differences—but if you saw mine this morning, and this one in the afternoon, it would be very difficult to notice them."

"Remember that the artisanship judges are all done now, and tomorrow morning the tone judging starts with a completely different set of judges."

"Exactly," Eric said, placing the Jackson in Goodman's case. "Now all you have to do is get this into the competition hall, and we'll be all set."

"Perfect! I'll see you downstairs." Goodman stepped out into the hallway, closing the door behind him.

Eric sat in the quiet of the room for a moment, alone with his thoughts. It did bother him to be in bed with someone like Phil Goodman, and he still harbored some moral discomfort with the whole plan, but not enough to stop him.

Well. In any case, it's too late to worry about that now. Time to clean the hair spray off the camera and get back downstairs.

CHAPTER 21

THURSDAY, 5:20 P.M.

Eric began to breathe more normally once he got outside the hotel doors and settled on the hard orange seat of the shuttle bus. *I did it. I can't believe I've actually gotten away with it,* he thought to himself. *Now I just wait for Goodman's buyer, whoever it is, to get on the shuttle. I verify the money has been transferred into my account, give them the Jackson, and we go our separate ways when we get to the airport.* Shortly after that, he'd be on his flight home, safe, rich, and avenged.

"Where are you headed?" A young man sitting beside him, obviously half of a couple, asked.

"I'm headed home to London. You?"

"We're headed to visit some friends who live in Paris. It will be the first time either of us has been there," the woman said.

"We just got married," the man said. "This will be kind of a combination visit with friends and honeymoon."

"Well, congratulations!" Eric said. "And I promise you're going to love Paris," he assured them. The couple detailed all the places they were planning to see once they'd arrived. He smiled at their youthful enthusiasm. *They've got their whole life ahead of them. The world hasn't worn them down yet. For their sake, I hope it never does.* As they shared their plans with him, he felt more like a third-party observer of the conversation than a participant. *They seem like a nice couple. If they only knew the average-looking person they're chatting with was a high-end thief who has just betrayed the very highest level of trust. If they only knew they were sitting next to a stolen violin worth millions of dollars.*

"So I assume you're a violinist?" the man asked as he pointed to the case on Eric's lap. "Me, too!" he said, pointing to a black violin case sitting on the floor between his feet. "Well, not a very good one. I can't play anything too complicated, but I still enjoy it."

"Oh, well, yes," Eric said, "I do play the violin, but mostly, I'm a violin maker."

"Really? How cool," the man said, "I don't think I've ever met a violin maker before."

Eric smiled politely as he noticed the shuttle passing by two different hotels without stopping. "Well, I guess you can scratch that one off your list; you've met one now."

The man's wife leaned over. "Did you make that one?" she asked enthusiastically.

Eric hesitated for a moment but then said, "Well, yes, I did."

"Cool, could we see it?"

Why not? You'll only be able to show it off to anyone for a few more minutes, and it would look odd if I told them no.

"Sure." Eric said. He opened the case, gently slid the violin out of its velvet cover, and showed it to the couple.

"May I?" the man asked, and after reminding the man how to hold it, Eric gently handed it over to him.

"It's really beautiful," the woman said while looking at it as the man held it.

"Thank you very much," Eric said as the man handed it back to him. He put it back in is cover, tucked it into the case, and set it between his feet. He leaned his head back and closed his eyes, hoping for a short nap, and offering a polite signal that he wanted to disengage from the conversation.

"I'm very sorry, sir," the front desk clerk told Luis. "It looks like you just missed Mr. Morrison. He checked out of his room at 5:15. Our concierge had booked a shuttle back to the airport for him; it left just five or ten minutes ago. He must have come downstairs right after the big excitement you were all involved in a little while ago."

Kavanaugh asked Luis, "You think that Goodman and Morrison were working together on whatever all this is?"

"Yes, I do. I think that what we're looking at here is how the Jackson was stolen. I don't have all the details worked out yet, but I think they used this instrument to get the violin off-site without suspicion. It's the only explanation I can come up with for Eric Morrison knowingly walking away with a violin other than his own."

"Because he knew he was walking away with mine!" Bill Sloan had come up behind them and heard what Luis was saying.

Luis nodded his head. "I'm thinking that's a distinct possibility, Dr. Sloan. We need to find out where Eric Morrison is right now, and get in front of him, fast. With any luck, that shuttle is still making pickups at other hotels and hasn't even started to head toward the airport."

While Kavanaugh arranged for a police cruiser to pick up Goodman and hold him for questioning, Luis contacted the shuttle dispatcher and explained the situation.

"Yes, that shuttle is still making rounds at hotels right around you," the dispatcher said. "It hasn't reached the airport yet."

"Good. Can you communicate with the driver in a way that the passengers can't hear?"

"Yes, we do," the dispatcher explained. "We just use a numerical code that tells the driver we need to speak privately, and they switch the radio speaker off and use the headset."

"Great. Privately tell your driver that there's a suspect on board. Tell them not to worry, they aren't considered dangerous, but while acting as naturally as possible, tell them to continue driving without stopping for more pickups. I'm sorry if you'll need to send other drivers to pick other passengers up, but this is important."

After getting off the phone, Luis told the others, "Assuming I'm right and that Morrison has the Jackson, now that he's off-site he could be meeting with his buyer anywhere, anytime. We want to limit his potential contacts and movement as much as possible until we can get to him."

"So now what happens?" Bill asked.

"Now, Dr. Sloan, you come with me. We're going to track down that shuttle bus, and I'll need you to identify the Jackson if we retrieve it."

"And us, too," Dan said. "Come on, Luis, at this point, we've come too far to not see this through."

Recognizing that the situation wasn't likely dangerous or potentially violent, Luis quickly said, "OK, but we don't have any time to waste!"

Dan, Greg, and Bill followed Luis out to his car, while Kavanaugh took his own, with Eric's trashed violin still in the backseat. The two vehicles rushed to where the dispatcher told them the shuttle was at that moment. A few minutes later, they were nearing the shuttle's location.

"There it is, up ahead!" Greg shouted, pointing up ahead of them. Kavanaugh had called for backup from the police department, and the cruisers were just moving into place to the front, left side, and rear of the shuttle. They were slowing the shuttle down and forcing it to pull over, all sirens blazing.

Eric's eyes opened abruptly at the sound: the shuttle was surrounded by police cruisers. With nowhere else to go, the shuttle abruptly turned onto the circular ramp leading from Harbor Boulevard onto the Santa Ana Freeway, swerving to the right and veering off the road, up onto a wide concrete walkway that ran alongside it, bouncing passengers out of their seats and luggage off the storage rack in the process. Almost before the shuttle had come to a stop, it was surrounded by police officers, with Luis's and Kavanaugh's cars pulling off the road right behind them. Luis rushed toward the shuttle with the others right behind. He scrambled onto the shuttle and strode toward Eric, who was still sitting in his seat.

"Mr. Morrison, you need to come with me. Let's go, right now."

Well, that's it, I guess. It's over. It's all over. Eric realized that despite his best efforts and plans, something had gone wrong and he'd been caught. Resigned, he stood, picked up the violin case and following Luis off the bus. As he started down the aisle, he looked down the young couple. "You're going to have a great story to tell your friends about how your honeymoon started," he said as they stared silently at him.

Once off the bus, Bill, Dan, and Greg drew near. Kavanaugh came up alongside them.

"Dr. Sloan, come here, please," Luis instructed. Bill came closer, staring at Eric with a combination of hurt, betrayal, and anger.

"Open the case, Mr. Morrison." Eric unfastened the case and lifted the lid, pulled the velvet bag out and slipped the violin out of it as Bill stepped even closer.

"Wait—no! This isn't the Jackson!"

Greg quickly moved in to look at the violin, also. "No, there's no way! This is just some low-end, mass-produced violin!"

Eric looked down at the violin with genuine surprise. Indeed, the violin in the case wasn't the Jackson. Then he realized that even though it was virtually identical, it wasn't even his case.

As Luis and Kavanaugh discussed the unexpected development, Eric put the violin away in the case and set it on the ground next to him. As he did, he noticed a new text message on his phone:

Nice chatting with you. Thanks for the wedding gift. Just sent you something, too. We'll give your regards to Paris.

Then it dawned on him. *That couple must be the buyer! I was waiting for them to get on after me, and they'd been there all along.* Goodman had apparently arranged for the buyer to have a matching case, and once they'd seen Eric really had the Jackson, they'd switched cases while he was napping.

After a moment, Eric regained his composure, and even a bit of courage. "I'm really not sure what's going on here, agent," he said to Luis, "but I didn't steal the Jackson. Honestly, I'm offended that you'd even think that I did. If you're done with me, I really have to get to the airport or I'm going to miss my flight."

Before they could even think to ask why he was carrying the cheap violin, their attention was diverted. "Hey! Hey! Over here, come over here!" Standing beside the front door of the shuttle bus was Bandit, the same operator who had driven Greg and Dan earlier in the week. She yelled over to them, "You need to get back on this bus. That man sitting back there switched out cases with the guy you have out here. He didn't think anyone saw him do it, but I saw him in my mirror!"

Luis beat Kavanaugh to the rear door and vaulted onto the bus. The couple had heard the driver and immediately jumped up, instinctively running down the aisle toward the front entry, where they literally came crashing into Bandit's imposing physical presence.

"Oh, no you don't!" she yelled as they bounced off her, falling backward onto the floor. Bandit stepped aside, and they were scooped up by uniformed police officers.

"Damn! What is it with me and violin people this week?" Bandit said as the police led the two away.

Luis walked back down the aisle and retrieved the violin case, which was still beneath the couple's seat. Stepping back off the shuttle, he walked over to Bill, Dan, and Greg.

"Dr. Sloan, I'm pretty sure this belongs to you." He set the nondescript, black case onto the hood of his car and unfasted the latch. Bill removed the protective pouch, revealing the Jackson— still fitted with Eric Morrison's decoys, but the genuine fittings were also inside the velvet pouch, ready for reinstallation.

"Thank God we got it back!" Bill said, carefully placing it back into the case.

"Bill, this is fantastic!" Greg exclaimed. "I'm so happy for you! It looks like it's going to need some careful restoration work, but before long, it should be as good as it was."

After a moment, Dan said, "Well, I guess that's it—case opened; case closed."

Greg groaned. "That was really bad, even for you."

Dan didn't say anything but offered an ornery smile.

"All right folks, show's over," Bandit called out to her riders. "Now, let's get the rest of you all to your gates and you can get on your way."

CHAPTER 22

THURSDAY, 6:50 P.M.

Hardly more than an hour later, Dan and Greg stood in their guestroom after quick showers and changes, about to head downstairs to the banquet. "It's still hard for me to believe that Eric Morrison actually stole the Jackson," Greg said.

Recognizing the time limitations, Dan fought the urge to delve into a sermon on the universal brokenness of humanity and simply offered, "I guess Malcolm Stewart's emotional abuse distorted Eric's psyche so much that eventually, his own nice guy persona became just as much a facade as Stewart's."

They gave each other a quick visual once-over before leaving their room. Dan's necktie and Greg's bow tie were tied nice and straight, there weren't any stray threads hanging anywhere, and hair was sufficiently neat. Greg's had a tendency to flip up in the middle, a sort-of Mohawk look that Dan teasingly referred to as a "Greghawk," but all was in order this evening.

"It's unreal, you know," Greg said thoughtfully. "I've been living and breathing the competition for months, but with everything happening today, I've hardly even thought about it."

Dan smiled. "Well, it's here now, and whatever's going to happen will happen. So let's go downstairs and have a nice, quiet meal with 200 of our closest friends."

Entering the banquet hall a few minutes later, they found their seats at a table shared with Bill Sloan, Konstantin Pappas, Hanna Sullenberger, Chloé Lavigne, Chase Reinhold, and Ping Yi. In short order, they were enjoying a meal that probably wouldn't have impressed Chet Hogarth, but it was decidedly a cut above standard banquet fare.

Once most of the attendees had moved on to dessert and after-dinner coffee, the president of the VSA and master of ceremonies for the evening came to the podium. "Friends, we all know that this has been a highly unusual convention. We were all shocked and horrified when the Jackson Stradivarius was stolen, and we were all delighted to learn just a short while ago that it's been safely recovered and returned to Dr. Bill Sloan."

The roar of applause and cheers didn't subside until Bill was coaxed to stand, which he did, as tipping his Trilby hat to the crowd.

"As exciting as that has been," the master of ceremonies

continued, "it's now time to move to another exciting part of our week, as we announce the awards conferred as part of this year's competition."

Dan glanced over at Greg. His husband had a particular smile plastered across his face, the one Dan had come to recognize as a cover for nervousness.

"This year, the competition was particularly intense," he stated. "The quality of entries has never been higher, so congratulations to all who submitted entries for an incredible body of work."

The VSA awards gold medals, silver medals, and certificates of merit in its competitions. An instrument receives a gold medal if it is recommended by the judges for a gold medal in at least one category—tone or artisanship—and receives at least a certificate of merit in the other.

An instrument receives a silver medal, for either artisanship or tone, if judges recommend a gold medal be awarded in one or the other category, but the instrument does not receive at least a certificate of merit in the other category.

The VSA awards a certificate of merit for artisanship or tone, or possibly both, to any instrument that reaches the medal round of competition but does *not* receive either a gold or silver medal.

Glancing at Greg, Dan worried, too. Would he win something this year? Would his dry spell finally be broken? Or were his fears valid? *Is my presence in Greg's life hurting his work?*

The awards moved through the various categories: bows, quartets, then individual instruments—double bass, cello, viola, and finally, violin. Each category slowly progressed through the presentation of certificates of merit, silver medals, and gold medals.

It seemed to go on forever. When the awards reached the violin category, Dan listened with increasing nervousness to the names of various makers, most of whom he knew, whose instruments had been awarded certificates of merit for tone. He was happy when he heard the master of ceremonies call out "Konstantin Pappas . . . Hanna Sullenberg . . ." and finally, ". . . Greg Zhu."

Dan embraced him, and several of Greg's friends, who had predicted he'd win something this year, began chanting, "Greg! Greg! Greg!" Greg beamed and made his way to the front of the hall to receive his certificate with as much calm as he could muster, which, honestly, wasn't much.

Dan's happiness for his husband came with some disappointment, too. *If he was awarded a certificate, it means he didn't get a gold or silver medal. Still, he's won something.* The post-marital drought was over. The spell was broken.

A few minutes later, the master of ceremonies moved on to certificates for artisanship, and again, Dan sat nervously as the list proceeded alphabetically: "Konstantin Pappas . . . Hanna Sullenberger . . ."

Wait for it. . . . Wait for it. . . . Yes? No?

"Greg Zhu."

This time, Greg didn't even try to be calm as he jumped up from the table and went forward to receive his second certificate of the evening.

Thank God! Dan thought as he applauded for his husband. *We can both breathe again. A pattern for him, and it wins high accolades for both tone and artisanship in probably the most prestigious luthiers' competition in the world.*

"So what do you think?" Dan asked after they had crawled into bed. "I imagine you must be feeling pretty good right about now."

Greg smiled and cuddled up next to his husband. "Oh, I can't begin to tell you how good it feels." A moment later, he said, "I know you were really hoping that I'd earn a gold medal this year, but while I didn't, I got as close to it as possible. Most of all, though, I just feel really humbled and honored. The judges were all highly regarded professionals, and it's really validating to know that they consider my work to be at this level."

"Well," Dan added, "I'm obviously very proud of you—not just for tonight, but for everything about you, and about your work. I really believe that 300 years from now, people will still be playing violins that you made, and they'll be studying your work just like you study the work of old masters now."

"Well, I don't know about that," Greg said, "but it would be kind of cool, wouldn't it?"

After a moment, Greg continued thoughtfully. "You know, if I wasn't going to gold, I think I'd actually rather double-certificate than get a silver. I think that's really more indicative of being a better all-around instrument."

"Well, I've told you before that I think it's silly that an instrument getting double certificates can actually have a higher overall score than one that gets a silver medal."

Greg shrugged his shoulders. "I know, but that's just one of our idiosyncrasies. Every professional world has its own particular weirdness, and that's just one of ours that's developed over time."

Dan rolled his eyes. "Sounds like that old church line all pastors cringe over when they ask why a congregation does some crazy thing or another. The answer is always the same: 'That's just the way we've always done it.'"

Greg grinned. "See, you understand perfectly." After a pause, he continued. "Anyway, as far as a gold medal, there's always the next competition. And I've been thinking about a really interesting idea for a new design that I want to experiment with. I think it could have real potential to be an excellent, award-winning model. I'm going to start with the Amati Grand Pattern and then blend in a modified arching based on the 1742. . . ."

Greg continued explaining the concept in almost excruciating detail for at least another 10 minutes before realizing that Dan had fallen asleep. He smiled and within minutes he'd drifted off himself, experiencing the contented slumber of someone who had received both the approval of his colleagues and the undying love of his spouse.

CHAPTER 23

FRIDAY, 9:00 A.M.

"Well Greg, I guess I'll see you next summer at Oberlin," Bill said between bites of scrambled egg and sips of coffee as he, Konstantin, Greg, and Dan shared a final breakfast together.

"Yep," Greg said, "but when we get together then, I hope it will be a whole lot more uneventful than this week."

"Definitely," Konstantin agreed. "I've had enough excitement this past week for at least a year."

They were still eating when Luis Romero and Bill Kavanaugh entered the hotel and walked over to their table.

"Dr. Sloan," Luis said as he reached out his hand, "I just wanted to say again that I'm very glad we were able to recover your violin, even if it will need a bit of work to remove some of the camouflage that Eric Morrison applied to it. For what it's worth, Morrison and Goodman have confessed to their plot. We'll obviously be speaking more as we prepare for their court dates, but for now, I want to tell you that it was a pleasure getting to know you, even if under these circumstances."

Bill replied, "Luis, I'm so grateful for all you've done for me; thank you very much!"

"So, out of curiosity," Luis asked, "where will you go to have the work done? I'm going to guess that you aren't going to take it back to Malcolm Stewart's shop."

Bill chuckled. "No, let's just say that I've lost a lot of trust in Mr. Stewart and his operation, and that I'll be looking for a new company to take care of the Jackson."

"I'm not at all surprised."

"Yes," Bill continued, "Malcolm Stewart has lost his top employee and a large chunk of his reputation, and bragging rights that he takes care of the Jackson, on top of all that."

"It's interesting," Dan interjected. "Stewart's arrogance and abuse poisoned Eric Morrison, driving him to do things he'd never have done otherwise. In the process, he ended up destroying not only Eric, but most likely, himself."

"Sounds like there's a sermon somewhere in there," Luis joked.

Dan smiled. "One or two, anyway."

"Well in any case," Bill added, "Luis, I'll always be glad that you were assigned to this case. I really don't think we'd have gotten the

Jackson back without you."

Jim Kavanaugh had been standing by quietly. He bristled at Bill's comment, but he conceded. "Luis, I'm not going to lie—you know I didn't want you on this case. I honestly thought that I could have gotten the Jackson back without you, and I still do. But I'll admit you offered valuable help. You did good work, and I enjoyed working with you. You're a good guy."

"Yes, he is," said a voice behind Kavanaugh. It was Josh. "He also has the day off, and we've got a full day planned." Josh leaned over and gave Luis a peck on the cheek. "Are you ready to go, honey?"

"Wait," Kavanaugh said with a mixture of disbelief and confusion. "You mean to tell me that you're gay?"

"Well, he'd better be, since he's married to me," Josh said with a smile. "And for what it's worth, I can assure you: yes, he's very, very gay."

"But Romero, that doesn't make any sense," Kavanaugh said, still in a state of disbelief. "Why didn't you tell me you were gay, when I said, well, you know, some of the things I've said to you this week?"

"You never asked, you just assumed I was straight," Luis said. "I didn't tell you because I figured it would get in the way of our working together, and clearly, I was right."

"But, I mean, look at you! You're a strong, good-looking guy, a real man's man!"

"Yes, he is," Josh interjected. "But hands off, detective, he's already spoken for."

Kavanaugh shook his head. "I'm sorry, I try. I really do. And I was serious, Romero, I really enjoyed working with you. But anymore, everywhere you turn you bump into gays, and lesbians, and now it's transgender people, too. You used to be able to assume that most of the people around you were just normal, regular people. Now, you people are everywhere."

Just as Eric Morrison had hit a point beyond which he'd snapped, Greg Zhu had just hit one of his own.

"You people? You people?" Greg's face went red and he jumped up from the table and jabbed his finger into Kavanaugh's chest, not quite yelling but not far from it. "Listen, detective, as far as 'normal' is concerned, we're just as normal or abnormal as straight people are. And whether you've recognized us or not, we've always been here, and we always will be. We're police officers, and FBI agents, and ministers, and luthiers, and everything else under the sun. We're parents, and children, and relatives and friends. Whatever we are, we aren't going anywhere. And if you don't like that, you can kiss my smooth Asian ass!"

Everyone around the table looked at Greg in shocked silence. They had never heard anything like this come out of their diminutive, perpetually good-natured and polite friend. It was the most un-Greg verbal explosion imaginable.

Dan finally broke the silence, glancing over at his husband in mock horror and remarking simply, "Well that wasn't very nice."

Looking over the top of his glasses at Dan, Greg grinned and simply said, "Screw you."

Dan Randolph had rarely been prouder of his husband.

"You guys have certainly had an exciting week," Dan's daughter Nicole said over the phone. He and Greg were just boarding their flight home when she called, and now they were in their seats while the other passengers continued boarding. "We were following the news about it online—it all seemed pretty crazy."

"Oh, it really was," Dan said. Just wait 'till I tell you all the details. It turns out that the couple that was arrested on the shuttle bus were front people working for some rich collector in China who was going to buy it for his private collection."

"Crazy stuff. Well, I'm glad your friend got his violin back; I really enjoyed meeting him at your wedding."

"He and Judy asked how you're doing; they enjoyed meeting you, too. So yeah, after this week, we're going to feel like we need a vacation to recover from our vacation. In any case, we'll be home by this evening. We're fully boarded now and will be taking off shortly. I'll talk with you again soon. Love you, honey."

"Love you too, Dad. Tell Greg we said congratulations; talk with you later."

As Dan ended the call, a clean-scrubbed young man with short blond hair plopped down in the seat next to him. He was wearing black slacks, a short-sleeved white dress shirt, black tie, and a name tag identifying him as Elder Leavitt.

"Good afternoon, sir, do you mind if I ask where you're traveling to?" the young man asked Dan enthusiastically.

"Oh, I'm headed back home to Louisville after being out here all week," Dan replied.

"Oh, that's nice; I hope you had an enjoyable visit. Louisville is a very nice place." The man asked. "So, may I ask what do you do you do for a living?"

Crap. Remembering his conversation earlier in the week, Dan answered, "Oh, I'm a . . . social worker."

"That's a very noble calling. I'm sure that you help a lot of people in your work."

"I hope so, but in my line of work, sometimes it can be hard to tell," Dan said truthfully. "So, after this weekend and your travels, are you looking forward to 'P Day' on Monday?" Dan was referring to "Preparation Day," a day off for most LDS missionaries that is most typically observed on Mondays.

The young man gave Dan a surprised look. "Oh, you know about our church organization. Are you one of the brethren?"

"Oh, no, not me," Dan said, "but my husband went to violin-making school in Salt Lake City, and while he lived there, he learned a lot about your church. I guess some of that knowledge just rubbed off on me." He patted Greg's hand on the adjacent armrest.

"Your . . . husband."

Dan leaned back and closed his eyes, enjoying the remainder of the flight in relative silence.

CHAPTER 24

LOUISVILLE, SUNDAY, 5:30 P.M.

"Oh, look, it's the TV stars!" Liz Findlay exclaimed as Dan and Greg walked in the door for dinner chez Thad. "We've seen you in the background of all sorts of news stories this week."

"Look, here's my favorite one," Jim Findlay said. He started streaming a video showing Luis Romero talking to Bill Sloan and holding the Jackson, with Dan and Greg standing alongside them.

"It's OK, Liz," Dan joked as they grabbed a drink and sat down. "No matter how famous we get, we'll always have time for the little people."

"So, how was church this morning?" Liz asked.

"It was very good," Dan said thoughtfully. "It was a Communion Sunday for us, and even though I've always got my eye on everyone else's worship experience, Communion Sundays are often the times when I actually feel more spiritually connected, myself. The communal prayers and the ritual, combined with the intimacy of serving each person the elements, helps me to experience gratitude and to feel the presence of the divine as my most open, authentic self, without facade, deception, pretense."

"Pfft! Touchy-feely liberal heresy," Chet mock-scolded from behind the kitchen counter. "I told you before; it's all about preaching the Bible: convict them of their sin, have an altar call, get them to pray the Sinner's Prayer and accept Jesus as their personal Lord and Savior. Everything else is just new age psychobabble!"

Dan laughed. "Oh, wait, I almost forgot." He reached into his pocket and pulled out a small, sealed tan paper packet and tossed it onto the granite countertop in front of Chet, whose arms were folded across his worn, favorite Warren Zevon T-shirt. Chet's eyes lit up when he saw the packet.

"My winter savory! Fantastic! I just assumed with everything else that was going on, you guys would have forgotten about it. Thanks!" He looked like an eight-year-old on Christmas morning.

"Oh no, we wouldn't have forgotten," Greg laughed. "If we had, we'd have never been invited back to dinner."

"Nah, you know you guys have a standing invitation to dinner every week, winter savory or not. But now that we have some, I can tell you that whatever else we're having next week, there will be a nice dish of fava beans seasoned with winter savory!"

Feeling ornery, Dan casually commented, "I still don't know

what the big deal is between winter savory and summer savory. Really, they can't be all that different."

Chet scowled. "Even more heresy from you, 'reverend,' " he said, framing the word in air quotes. "But then again, I've come to expect that. Here," he said, striding across the kitchen. He pulled a stack of small white bowls from a cabinet and quickly placed two of them in front of everyone there. "Now, here's a little taste of summer savory, and here's winter savory," he said, shaking samples of each into the bowls. "Now you taste those and tell me you can't tell the difference."

Shelly Hogarth and Cathy Findlay shot weary glances across the table at Dan. "Really?" Shelly asked. "Do you have to encourage him?"

"Exactly," Cathy added. "Maybe I'll set Greg off the same way by saying that no modern violin could ever sound as good as the old ones."

"That just isn't true," Greg said. "The double-blind Paris Experiment, pitting antique and modern instruments against each other, showed there was no real discernible difference."

Dan put his hand on Greg's. "Honey, she's just baiting you." Cathy winked.

"Oh, I know, but still."

The Hogarths' pug sniffed under his chair, and Dan's mind wandered to the events of the past week. He remembered his chance encounter with the Irvings in the airport, and his thoughts about the mystery movie they'd discussed. Sometimes, the villain in a mystery is the least likely suspect, and sometimes it's someone you'd most suspect. *And apparently sometimes*, Dan thought, *it's both.*

It also dawned on him that a common thread running through the week's events was deception. Whether a violin, a situation, or a person, things aren't always what they seem. Plausible or otherwise, deception is often wrong, occasionally necessary, and sometimes even kind. *For better or worse, though, it will always be a part of human experience.*

Dan's attention returned to the conversation around the table. As Chet continued to detail the subtle and complex differences between winter and summer savory, Dan licked his fingertip and stuck it into each of the bowls in front of him, sampling the two spices in succession. "Oh, absolutely," he said, thoughtfully nodding his head. "Now I get it! There's a huge difference between these two. No one would ever confuse one of them for the other!"

ACKNOWLEDGMENTS

I would like to offer particular thanks to the following:

The Violin Society of America, for allowing use of its name in this story, for having provided the underlying setting from which this story developed, and for allowing me to be a fly on the wall at a number of their events and workshops over the years.

Concertmaster Gabriel Lefkowitz and Assistant Concertmaster Julia Noone of the Louisville Orchestra, who helped to provide Alana Marino's "voice" in Chapter 4 as she explained the concept of tone and what a professional violinist looks for in an instrument.

Dianne Bellis, my editor. This book originally began as an attempt to tell parts of my own life's story, all somewhat held together by an underlying mystery. Dianne's advice gently and deftly allowed me to see that in fact, my life was actually pretty boring—at least, it was not the stuff that books are written about—and that readers would consider many of those autobiographical bits to be uninteresting speed bumps in what had potential to actually be a pretty good mystery. Faced with that, I needed to decide whether to write a book about me that virtually no one would be interested in reading or to strip much of myself out of the story and write a mystery that people might actually enjoy. What you're about to read is the result of my having largely chosen option B.

The real-life Greg Zhu—my husband, master luthier George Yu—for utterly invaluable musical, technical, and historical assistance, immense patience, love, companionship, and the constant emotional support that he provided during the writing of this book—which you'll probably recognize is actually just an extended love letter to him.

Dr. Bill Sloan, for allowing himself and his family to be portrayed and for supporting the idea of the book, but mostly for simply being someone George and I both consider a dear and valued friend.

PHOTOGRAPHS

The 'Leonora Jackson' Stradivari, 1714 (front cover).

Photo: George Yu

The 'Leonora Jackson' Stradivari, 1714 (front, page vii; rear, page 319; scrollwork, page 63). Photos: Jan Röhrmann, 'Antonius Stradivarius Vol. I-IV': Wikimedia Commons, free use—free use—link to license: https://creativecommons.org/licenses/by-sa/4.0/

Violin rib structure, page 19 and Vieuxtemps Amati (page 61).

Photos: George Yu

Author portrait, page 320. Photo: Jon Cherry

Author and Jackson Stradivarius (page 318, top).

Photo: Dr. Bill Sloan

George Yu and Dr. Bill Sloan, (page 318, bottom).

Photo: Dwain Lee

ILLUSTRATIONS

Violin cross section (page 127). Diagram: Amitchell 125, Interior of a violin: Wikimedia, Creative Commons free use—link to license: https://creativecommons.org/licenses/by-sa/4.0/

Front and side view of a violin (page viii). Diagram: John Waddle and Steve Sirr

All photographs and illustrations are used with permission.

The author with the Jackson Stradivarius

The author's husband, George Yu, playing the "Bach Double" with Dr. Bill Sloan—George on the Jackson, Bill on his 1742 Guarneri del Gesù

ABOUT THE AUTHOR

 DWAIN LEE is a Presbyterian minister and pastor. Before entering the ministry, he was an architect in private practice in Columbus, Ohio, for many years. He and his husband now live in Louisville, Kentucky, where he works, writes, and is active in social justice advocacy. He has two daughters and enjoys travel, gardening, home repair, camping, and yoga.